My
Brilliant
Career

STELLA MARIA MILES FRANKLIN lived from 1879 to 1954. She was raised in mountainous New South Wales, Australia, and wrote *My Brilliant Career* when she was only sixteen. She was twenty-one when it was first published in Edinburgh, Scotland. Distressed by critical attention that viewed the book as pure autobiography, the author kept it out of print for the rest of her life. It was finally reissued in Australia, to much acclaim, in 1966. Miles Franklin wrote eleven other novels and was also active in the feminist and socialist movements in America, England, and finally, Australia, where she returned toward the end of her life, after thirty years of self-exile.

MILES FRANKLIN

My Brilliant Career

WASHINGTON SQUARE PRESS
PUBLISHED BY POCKET BOOKS NEW YORK

A Washington Square Press Publication of
POCKET BOOKS, a Simon & Schuster division of
GULF & WESTERN CORPORATION
1230 Avenue of the Americas, New York, N.Y. 10020

First published in Edinburgh, 1901
First published by Angus & Robertson Publishers,
Australia, 1965

Published by arrangement with St. Martin's Press
Library of Congress Catalog Card Number: 80-52658

ISBN: 0-671-42736-9

First Washington Square Press printing September, 1981

10 9 8 7 6 5 4 3 2 1

WASHINGTON SQUARE PRESS, WSP and colophon are
trademarks of Simon & Schuster.

Printed in the U.S.A.

PREFACE

A few months before I left Australia I got a letter from the bush signed "Miles Franklin," saying that the writer had written a novel, but knew nothing of editors and publishers, and asking me to read and advise. Something about the letter, which was written in a strong original hand, attracted me, so I sent for the MS., and one dull afternoon I started to read it. I hadn't read three pages when I saw what you will no doubt see at once—that the story had been written by a girl. And as I went on I saw that the work was Australian—born of the bush. I don't know about the girlishly emotional parts of the book—I leave that to girl readers to judge; but the descriptions of bush life and scenery came startlingly, painfully real to me, and I know that, as far as they are concerned, the book is true to Australia—the truest I ever read.

I wrote to Miles Franklin, and she confessed that she was a girl. I saw her before leaving Sydney. She is just a little bush girl, barely twenty-one yet, and has scarcely ever been out of the bush in her life. She has lived her book, and I feel proud of it for the sake of the country I came from, where people toil and bake and suffer and are kind; where every second sun-burnt bushman is a sympathetic humorist, with the sadness of the bush deep in his eyes and a brave grin for the worst of times, and where every third bushman is a poet, with a big heart that keeps his pockets empty.

HENRY LAWSON

England, April 1901

NEW INTRODUCTION

Stella Maria Sarah Miles Franklin was born on October 14, 1879. Of Irish descent on her father's side, of German and English descent on her mother's, she was a fifth-generation Australian, her maternal great-great-grandfather Edward Miles arriving at Sydney Cove in 1788 with the First Fleet. Her family were pioneers, mountain squatters settled in the rough and beautiful mountain-guarded valleys of the Australian Alps in New South Wales, on the Western edge of what is now the Australian Capital Territory. Miles Franklin spent her first ten years on her father's cattle station, "Brindabella," growing up with her six younger brothers and sisters, sharing with them and neighboring cousins a Scottish tutor—a remittance man often the worse for drink—who nevertheless gave her a grounding in composition and a love of literature advanced for her years. "Shakespeare, the Bible, Dickens, Aesop's fables— that's what I was brung (or drugged up) on." When Stella Franklin was ten her family moved down from the mountains, first to a dairying selection, then to a small property, "Stillwater" ("Possum Gully" in *My Brilliant Career*). Stella Franklin was deeply affected by this change, and the harsh conditions of a pioneering selector's life, and these years were a period of growing rebellion. She did not get on with her austere mother, and was jealous of her younger and prettier sister who was allowed to spend some years with their maternal grandmother on the beautiful family property, "Talbingo" ("Caddagat" in *My Brilliant Career*). Stella Franklin was a born horsewoman, famous as a local showrider in the district; she loved music and wanted to be a singer. Reduced family circumstances making this impossible, she turned her attention to writing. When she was only sixteen she wrote *My Brilliant Career*—"conceived and tossed off in a matter of weeks."

Family life in the Australian bush was not the only influence on Stella Franklin's writing. She was acutely affected too by the decade in which she grew up—the 1890s, a period of political and artistic ferment in Australia. Politically the movement to federate the six Australian states was at its peak in those years, leading to the establishment of Australia as an independent Commonwealth on January 1, 1901, the year in which *My Brilliant Career* was first published. Artistically the nineties saw the emergence of aggressive nationalism in literature too. The writers of this decade, encouraged by the famous Australian weekly *The Bulletin,* struggled to give depth and definition to a new and different race of people living in a new and different country. These writers were exuberant, masculine, openly chauvinistic both politically and sexually, resentful of the old world with its hereditary privileges, its landlordism, its class distinctions. "We have nothing in common with the English people except our language," wrote Henry Lawson, the most typical of this group (he provided a preface to the first edition of *My Brilliant Career*). These writers, Lawson, "Banjo" Paterson, Will Ogilvie and many others gave a literary soul to Australia, presenting its population—predominantly urban then as now—with an image of the Bush as the "real Australia," celebrating as the only "real Australian" the country bushman, with his code of "mateship," his independence, his belief in the fellowship of the working man. "Man" is the operative word in this ethos, and indeed it had little place for or interest in its womenfolk, except as the suffering and passive recipients of the lives allotted them by the brave men with whom they lived, and the tough circumstances of Australian bush life.

Miles Franklin absorbed and shared the intense nationalism and socialism of her male contemporary mentors, as is made abundantly and sometimes gratingly clear in the pages of *My Brilliant Career*. But she revolted then and forever against the role of women in their scheme of things, against the "dullness and tame hennishness" of women's lives. It is interesting that *My Brilliant Career*, published two years before the novel which best expresses the sentiments of nineties Australian nationalism, Joseph Furphy's *Such Is Life*, remained out of print from 1901 until 1966. This was Miles Franklin's own wish, but it is obvious too that as a woman, expressing a woman's view of those halcyon days, she had no place in any establishment view of the "great" Australian literature of the nineties.

There were other reasons why Stella Franklin refused to keep the book in print. Like most of her female contemporaries, she chose to publish under a male pseudonym (Henry Handel Richardson did the same and it is no coincidence that Laura, the heroine of *The Getting Of Wisdom*, is in many ways a literary twin of Sybylla). Initially she submitted her manuscript to *The Bulletin*, through them Henry Lawson read it and advised her to send it to his publishers, Blackwoods in Edinburgh. Using her great-great-grandfather's name, Miles, did not help when *My Brilliant Career* was finally published in 1901. Publication brought Miles Franklin instant fame and unwelcome notoriety, most particularly in the district in which she had to live, where it was received as fact, not fiction. Miles Franklin insisted that it was merely a "girl's story," and that she withdrew it from publication because of the "stupid literalness" with which it was taken to be her own autobiography. However, there is a supposition that she was influenced too by the critical comments of Havelock Ellis who lived in Australia from 1875-9, and who reviewed the book for the *Weekly Critical Review* (Paris 1903). He described it as a "vivid and sincere book, certainly the true reflection of the life around her. Such a book has psychological in-

terest, the interest that belongs to the confessions of a
Marie Bashkirtseff of the bush." He was critical of
its crudity though, of its "embittered and egotistical
mood," which he interpreted as unconscious abnor-
mality.

It is difficult now to assess which of these depressing
reactions was responsible for the disappearance of *My
Brilliant Career* for over sixty years. Certainly in the
sequel to *My Brilliant Career, My Career Goes Bung,*
Miles Franklin refers with contempt to "the dubious
guesses of psychoanalysis." Whatever her reactions to
psychological analysis and family disapproval, now one
cannot but think that Miles Franklin was decades ahead
of her time and that *My Brilliant Career* was written
for an audience not yet born.

For in the character of Sybylla Melvyn, Miles Franklin created a character who mouths with incredible
charm but deadly accuracy the fears, conflicts and torments of every girl, with an understanding usually asso-
ciated with writers of the 1960s and '70s. Sybylla is a
girl in a man's world, a girl who "being so very plain"
knows she is "not a valuable article in the marriage
market," but despises the slavery which respectable
marriage will bring. She will never "perpetrate matrimony," will not be a "participant" in that "degradation"—this is astounding stuff from a sixteen-year-old
living in the outback in 1885. She has ideas about
politics, about writing and music, and she sees quite
clearly the life of loneliness this will mean for her because she is a woman—"a man with these notions
is a curse to himself but a woman . . . she is not merely
a creature out of her sphere—she is a creature without
a sphere—a lonely being!" And yet Sybylla knows the
value of love between man and woman—"our greatest
heart-treasure is a knowledge that there is in creation
an individual to whom our existence is necessary—
someone who is part of our life as we are part of theirs,
someone in whose life we feel assured our death would
leave a gap for a day or two. And who can be this but
a husband or wife?"

Sybylla is the product of unsophisticated genius, a creation of tremendous energy, whose ebullient outpourings place this novel well above and outside the nostalgic portrayals of Miles Franklin's literary contemporaries. Not only does she fictionalize the conflicts of adolescence and of every woman's life, more, in Sybylla Miles Franklin has created a literary personality which truly lives. For Sybylla is no mere "whinger." She laughs and flirts and battles and endlessly sends herself up; she cuts herself down to size in the most endearing way, so that despite its juvenile prose, the adolescent fantasies which constitute the plot, its rampant and irritating Australian nationalism, the emotion one feels when reading *My Brilliant Career* is one of passionate identification with Sybylla and her rags to riches story. At the moment when Sybylla tells her suitor Harry of her final decision, one can hear a million female voices saying "Oh no," but then adding "Yes, you're right, and good luck to you." *My Brilliant Career* presents one of the most encouraging heroines in fiction, because Sybylla *knows what her problems are*. One can hardly restrain oneself from leaping back in time to tell Miles Franklin, "Sybylla is me."

In 1901 however, Miles Franklin was so distressed by the reaction to her novel that she left home, moving in 1904 to Sydney. There she worked as a domestic servant for a year, writing for *The Bulletin* under the pseudonym of Mary Anne (the second of her literary masks) and preparing the novel she'd begun in the intervening years: *My Career Goes Bung*. At this time she met the Australian suffragist Rose Scott whose salon, a center for feminist and intellectual discussion, Miles Franklin often visited. *My Career Goes Bung,* intended as a corrective to *My Brilliant Career,* was rejected by publishers as too outspoken (it was finally published, unaltered, in 1946). Disillusioned, Miles Franklin decided to go to America, an exile from her native land which was to last for nearly thirty years. She never returned to the bush country of her childhood, but her memories of it are the cornerstone of all her later writing.

In America Miles Franklin joined the Australian feminist and labor leader Alice Henry. For the next ten years she worked with her for the Women's Trade Union League, managing its national office in Chicago and editing its magazine *Life and Labor*. During those years she wrote only one book, *Some Everyday Folk And Dawn* (1909), dedicated to "English *men* who believe in votes for *women*," its heroine Dawn a more mature Sybylla. In a later novel *Cockatoos* (written 1927/8, published 1945), Miles Franklin fictionalized the artistic frustration and homesickness she felt in those years.

With the outbreak of the First World War she went to London, at first working in slum nurseries and then joining the Scottish Women's Hospital Unit which was stationed at Salonika in the Balkans. This extraordinary hospital unit was the brainchild of Elsie Inglis, the Scottish surgeon, Suffragist and hospital administrator. By August 1914 this redoubtable woman had collected expert women physicians, surgeons, nurses and drivers to go to the Front. She had also collected £25,000, but the War Office replied with "My good lady, go home and sit still." The French immediately accepted her offer, and later Dr. Inglis took her unit to Serbia. Here Miles Franklin joined them, serving from 1917-18.

After the war she returned to London where she worked as a political secretary for the National Housing Council in Bloomsbury, making two brief trips to Australia in 1924 and 1930. About this fascinating period of her life little is known. She published only three novels in these years, two of them part of a sequence of six novels which were published between 1928 and 1956 under yet another pseudonym, "Brent of Bin Bin." The Bin Bin novels, published out of order but interconnected, form a saga of Australian pioneering life, telling the story of a group of pastoral families from the 1850s to the 1930s. Written in

London between 1925-1931, Miles Franklin released into them a flood of childhood memories, writing about the people she'd known and the bush she'd loved as a child. In her lifetime Miles Franklin refused to admit that she was Brent of Bin Bin, that old reaction to *My Brilliant Career* standing permanently as a barrier between her creative capacity and the works she wished to write. Return to Australia in 1933 seems to have exorcised that ghost, for in 1936 she published, under her own name, another heroic account of pioneer life, *All That Swagger* (1936). This novel and the Bin Bin sequence have been critically considered her greatest literary works.

CONTENTS

Contents

INTRODUCTION

Possum Gully, near Goulburn,
N.S. Wales, Australia, 1st March, 1899

MY DEAR FELLOW AUSTRALIANS,

Just a few lines to tell you that this story is all about myself—for no other purpose do I write it.

I make no apologies for being egotistical. In this particular I attempt an improvement on other autobiographies. Other autobiographies weary one with excuses for their egotism. What matters it to you if I am egotistical? What matters it to you though it should matter that I am egotistical?

This is not a romance—I have too often faced the music of life to the tune of hardship to waste time in sniveling and gushing over fancies and dreams; neither is it a novel, but simply a yarn—a *real* yarn. Oh! as real, as really real—provided life itself is anything beyond a heartless little chimera—it is as real in its weariness and bitter heartache as the tall gum-trees, among which I first saw the light, are real in their stateliness and substantiality.

My sphere in life is not congenial to me. Oh, how I hate this living death which has swallowed all my teens, which is greedily devouring my youth, which will sap my prime, and in which my old age, if I am cursed with any, will be worn away! As my life creeps on for ever through the long toil-laden days with its agonizing monotony, narrowness, and absolute uncongeniality, how my spirit frets and champs its unbreakable fetters —all in vain!

SPECIAL NOTICE

You can dive into this story head first as it were. Do not fear encountering such trash as descriptions of beautiful sunsets and whisperings of wind. We (999 out of every 1000) can see nought in sunsets save as signs and tokens whether we may expect rain on the morrow or the contrary, so we will leave such vain and foolish imagining to those poets and painters—poor fools! Let us rejoice that we are not of their temperament!

Better be born a slave than a poet, better be born a black, better be born a cripple! For a poet must be companionless—alone! *fearfully* alone in the midst of his fellows whom he loves. Alone because his soul is as far above common mortals as common mortals are above monkeys.

There is no plot in this story, because there has been none in my life or in any other life which has come under my notice. I am one of a class, the individuals of which have not time for plots in their life, but have all they can do to get their work done without indulging in such a luxury.

CHAPTER ONE

I Remember, I Remember

"Boo, hoo! Ow, ow; Oh! oh! Me'll die. Boo, hoo. The pain, the pain! Boo, hoo!"

"Come, come, now. Daddy's little mate isn't going to turn Turk like that, is she? I'll put some fat out of the dinner-bag on it, and tie it up in my hanky. Don't cry any more now. Hush, you must not cry! You'll make old Dart buck if you kick up a row like that."

That is my first recollection of life. I was barely three. I can remember the majestic gum-trees surrounding us, the sun glinting on their straight white trunks, and falling on the gurgling fern-banked stream, which disappeared beneath a steep scrubby hill on our left. It was an hour past noon on a long clear summer day. We were on a distant part of the run, where my father had come to deposit salt. He had left home early in the dewy morning, carrying me in front of him on a little brown pillow which my mother had made for the purpose. We had put the lumps of rock-salt in the troughs on the other side of the creek. The stringy-bark roof of the salt-shed which protected the troughs from rain peeped out picturesquely from the musk and peppercorn shrubs by which it was densely surrounded, and was visible from where we lunched. I refilled the quart-pot in which we had boiled our tea with water from the creek, father doused our fire out with it, and then tied the quart to the D of his saddle with a piece of green hide. The green-hide bags in which the salt had been carried were hanging on the hooks of the pack-saddle which encumbered the bay pack-horse. Father's saddle and the brown pillow were on Dart, the big gray horse on which he generally carried me, and we were on the point of making tracks for home.

Preparatory to starting, father was muzzling the dogs which had just finished what lunch we had left. This process, to which the dogs strongly objected, was rendered necessary by a cogent reason. Father had brought his strychnine flask with him that day, and in hopes of causing the death of a few dingoes, had put strong doses of its contents in several dead beasts which we had come across.

While the dogs were being muzzled, I busied myself in plucking ferns and flowers. This disturbed a big black snake which was curled at the butt of a tree fern. "Bitey! bitey!" I yelled, and father came to my rescue, dispatching the reptile with his stock-whip. He had been smoking, and dropped his pipe on the ferns. I picked it up, and the glowing embers which fell from it burnt my dirty little fat fists. Hence the noise with which my story commences.

In all probability it was the burning of my fingers which so indelibly impressed the incident on my infantile mind. My father was accustomed to take me with him, but that is the only jaunt at that date which I remember, and that is all I remember of it. We were twelve miles from home, but how we reached there I do not know.

My father was a swell in those days—held Bruggabrong, Bin Bin East, and Bin Bin West, which three stations totaled close on 200,000 acres. Father was admitted into swelldom merely by right of his position. His pedigree included nothing beyond a grandfather. My mother, however, was a full-fledged aristocrat. She was one of the Bossiers of Caddagat, who numbered among their ancestry one of the depraved old pirates who pillaged England with William the Conqueror.

"Dick" Melvyn was as renowned for hospitality as joviality, and our comfortable, wide-verandaed, irregularly built, slab house in its sheltered nook amid the Timlinbilly Ranges was ever full to overflowing. Doctors, lawyers, squatters, commercial travelers, bankers, journalists, tourists, and men of all kinds and classes crowded our well-spread board; but seldom a female face, except mother's, was to be seen there, Bruggabrong being a very out-of-the-way place.

I was both the terror and the amusement of the station. Old boundary-riders and drovers inquire after me with interest to this day.

I knew everyone's business, and was ever in danger of publishing it at an inopportune moment.

In flowery language, selected from slang used by the station hands, and long words picked up from our visitors, I propounded unanswerable questions which brought blushes to the cheeks of even tough old wine-bibbers.

Nothing would induce me to show more respect to an appraiser of the runs than to a boundary-rider, or to a clergyman than a drover. I am the same to this day. My organ of veneration must be flatter than a pancake, because to venerate a person simply for his position I never did or will. To me the Prince of Wales will be no more than a shearer, unless when I meet him he displays some personality apart from his princeship—otherwise he can go hang.

Authentic record of the date when first I had a horse to myself has not been kept, but it must have been early, as at eight I was fit to ride anything on the place. Side-saddle, man-saddle, no-saddle, or astride were all the same to me. I rode among the musterers as gamely as any of the big sunburnt bushmen.

My mother remonstrated, opined I would be a great unwomanly tomboy. My father poohed the idea.

"Let her alone, Lucy," he said, "let her alone. The rubbishing conventionalities which are the curse of her sex will bother her soon enough. Let her alone!"

So, smiling and saying, "She should have been a

boy," my mother let me alone, and I rode, and in comparison to my size made as much noise with my stockwhip as any one. Accidents had no power over me, I came unscathed out of droves of them.

Fear I knew not. Did a drunken tramp happen to kick up a row, I was always the first to confront him, and, from my majestic and roly-poly height of two feet six inches, demand what he wanted.

A digging started near us and was worked by a score of two dark-browed sons of Italy. They made mother nervous, and she averred they were not to be trusted, but I liked and trusted them. They carried me on their broad shoulders, stuffed me with lollies and made a general pet of me. Without the quiver of a nerve I swung down their deepest shafts in the big bucket on the end of a rope attached to a rough windlass, which brought up the miners and the mullock.

My brothers and sisters contracted mumps, measles, scarlatina, and whooping-cough. I rolled in the bed with them yet came off scot-free. I romped with dogs, climbed trees after birds' nests, drove the bullocks in the dray, under the instructions of Ben, our bullocky, and always accompanied my father when he went swimming in the clear, mountain, shrub-lined stream which ran deep and lone among the weird gullies, thickly carpeted with maidenhair and numberless other species of ferns.

My mother shook her head over me and trembled for my future, but father seemed to consider me nothing unusual. He was my hero, confidant, encyclopedia, mate, and even my religion till I was ten. Since then I have been religionless.

Richard Melvyn, you were a fine fellow in those days! A kind and indulgent parent, a chivalrous husband, a capital host, a man full of ambition and gentlemanliness.

Amid these scenes, and the refinements and pleasures of Caddagat, which lies a hundred miles or so farther Riverinawards, I spent the first years of my childhood.

CHAPTER TWO

An Introduction to Possum Gully

I was nearly nine summers old when my father conceived the idea that he was wasting his talents by keeping them rolled up in the small napkin of an out-of-the-way place like Bruggabrong and the Bin Bin stations. Therefore he determined to take up his residence in a locality where he would have more scope for his ability.

When giving his reason for moving to my mother, he put the matter before her thus: The price of cattle and horses had fallen so of late years that it was impossible to make much of a living by breeding them. Sheep were the only profitable article to have nowadays, and it would be impossible to run them on Bruggabrong or either of the Bin Bins. The dingoes would work havoc among them in no time, and what they left the duffers would soon dispose of. As for bringing police into the matter, it would be worse than useless. They could not run the offenders to earth, and their efforts to do so would bring down upon their employer the wrath of the duffers. Result, all the fences on the station would be fired for a dead certainty, and the destruction of more than a hundred miles of heavy log fencing on rough country like Bruggabrong was no picnic to contemplate.

This was the feasible light in which father shaded

his desire to leave. The fact of the matter was that the heartless harridan, discontent, had laid her claw-like hand upon him. His guests were ever assuring him he was buried and wasted in Timlinbilly's gullies. A man of his intelligence, coupled with his wonderful experience among stock, would, they averred, make a name and fortune for himself dealing or auctioneering if he only liked to try. Richard Melvyn began to think so too, and desired to try. He did try.

He gave up Bruggabrong, Bin Bin East and Bin Bin West, bought Possum Gully, a small farm of one thousand acres, and brought us all to live near Goulburn. Here we arrived one autumn afternoon. Father, mother, and children packed in the buggy, myself, and the one servant-girl, who had accompanied us, on horseback. The one man father had retained in his service was awaiting our arrival. He had preceded us with a bullock-drayload of furniture and belongings, which was all father had retained of his household property. Just sufficient for us to get along with, until he had time to settle and purchase more, he said. That was ten years ago, and that is the only furniture we possess yet—just enough to get along with.

My first impression of Possum Gully was bitter disappointment—an impression which time has failed to soften or wipe away.

How flat, common, and monotonous the scenery appeared after the rugged peaks of the Timlinbilly Ranges!

Our new house was a ten-roomed wooden structure, built on a barren hillside. Crooked stunted gums and stringybarks, with a thick underscrub of wild cherry, hop, and hybrid wattle, clothed the spurs which ran up from the back of the detached kitchen. Away from the front of the house were flats, bearing evidence of cultivation, but a drop of water was nowhere to be seen. Later, we discovered a few round, deep, weedy waterholes down on the flat, which in rainy weather swelled to a stream which swept all before it. Possum Gully is one of the best watered spots in the district, and in that respect has stood to its guns in the bitterest drought. Use and knowledge have taught us the full value of its fairly clear and beautifully soft water. Just then, however, coming from the mountains where every gully had its limpid creek, we turned in disgust from the idea of having to drink this water.

I felt cramped on our new run. It was only three miles wide at its broadest point. Was I always, always, always to live here, and never, never, never to go back to Bruggabrong? That was the burden of the grief with which I sobbed myself to sleep on the first night after our arrival.

Mother felt dubious of her husband's ability to make a living off a thousand acres, half of which were fit to run nothing but wallabies, but father was full of plans, and very sanguine concerning his future. He was not going to squat henlike on his place as the cockies around him did. He meant to deal in stock, making of Possum Gully merely a depot on which to run some of his bargains until reselling.

Dear, oh dear! It was terrible to think he had wasted the greater part of his life among the hills where the mail came but once a week, and where the nearest town, of 650 inhabitants, was forty-six miles distant. And the road had been impassable for vehicles. Here, only seventeen miles from a city like Goulburn, with splendid roads, mail thrice weekly, and a railway platform only eight miles away, why, man, my fortune is made! Such were the sentiments to which he gave birth out of the fullness of his hopeful heart.

Ere the diggings had broken out on Bruggabrong, our nearest neighbor, excepting, of course, boundary-riders, was seventeen miles distant. Possum Gully was a thickly populated district, and here we were surrounded by homes ranging from half a mile to two and three miles away. This was a new experience for us, and it took us some time to become accustomed to the advantage and disadvantage of the situation. Did we require an article, we found it handy, but decidedly the reverse when our neighbors borrowed from us, and, in the greater percentage of cases, failed to return the loan.

CHAPTER THREE

A Lifeless Life

Possum Gully was stagnant—stagnant with the narrow stagnation prevalent in all old country places.

Its residents were principally married folk and children under sixteen. The boys, as they attained manhood, drifted outback to shear, drove, or to take up land. They found it too slow at home, and besides there was not room enough for them there when they passed childhood.

Nothing ever happened there. Time was no object, and the days slid quietly into the river of years, distinguished one from another by name alone. An occasional birth or death was a big event, and the biggest event of all was the advent of a new resident.

When such a thing occurred it was customary for all the male heads of families to pay a visit of inspection, to judge if the new-comers were worthy of admittance into the bosom of the society of the neighborhood. Should their report prove favorable, then their wives finished the ceremony of inauguration by paying a friendly visit.

After his arrival at Possum Gully father was much

away on business, and so on my mother fell the ordeal of receiving the callers, male and female.

The men were honest, good-natured, respectable, common bushmen farmers. Too friendly to pay a short call, they came and sat for hours yarning about nothing in particular. This bored my gentle mother excessively. She attempted to entertain them with conversation of current literature and subjects of the day, but her efforts fell flat. She might as well have spoken in French.

They conversed for hours and hours about dairying, interspersed with pointless anecdotes of the man who had lived there before us. I found them very tame.

After graphic descriptions of life on big stations outback, and the dashing snake yarns told by our kitchenfolk at Bruggabrong, and the anecdotes of African hunting, travel, and society life which had often formed our guests' subject of conversation, this endless fiddle-faddle of the price of farm produce and the state of crops was very fatuous.

Those men, like everyone else, only talked shop. I say nothing in condemnation of it, but merely point out that it did not then interest us, as we were not living in that shop just then.

Mrs. Melvyn must have found favor in the eyes of the specimens of the lords of creation resident at Possum Gully, as all the matrons of the community hastened to call on her, and vied with each other in a display of friendliness and good-nature. They brought presents of poultry, jam, butter, and suchlike. They came at two o'clock and stayed till dark. They inventoried the furniture, gave mother cookery recipes, described minutely the unsurpassable talents of each of their children, and descanted volubly upon the best way of setting turkey hens. On taking their departure they cordially invited us all to return their visits, and begged mother to allow her children to spend a day with theirs.

We had been resident in our new quarters nearly a month when my parents received an intimation from the teacher of the public school, two miles distant, to the effect that the law demanded that they should send their children to school. It upset my mother greatly. What was she to do?

"Do! Bundle the nippers off to school as quickly as possible, of course," said my father.

My mother objected. She proposed a governess now and a good boarding-school later on. She had heard such dreadful stories of public schools! It was terrible to be compelled to send her darlings to one; they would be ruined in a week!

"Not they," said father. "Run them off for a week or two, or a month at the outside. They can't come to any harm in that time. After that we will get a governess. You are in no state of health to worry about one just now, and it is utterly impossible that I can see about the matter at present. I have several specs. on foot that I must attend to. Send the youngsters to school down here for the present."

We went to school, and in our dainty befrilled pinafores and light shoes were regarded as great swells by the other scholars. They for the most part were the children of very poor farmers, whose farm earnings were augmented by road-work, wood-carting, or any such labor which came within their grasp. All the boys went barefooted, also a moiety of the girls. The school was situated on a wild scrubby hill, and the teacher boarded with a resident a mile from it. He was a man addicted to drink, and the parents of his scholars lived in daily expectation of seeing his dismissal from the service.

It is nearly ten years since the twins (who came next to me) and I were enrolled as pupils of the Tiger Swamp public school. My education was completed there; so was that of the twins, who are eleven months younger than I. Also my other brothers and sisters are quickly getting finishedwards; but that is the only school any of us have seen or known. There was even a time when father spoke of filling in the free forms for our attendance there. But mother—a woman's pride bears more wear than a man's—would never allow us to come to that.

All our neighbors were very friendly; but one in particular, a James Blackshaw, proved himself most desirous of being comradely with us. He was a sort of self-constituted sheik of the community. It was usual for him to take all new-comers under his wing, and with officious good-nature endeavor to make them feel at home. He called on us daily, tied his horse to the paling fence beneath the shade of a sallic-tree in the backyard, and when mother was unable to see him he was content to yarn for an hour or two with Jane Haizelip, our servant-girl.

Jane disliked Possum Gully as much as I did. Her feeling being much more defined, it was amusing to hear the flat-out opinions she expressed to Mr. Blackshaw, whom, by the way, she termed "a mooching hen of a chap."

"I suppose, Jane, you like being here near Goulburn, better than that out-of-the-way place you came from," he said one morning as he comfortably settled himself on an old sofa in the kitchen.

"No jolly fear. Out-of-the-way place! There was more life at Bruggabrong in a day than you crawlers 'ud see here all yer lives," she retorted with vigor, energetically pommelling a batch of bread which she was mixing.

"Why, at Brugga it was as good as a show every week. On Saturday evening all the coves used to come in for their mail. They'd stay till Sunday evenin'. Splitters, boundary-riders, dog-trappers—every man-jack of 'em. Some of us wuz always good fer a toon on the concertina, and the rest would dance. We had fun to no end. A girl could have a fly round and a lark or two there I tell you; but here," and she emitted a snort of contempt, "there ain't one bloomin' feller to do a mash with. I'm full of the place. Only I promised to stick to the missus a while, I'd scoot tomorrer. It's the dead-and-alivest hole I ever seen."

"You'll git used to it by and by," said Blackshaw.

"Used to it! A person 'ud hev to be brought up onder a hen to git used to the dullness of this hole."

"You wasn't brought up under a hen, or it must have been a big Bramer Pooter, if you were," replied he, noting the liberal proportions of her figure as she hauled a couple of heavy pots off the fire. He did not offer to help her. Etiquette of that sort was beyond his ken.

"You oughter go out more and then you wouldn't find it so dull," he said, after she had placed the pots on the floor.

"Go out! Where 'ud I go to, pray?"

"Drop in an' see my missus again when you git time. You're always welcome."

"Thanks, but I had plenty of goin' to see your missus last time."

"How's that?"

"Why, I wasn't there harf an hour when she had to strip off her clean duds an' go an' milk. I don't think much of any of the men around here. They let the women work too hard. I never see such a tired wore-out set of women. It puts me in mind ev the time wen the black fellers made the gins do all the work. Why, on Bruggabrong the women never had to do no out-side work, only on a great pinch wen all the men were away at a fire or a muster. Down here they do every-thing. They do all the milkin', and pig-feedin', and poddy-rarin'. It makes me feel fit to retch. I don't know whether it's because the men is crawlers or whether it's dairyin'. I don't think much of diaryin'. It's slavin', an' delvin', an' scrapin' yer eyeballs out from mornin' to night, and nothink to show for your pains; and now you'll oblige me, Mr. Blackshaw, if you'll lollop some-where else for a minute or two. I want to sweep under that sofer."

This had the effect of making him depart. He said good morning and went off, not sure whether he was most amused or insulted.

CHAPTER FOUR

A Career Which Soon Careered to an End

While mother, Jane Haizelip, and I found the days long and life slow, father was enjoying himself immensely.

He had embarked upon a lively career—that gambling trade known as dealing in stock.

When he was not away in Riverina inspecting a flock of sheep, he was attending the Homebush Fat Stock Sales, rushing away out to Bourke, or tearing off down the Shoalhaven to buy some dairy heifers.

He was a familiar figure at the Goulburn sale-yards every Wednesday, always going into town the day before and not returning till a day, and often two days, afterwards.

He was in great demand among drovers and auctioneers; and in the stock news his name was always mentioned in connection with all the principal sales in the colony.

It takes an astute, clear-headed man to keep himself off shore in stock dealing. I never yet heard of a dealer who occasionally did not temporarily, if not totally, go to the wall.

He need not necessarily be downright unscrupulous, but if he wishes to profit he must not be overburdened with niceties in the point of honor. That is where Richard Melvyn fell through. He was crippled with too many Utopian ideas of honesty, and was too soft ever

13

to come off anything but second-best in a deal. He might as well have attempted to make his fortune by scraping a fiddle up and down Auburn Street, Goulburn. His dealing career was short and merry. His vanity to be considered a socialistic fellow, who was as ready to take a glass with a swaggie as a swell, and the lavish shouting which this principle incurred, made great inroads on his means. Losing money every time he sold a beast, wasting stamps galore on letters to endless auctioneers, frequently remaining in town half a week at a stretch, and being hail-fellow to all the spongers to be found on the trail of such as he, quickly left him on the verge of bankruptcy. Some of his contemporaries say it was grog that did it all.

Had he kept clear-headed he was a smart fellow, and gave promise of doing well, but his head would not stand alcohol, and by it he was undermined in no time. In considerably less than a twelvemonth all the spare capital in his coffers from the disposal of Bruggabrong and the Bin Bins had been squandered. He had become so hard up that to pay the drovers in his last venture he was forced to sell the calves of the few milch-cows retained for household uses.

At this time it came to my father's knowledge that one of our bishops had money held in trust for the Church. On good security he was giving this out for usury, the same as condemned in the big Bible, out of which he took the text of the dry-hash sermons with which he bored his fashionable congregations in his cathedral on Sundays.

Father took advantage of this Reverend's inconsistency and mortgaged Possum Gully. With the money thus obtained he started once more and managed to make a scant livelihood and pay the interest on the bishop's loan. In four or five years he had again reached loggerheads. The price of stock had fallen so that there was nothing to be made out of dealing in them.

Richard Melvyn resolved to live as those around

him—start a dairy; run it with his family, who would also rear poultry for sale.

As instruments of the dairying trade he procured fifty milch-cows, the calves of which had to be "poddied," and a hand cream-separator.

I was in my fifteenth year when we began dairying; the twins Horace and Gertie were, as you already know, eleven months younger. Horace, had there been any one to train him, contained the makings of a splendid man; but having no one to bring him up in the way he should go, he was a churlish and trying bully, and the issue of his character doubtful.

Gertie milked thirteen cows, and I eighteen, morning and evening. Horace and mother, between them, milked the remaining seventeen.

Among the dairying fraternity little toddlers, ere they are big enough to hold a bucket, learn to milk. Thus their hands become inured to the motion, and it does not affect them. With us it was different. Being almost full grown when we started to milk, and then plunging heavily into the exercise, it had a painful effect upon us. Our hands and arms, as far as the elbows, swelled, so that our sleep at night was often disturbed by pain.

Mother made the butter. She had to rise at two and three o'clock in the morning, in order that it would be cool and firm enough to print for market.

Jane Haizelip had left us a year previously, and we could afford no one to take her place. The heavy work told upon my gentle, refined mother. She grew thin and careworn, and often cross. My father's share of the work was to break in the wild cows, separate the milk, and take the butter into town to the grocer's establishment where we obtained our supplies.

Dick Melvyn of Bruggabrong was not recognizable in Dick Melvyn, dairy farmer and cocky of Possum Gully. The former had been a man worthy of the name. The latter was a slave of drink, careless, even dirty and bedraggled in his personal appearance. He disregarded all manners, and had become far more plebeian and

common than the most miserable specimen of humanity around him. The support of his family, yet not its
support. The head of his family, yet failing to fulfill the
obligations demanded of one in that capacity. He
seemed to lose all love and interest in his family, and
grew cross and silent, utterly without pride and pluck.
Formerly so kind and gentle with animals, now he was
the reverse.

His cruelty to the young cows and want of patience
with them I can never forget. It has often brought upon
me the threat of immediate extermination for volunteering scathing and undesired opinions on his conduct.

The part of the dairying that he positively gloried in
was going to town with the butter. He frequently remained in for two or three days, as often as not spending all the money he got for the butter in a drunken
spree. Then he would return to curse his luck because
his dairy did not pay as well as those of some of our
neighbors.

The curse of Eve being upon my poor mother in
those days, she was unable to follow her husband.
Pride forbade her appealing to her neighbors, so on me
devolved the duty of tracking my father from one pub
to another and bringing him home.

Had I done justice to my mother's training I would
have honored my paternal parent in spite of all this,
but I am an individual ever doing things I oughtn't at
the time I shouldn't.

Coming home, often after midnight, with my drunk-
en father talking maudlin conceited nonsense beside
me, I developed curious ideas on the fifth commandment. Those journeys in the spring-cart through the
soft faint starlight were conducive to thought. My
father, like most men when under the influence of
liquor, would allow no one but himself to handle the
reins, and he was often so incapable that he would
keep turning the horse round and round in the one
place. It is a marvel we never met with an accident. I
was not nervous, but quite content to take whatever
came, and our trusty old horse fulfilled his duty, ever

faithfully taking us home along the gum-tree-lined road.

My mother had taught me from the Bible that I should honor my parents, whether they were deserving of honor or not.

Dick Melvyn being my father did not blind me to the fact that he was a despicable, selfish, weak creature, and as such I despised him with the relentlessness of fifteen, which makes no allowance for human frailty and weakness. Disgust, not honor, was the feeling which possessed me when I studied the matter.

Toward mother I felt differently. A woman is but the helpless tool of man—a creature of circumstances.

Seeing my father beside me, and thinking of his infant with its mother, eating her heart out with anxiety at home, this was the reasoning which took possession of me. Among other such inexpressible thoughts I got lost, grew dizzy, and drew back appalled at the spirit which was maturing within me. It was a grim lonely one, which I vainly tried to hide in a bosom which was not big or strong enough for its comfortable habitation. It was a climbing plant without a pole—it groped about the ground, bruised itself, and became hungry searching for something strong to which to cling. Needing a master-hand to train and prune, it was becoming rank and sour.

CHAPTER FIVE

Disjointed Sketches and Grumbles

It was my duty to "rare the poddies." This is the most godless occupation in which it has been my lot to engage. I did a great amount of thinking while feeding them—for, by the way, I am afflicted with the power of thought, which is a heavy curse. The less a person thinks and inquires regarding the why and the wherefore and the justice of things, when dragging along through life, the happier it is for him, and doubly, trebly so, for her.

Poor little calves! Slaves to the greed of man! Bereft of the mothers with which Nature has provided them, and compelled to exist on milk from the separator, often thick, sour, and icy cold.

Besides the milking I did, before I went to school every morning, for which I had to prepare myself and the younger children, and to which we had to walk two miles, I had to feed thirty calves and wash the breakfast dishes. On returning from school in the afternoon, often in a state of exhaustion from walking in the blazing sun, I had the same duties over again, and in addition boots to clean and home lessons to prepare for the morrow. I had to relinquish my piano practice for want of time.

Ah, those short, short nights of rest and long, long days of toil! It seems to me that dairying means slavery in the hands of poor people who cannot afford hired labor. I am not writing of dairy-farming, the genteel and artistic profession as eulogized in leading articles of agricultural newspapers and as taught in agricultural colleges. I am depicting practical dairying as I have lived it, and seen it lived, by dozens of families around me.

It takes a great deal of work to produce even one pound of butter fit for market. At the time I mention it was 3d. and 4d. per lb., so it was much work and small pay. It was slaving and delving from morning till night—Sundays, week-days, and holidays, all alike were work-days to us.

Hard graft is a great leveler. Household drudgery, wood-cutting, milking, and gardening soon roughen the hands and dim the outside polish. When the body is wearied with much toil the desire to cultivate the mind, or the cultivation it has already received, is gradually wiped out. Thus it was with my parents. They had dropped from swelldom to peasantism. They were among and of the peasantry. None of their former acquaintances came within their circle now, for the iron ungodly hand of class distinction has settled surely down upon Australian society—Australia's democracy is only a tradition of the past.

I say naught against the lower life. The peasantry are the bulwarks of every nation. The life of a peasant is, to a peasant who is a peasant with a peasant's soul, when times are good and when seasons smile, a grand life. It is honest, clean, and wholesome. But the life of a peasant to me is purgatory. Those around me worked from morning till night and then enjoyed their well-earned sleep. They had but two states of existence—work and sleep.

There was a third part in me which cried out to be fed. I longed for the arts. Music was a passion with me. I borrowed every book in the neighborhood and stole hours from rest to read them. This told upon me and made my physical burdens harder for me than for other children of my years around me. That third was

the strongest part of me. In it I lived a dream-life with
writers, artists, and musicians. Hope, sweet, cruel, delu-
sive Hope, whispered in my ear that life was long with
much by and by, and in that by and by my dream-life
would be real. So on I went with that gleaming lake in
the distance beckoning me to come and sail on its silver
waters, and Inexperience, conceited, blind Inexperience, failing to show the impassable pit between it and
me.

To return to the dairying.

Old and young alike we earned our scant livelihood
by the heavy sweat of our brows. Still, we *did* gain an
honest living. We were not ashamed to look day in the
face, and fought our way against all odds with the
stubborn independence of our British ancestors. But
when 1894 went out without rain, and '95, hot, dry,
pitiless '95, succeeded it, there came a time when it
was impossible to make a living.

The scorching furnace-breath winds shriveled every
blade of grass, dust and the moan of starving stock
filled the air, vegetables became a thing of the past.
The calves I had reared died one by one, and the cows
followed in their footsteps.

I had left school then, and my mother and father
and I spent the days in lifting our cows. When our
strength proved inadequate, the help of neighbors had
to be called in, and father would give his services in
return. Only a few of our more well-to-do neighbors
had been able to send their stock away, or had any
better place to which to transfer them. The majority of
them were in as tight a plight as ourselves. This cow-
lifting became quite a trade, the whole day being spent
in it and in discussing the bad prospect ahead if the
drought continued.

Many an extra line of care furrowed the brows of the
disheartened bushmen then. Not only was their living
taken from them by the drought, but there is nothing
more heartrending than to have poor beasts, especially
dairy cows, so familiar, valued, and loved, pleading for

food day after day in their piteous dumb way when one has it not to give.

We shore ourselves of all but the bare necessities of life, but even they for a family of ten are considerable, and it was a mighty tussle to get both ends within cover of meeting. We felt the full force of the heavy hand of poverty—the most stinging kind of poverty too, that which still holds up its head and keeps an outside appearance. Far more grinding is this than the poverty inherited from generations which is not ashamed of itself, and has not as an accompaniment the wounded pride and humiliation which attacked us.

Some there are who argue that poverty does not mean unhappiness. Let those try what it is to be destitute of even one companionable friend, what it means to be forced to exist in an alien sphere of society, what it is like to be unable to afford a stamp to write to a friend; let them long as passionately as I have longed for reading and music, and be unable to procure it because of poverty; let poverty force them into doing work against which every fiber of their being revolts, as it has forced me, and then see if their lives will be happy.

My school life had been dull and uneventful. The one incident of any note had been the day that the teacher, better known as old Harris, "stood up" to the inspector. The latter was a precise, collar-and-cuffs sort of little man. He gave one the impression of having all his ideas on the subjects he thought worthy of attention carefully culled and packed in his brain-pan, and neatly labeled, so that he might without fluster pounce upon any of them at a moment's warning. He was gentlemanly and respectable, and discharged his duties punctiliously in a manner reflecting credit on himself and his position, but, comparing the mind of a philanthropist to the Murrumbidgee in breadth, his, in comparison, might be likened to the flow of a bucket of water in a dray-rut.

On the day in question—a precious hot one it was—he had finished examining us in most subjects, and was looking at our copy-books. He looked up from them, ahemed! and fastidiously straightened his waistcoat.

"Mr. Harris!"

"Yes, sir."

"Comparisons are odious, but, unfortunately, I am forced to draw one now."

"Yes, sir."

"This writing is much inferior to that of town scholars. It is very shaky and irregular. Also, I notice that the children seem stupid and dull. I don't like putting it so plainly, but, in fact, ah, they seem to be possessed with the proverbial stupidity of country people. How do you account for this?"

Poor old Harris! In spite of his drunken habits and inability to properly discharge his duties, he had a warm heart and much fellowshiply humanity in him. He understood and loved his pupils, and would not have aspersions cast upon them. Besides, the nip he had taken to brace himself to meet the inspector had been two or three, and they robbed him of the discretion which otherwise might have kept him silent.

"Si-r-r-r, I can and will account for it. Look you at every one of those children. Every one, right down to this little tot," indicating a little girl of five, "has to milk and work hard before and after school, besides walk on an average two miles to and from school in this infernal heat. Most of the elder boys and girls milk on an average fourteen cows morning and evening. You try that treatment for a week or two, my fine gentleman, and then see if your fist doesn't ache and shake so that you can't write at all. See if you won't look a trifle dozy. Stupidity of country people be hanged! If you had to work from morning till night in the heat and dust, and get precious little for it too, I bet you wouldn't have much time to scrape your finger-nails, read science notes, and look smart." Here he took off his coat and shaped up to his superior.

The inspector drew back in consternation.

"Mr. Harris, you forget yourself!"

At this juncture they went outside together. What

happened there we never knew. That is all we heard of the matter except the numerous garbled accounts which were carried home that afternoon.

A DROUGHT IDYLL

"Sybylla, what are you doing? Where is your mother?"

"I'm ironing. Mother's down at the fowl-house seeing after some chickens. What do you want?"

It was my father who addressed me. Time, 2 o'clock p.m. Thermometer hung in the shade of the veranda registering 105½ degrees.

"I see Blackshaw coming across the flat. Call your mother. You bring the leg-ropes—I've got the dog-leg. Come at once; we'll give the cows another lift. Poor devils—might as well knock 'em on the head at once, but there might be rain next moon. This drought can't last for ever."

I called mother, got the leg-ropes, and set off, pulling my sunbonnet closely over my face to protect my eyes from the dust which was driving from the west in blinding clouds. The dog-leg to which father had referred was three poles about eight or ten feet long, strapped together so they could be stood up. It was an arrangement father had devised to facilitate our labor in lifting the cows. A fourth and longer pole was placed across the fork formed by the three, and to one end of this were tied a couple of leg-ropes, after being placed round the beast, one beneath the flank and one around the girth. On the other end of this pole we would put our weight while one man would lift with the tail and another with the horns. New-chum cows would sulk, and we would have great work with them; but those used to the performance would help themselves, and up they'd go as nice as a daisy. The only art needed was to draw the pole back quickly before the cows could move, or the leg-ropes would pull them over again.

On this afternoon we had six cows to lift. We struggled manfully, and got five on their feet, and then proceeded to where the last one was lying, back down-

wards, on a shadeless stony spot on the side of a hill.
The men slewed her around by the tail, while mother
and I fixed the dog-leg and adjusted the ropes. We
got the cow up, but the poor beast was so weak and
knocked about that she immediately fell down again.
We resolved to let her have a few minutes' spell before
making another attempt at lifting. There was not a
blade of grass to be seen, and the ground was too dusty
to sit on. We were too overdone to make more than
one-worded utterances, so waited silently in the blazing
sun, closing our eyes against the dust.

Weariness! Weariness!

A few light wind-smitten clouds made wan streaks
across the white sky, haggard with the fierce relentless
glare of the afternoon sun. Weariness was written
across my mother's delicate careworn features, and
found expression in my father's knitted brows and
dusty face. Blackshaw was weary, and said so, as he
wiped the dust, made mud with perspiration, off his
cheeks. I was weary—my limbs ached with the heat
and work. The poor beast stretched at our feet was
weary. All nature was weary, and seemed to sing a
dirge to that effect in the furnace-breath wind which
roared among the trees on the low ranges at our back
and smote the parched and thirsty ground. All were
weary, all but the sun. He seemed to glory in his power,
relentless and untiring, as he swung boldly in the sky,
triumphantly leering down upon his helpless victims.

Weariness! Weariness!

This was life—my life—my career, my brilliant
career! I was fifteen—fifteen! A few fleeting hours and
I would be old as those around me. I looked at them as
they stood there, weary, and turning down the other
side of the hill of life. When young, no doubt they had
hoped for, and dreamed of, better things—had even
known them. But here they were. This had been their
life; this was their career. It was, and in all probability
would be, mine too. My life—my career—my brilliant
career!

Weariness! Weariness!

The summer sun danced on. Summer is fiendish, and life is a curse, I said in my heart. What a great dull hard rock the world was! On it were a few barren narrow ledges, and on these, by exerting ourselves so that the force wears off our finger-nails, it allows us to hang for a year or two, and then hurls us off into outer darkness and oblivion, perhaps to endure worse torture than this.

The poor beast moaned. The lifting had strained her, and there were patches of hide worn off her the size of breakfast-plates, sore and most harrowing to look upon.

It takes great suffering to wring a moan from the patience of a cow. I turned my head away, and with the impatience and one-sided reasoning common to fifteen, asked God what He meant by this. It is well enough to heap suffering on human beings, seeing it is supposed to be merely a probation for a better world, but animals—poor, innocent animals—why are they tortured so?

"Come now, we'll lift her once more," said my father. At it we went again; it is surprising what weight there is in the poorest cow. With great struggling we got her to her feet once more, and were careful this time to hold her till she got steady on her legs. Father and mother at the tail and Blackshaw and I at the horns, we marched her home and gave her a bran mash. Then we turned to our work in the house while the men sat and smoked and spat on the veranda, discussing the drought for an hour, at the end of which time they went to help someone else with their stock. I made up the fire and we continued our ironing, which had been interrupted some hours before. It was hot unpleasant work on such a day. We were forced to keep the doors and windows closed on account of the wind and dust. We were hot and tired, and our feet ached so that we could scarcely stand on them.

Weariness! Weariness!

Summer is fiendish and life is a curse, I said in my heart.

Day after day the drought continued. Now and again

there would be a few days of the raging wind before
mentioned, which carried the dry grass off the paddocks and piled it against the fences, darkened the air
with dust, and seemed to promise rain, but ever it dispersed whence it came, taking with it the few clouds it
had gathered up; and for weeks and weeks at a stretch,
from horizon to horizon, was never a speck to mar the
cruel dazzling brilliance of the metal sky.

Weariness! Weariness!

I said the one thing many times but, ah, it was a
weary thing which took much repetition that familiarity
might wear away a little of its bitterness!

CHAPTER SIX

Revolt

In spite of our pottering and lifting, with the exception
of five, all our cows eventually died; and even these
and a couple of horses had as much as they could do
to live on the whole of the thousand acres which, without reserve, were at their disposal. They had hardly any
grass—it was merely the warmth and water which kept
them alive. Needless to say, we were on our beam-ends
financially. However, with a little help from more for-
tunate relatives, and with the money obtained from the
sale of the cowhides and mother's poultry, we managed
to pay the interest on the money borrowed from the
bishop, and keep bread in our mouths.

Unfortunately for us, at this time the bishop's agent

proved a scoundrel and absconded. My father held receipts to show that to this agent he had regularly paid the interest of the money borrowed; but through some finicking point of law, because we had not money to contend with him, his lordship the bishop now refused to acknowledge his agent and one-time pillar of the cathedral, and, having law on his side, served a writ on us. In the face of our misfortunes this was too much: we begged for time, which plea he answered by putting in the bailiff and selling everything we possessed. Our five cows, two horses, our milk separator, plough, cart, dray, buggy, even our cooking utensils, books, pictures, furniture, father's watch—our very beds, pillows, and blankets. Not a thing besides what we stood up in was left us, and this was money for the payment of which my father held receipts.

But for the generosity of our relatives we would have been in a pretty plight. They sent us sufficient means to buy in everything, and our neighbors came to our rescue with enthusiasm and warm-hearted genuine sympathy. The bailiff—a gentleman to the core—seeing how matters stood, helped us to the utmost of his power.

Our goods were disposed of on the premises, and the neighbors arranged a mock sale, at which the bailiff winked. Our friends had sent the money, and the neighbors did the bidding—none bidding against each other—and thus our belongings went for a mere trifle. Every cloud has its silver lining, and the black cloud of poverty has a very bright silver lining.

In poverty you can get at the real heart of people as you can never do if rich. People are your friends from pure friendship and love, not from sponging self-interestedness. It is worth being poor once or twice in a lifetime just to experience the blessing and heartrestfulness of a little genuine reality in the way of love and friendship. Not that it is impossible for opulence to have genuine friends, but rich people, I fear, must ever have at their heart cankering suspicion to hint that the friendship and love lavished upon them is merely self-interestedness and sham, the implements of trade used by the fawning toadies who swarm around wealth.

In conjunction with the bishop's name, the approaching sale of our goods had been duly advertised in the local papers, and my father received several letters of sympathy from the clergy deploring the conduct of the bishop. These letters were from men unknown to father, who were unaware that Richard Melvyn was being sold off for a debt already paid.

By the generosity of relatives and the goodness of neighbors as kind as ever breathed, our furniture was our own again, but what were we to do for a living? Our crops were withering in the fields for want of rain, and we had but five cows—not an over-bright outlook. As I was getting to bed one night my mother came into my room and said seriously, "Sybylla, I want to have a talk with you."

"Talk away," I responded rather sullenly, for I expected a long sing-song about my good-for-nothingness in general—a subject of which I was heartily tired.

"Sybylla, I've been studying the matter over a lot lately. It's no use, we cannot afford to keep you at home. You'll have to get something to do."

I made no reply, and my mother continued, "I am afraid we will have to break up the home altogether. It's no use; your father has no idea of making a living. I regret the day I ever saw him. Since he has taken to drink he has no more idea of how to make a living than a cat. I will have to give the little ones to some of the relatives; the bigger ones will have to go out to service, and so will your father and I. That's all I can see ahead of us. Poor little Gertie is too young to go out in the world (she was not twelve months younger than I); she must go to your grandmother, I think."

I still made no reply, so my mother inquired, "Well, Sybylla, what do you think of the matter?"

"Do you think it absolutely necessary to break up the home?" I said.

"Well, you suggest something better if you are so clever," said mother, crossly. "That is always the way;

if I suggest a thing it is immediately put down, yet there is never any one to think of things but me. What would you do? I suppose you think you could make a living on the place for us yourself."

"Why can't we live at home? Blackshaw and Jansen have no bigger places than we, and families just as large, and yet they make a living. It would be terrible for the little ones to grow up separated; they would be no more to each other than strangers."

"Yes; it is all very well for you to talk like that, but how is your father to start again with only five cows in the world? It's no use, you never talk sense. You'll find my way is always the best in the end."

"Would it not be easier," I replied, "for our relations to each give a little toward setting us up again, than to be burdened with the whole responsibility of rearing a child? I'm sure they'd much prefer it."

"Yes, perhaps it would be better, but I think *you* will have to get your own living. What would they say about having to support such a big girl as you are?"

"I will go and earn my own living, and when you get me weeded out of the family you will have a perfect paradise. Having no evil to copy, the children will grow up saints," I said bitterly.

"Now, Sybylla, it is foolish to talk like that, for you know that you take no interest in your work. If you'd turn to and help me rear poultry and make dresses— and why don't you take to cooking?"

"Take to cooking!" I retorted with scorn. "The fire that a fellow has to endure on that old oven would kill a horse, and the grit and dirt of clearing it up grinds on my very nerves. Besides, if I ever do want to do any extra fancy cooking, we either can't afford the butter or the currants, or else the eggs are too scarce! Cook, be grannied!"

"Sybylla! Sybylla, you are getting very vulgar!"

"Yes, I once was foolish enough to try and be polite, but I've given it up. My style of talk is quite good enough for my company. What on earth does it matter whether I'm vulgar or not. I can feed calves and milk

and grind out my days here just as well vulgar as un-
vulgar," I answered savagely.

"There, you see you are always discontented about
your home. It's no use; the only thing is for you to earn
your own living."

"I will earn my own living."

"What will you do? Will you be examined for a
pupil-teacher? That is a very nice occupation for girls."

"What chance would I have in a competitive exam
against Goulburn girls? They all have good teachers
and give up their time to study. I only have old Harris,
and he is the most idiotic old animal alive; besides, I
loathe the very thought of teaching. I'd as soon go on
the wallaby."

"You are not old enough to be a general servant or
a cook; you have not experience enough to be a house-
maid; you don't take to sewing, and there is no chance
of being accepted as a hospital nurse: you must confess there is nothing you can do. You are really a very
useless girl for your age."

"There are heaps of things I could do."

"Tell me a few of them."

I was silent. The professions at which I felt I had the
latent power to excel, were I but given a chance, were
in a sphere far above us, and to mention my feelings
and ambitions to my matter-of-fact practical mother
would bring upon me worse ridicule than I was already
forced to endure day by day.

"Mention a few of the things you could do."

I might as well have named flying as the professions
I was thinking of. Music was the least unmentionable
of them, so I brought it forward.

"Music! But it would take years of training and great
expense before you could earn anything at that! It is
quite out of the question. The only thing for you to do
is to settle down and take interest in your work, and
help make a living at home, or else go out as a nurse-
girl, and work your way up. If you have any ability
in you it would soon show. If you think you could do
such strokes, and the home work is not good enough

for you, go out and show the world what a wonderful creature you are."

"Mother, you are unjust and cruel!" I exclaimed. "You do not understand me at all. I never thought I could do strokes. I cannot help being constituted so that grimy manual labor is hateful to me, for it *is* hateful to me, and I hate it more and more every day, and you can preach and preach till you go black in the face, and still I'll hate it more than ever. If I have to do it all my life, and if I'm cursed with a long life, I'll hate it just as much at the end as I do now. I'm sure it's not any wish of mine that I'm born with inclinations for better things. If I could be born again, and had the designing of myself, I'd be born the lowest and coarsest-minded person imaginable, so that I could find plenty of companionship, or I'd be born an idiot, which would be better still."

"Sybylla!" said my mother in a shocked tone. "It is a wonder God doesn't strike you dead; I never heard——"

"I don't believe there is a God," I said fiercely, "and if there is, He's not the merciful being He's always depicted, or He wouldn't be always torturing me for His own amusement."

"Sybylla, Sybylla! That I should ever have nurtured a child to grow up like this! Do you know that——"

"I only know that I hate this life. I hate it, I hate it, I hate it," I said vehemently.

"Talk about going out to earn your own living! Why, there's not a woman living would have you in her house above a day. You are a perfect she-devil. Oh God!" And my mother began to cry. "What have I done to be cursed with such a child? There is not another woman in the district with such a burden put upon her. What have I done? I can only trust that my prayers to God for you will soften your evil heart."

"If your prayers are answered, it's more than ever mine were," I retorted.

"*Your* prayers!" said my mother, with scorn. "The horror of a child not yet sixteen being so hardened. I don't know what to make of you, you never cry or ask forgiveness. There's dear little Gertie now, she is often naughty, but when I correct her she frets and worries and shows herself to be a human being and not a fiend."

So saying my mother went out of the room.

"I've asked for forgiveness once too often, to be sat upon for my pains," I called out.

"I believe you're mad. That is the only feasible excuse I can make for your conduct," she said as a parting shot.

"Why the deuce don't you two get to bed and not wrangle like a pair of cats in the middle of the night, disturbing a man's rest?" came in my father's voice from amid the bedclothes.

My mother is a good woman—a very good woman—and I am, I think, not quite all criminality, but we do not pull together. I am a piece of machinery which, not understanding, my mother winds up the wrong way, setting all the wheels of my composition going in creaking discord.

She wondered why I did not cry and beg forgiveness, and thereby give evidence of being human. I was too wrought up for tears. Ah, that tears might have come to relieve my overburdened heart! I took up the home-made tallow candle in its tin stick and looked at my pretty sleeping sister Gertie (she and I shared the one bed). It was as mother had said. If Gertie was scolded for any of her shortcomings, she immediately took refuge in tears, said she was sorry, obtained forgiveness, and straightaway forgot the whole matter. She came within the range of mother's understanding, I did not; she had feelings, mother thought, I had none. Did my mother understand me, she would know that I am capable of more depths of agony and more exquisite heights of joy in one day than Gertie will experience in her whole life.

Was I mad as mother had said? A fear took possession of me that I might be. I certainly was utterly different to any girl I had seen or known. What was the hot wild spirit which surged within me? Ah, that I might weep! I threw myself on my bed and moaned. Why was I not like other girls? Why was I not like Gertie? Why were not a new dress, everyday work, and an occasional picnic sufficient to fill my mind? My movements awakened Gertie.

"What is the matter, dear Sybylla? Come to bed. Mother has been scolding you. She is always scolding some one. That doesn't matter. You say you are sorry, and she won't scold any more. That's what I always do. Do get into bed. You'll be tired in the morning."

"What does it matter if I will be. I wish I would be dead. What's the good of a hateful thing like I am being alive. No one wants or cares for me."

"I love you, Sybylla, better than all the rest. I could not do without you," and she put her pretty face to mine and kissed me.

What a balm to the tempest-tossed soul is a little love, though it may be fleeting and fickle! I was able to weep now, with wild hot tears, and with my sister's arms around me I fell asleep without undressing further.

CHAPTER SEVEN

Was E'er a Rose Without Its Thorn?

I arose from bed next morning with three things in my head—a pair of swollen eyes, a heavy pain, and a fixed determination to write a book. Nothing less than a book. A few hours' work in the keen air of a late

autumn morning removed the swelling from my eyes
and the pain from my temples, but the idea of relieving
my feelings in writing had taken firm root in my brain.
It was not my first attempt in this direction. Two years
previously I had purloined paper and sneaked out of
bed every night at one or two o'clock to write a prodi-
gious novel in point of length and detail, in which a
full-fledged hero and heroine performed the duties of a
hero and heroine in the orthodox manner. Knowing
our circumstances, my grandmother was accustomed,
when writing to me, to enclose a stamp to enable me
to reply. These I saved, and with them sent my book
to the leading Sydney publisher. After waiting many
weeks I received a polite memo to the effect that the
story showed great ability, but the writer's inexperience
was too much in evidence for publication. The writer
was to study the best works of literature, and would
one day, no doubt, take a place among Australian
novelists.

This was a very promising opinion of the work of a
child of thirteen, more encouraging than the great writers got at the start of their literary career; but it seemed
to even my childish intelligence that the memo was a
stereotyped affair that the publisher sent in answer to
all the MSS. of fameless writers submitted to him, and
also sent in all probability without reading as much as
the name of the story. After that I wrote a few short
stories and essays; but now the spirit moved me to
write another book—not with any hope of success, as
it was impossible for me to study literature as advised.
I seldom saw a book, and could only spare time in tiny
scraps to read them when I did.

However, the few shillings I had obtained at odd
times I spent on paper, and in secret robbed from
much-needed rest a few hours weekly wherein to write.
This made me very weary and slow in the daytime, and
a sore trial to my mother. I was always forgetting
things I should not have forgotten, because my thoughts
were engaged in working out my story. The want of

rest told upon me. I continually complained of weariness, and my work was a drag to me.

My mother knew not what to make of it. At first she thought I was lazy and bad, and punished me in various ways; but while my book occupied my mind I was not cross, gave her no impudence, and did not flare up. Then she began to fear I must be ill, and took me to a doctor, who said I was much too precocious for my years, and would be better when the weather got warmer. He gave me a tonic, which I threw out the window. I heard no more of going out as nurse-girl: father had joined a neighbor who had taken a road contract, and by this means the pot was kept, if not quite, at least pretty near, boiling.

Life jogged along tamely, and, as far as I could see, gave promise of going to the last slip-rails without a canter, until one day in July 1896 mother received a letter from her mother which made a pleasant change in my life, though, like all sweets, that letter had its bitter drop. It ran as follows:—

My dear daughter, Lucy,

Only a short letter this time. I am pressed for time, as four or five strangers have just come and asked to stay for the night, and as one of the girls is away, I have to get them beds. I am writing about Sybylla. I am truly grieved to hear she is such a source of grief and annoyance to you. The girl must surely be ill or she would never act as you describe. She is young yet, and may settle down better by and by. We can only entrust her to the good God who is ever near. Send her up to me as soon as you can. I will pay all expenses. The change will do her good, and if her conduct improves, I will keep her as long as you like. She is young to mention in regard to marriage, but in another year she will be as old as I was when I married, and it might be the makings of her if she married early. At any rate she will be better away from Possum Gully, now that she is growing into womanhood, or she may be in danger of forming ties beneath her. She might do something good for herself up here: not that I would ever be a match-maker in the least degree, but Gertie will soon be coming on, and Sybylla, being so very plain, will need all the time she can get.

Your loving mother,
L. Bossier.

My mother gave me this letter to read, and, when I had finished perusing it, asked me would I go. I replied coldly:

"Yes. Paupers and beggars cannot be choosers, and grandmother might as well keep me at Caddagat as at Possum Gully"—for my grandmother contributed greatly to the support of our family.

As regards scenery, the one bit of beauty Possum Gully possessed was its wattles. Bowers of grown and scrubs of young ones adorned the hills and gullies in close proximity to the house, while groves of different species graced the flats. Being Sunday, on this afternoon I was at liberty for a few hours; and on receiving the intelligence contained in the letter, I walked out of the house over a low hill at the back into a gully, where I threw myself at the foot of a wattle in a favorite clump, and gave way to my thoughts.

So mother had been telling grandmother of my faults —my grandmother whom I loved so dearly. Mother might have had enough honor and motherly protection to have kept the tale of my sins to herself. Though this intelligence angered, it did not surprise me, being accustomed to mother telling every neighbor what a great trial I was to her—how discontented I was, and what little interest I took in my work. It was the last part of the letter which finished up my feelings. Oh heavens! Surely if my mother understood the wild pain, the days and hours of agony pure and complete I have suffered on account of my appearance, she would never have shown me that letter.

I was to be given more time on account of being

ugly—I was not a valuable article in the marriage market, sweet thought! My grandmother is one of the good old school, who believed that a girl's only proper sphere in life was marriage; so, knowing her sentiments, her purpose to get me married neither surprised nor annoyed me. But I was plain. Ah, bosh! Oh! Ah! I cannot express what kind of a feeling that fact gave me. It sank into my heart and cut like a cruel jagged knife—not because it would be a drawback to me in the marriage line, for I had an antipathy to the very thought of marriage. Marriage to me appeared the most horribly tied-down and unfair-to-women existence going. It would be from fair to middling if there was love; but I laughed at the idea of love, and determined never, never, never to marry.

The other side of the letter—the part which gave me joy—was the prospect of going to Caddagat.

Caddagat, the place where I was born! Caddagat, whereat, enfolded in grandmotherly love and petting which accrued therefrom, I spent some of my few sweet childish days. Caddagat, the place my heart fondly enshrines as home. Caddagat, draped by nature in a dream of beauty. Caddagat, Caddagat! Caddagat for me, Caddagat for ever! I say.

Too engrossed with my thoughts to feel the cold of the dull winter day, I remained in my position against the wattle-tree until Gertie came to inform me that tea was ready.

"You know, Sybylla, it was your turn to get the tea ready; but I set the table to save you from getting into a row. Mother was looking for you, and said she supposed you were in one of your tantrums again."

Pretty little peacemaker! She often did things like that for me.

"Very well, Gertie, thank you. I will set it two evenings running to make up for it—if I'm here."

"If you are here! What do you mean?"

"I am going away," I replied, watching her narrowly to see if she cared, for I was very hungry for love.

"Going to run away because mother is always scolding you?"

"No, you little silly! I'm going up to Caddagat to live with grannie."

"Always?"

"Yes."

"Really?"

"Yes."

"Honor bright?"

"Yes; really and truly and honor bright."

"Won't you ever come back again?"

"I don't know about *never* coming back again; but I'm going up for always, as far as a person can lay out ahead of her. Do you care?"

Yes she cared. The childish mouth quivered, the pretty blue-eyed face fell, the ready tears flowed fast. I noticed every detail with savage comfort. It was more than I deserved, for, though I loved her passionately, I had ever been too much wrapped in self to have been very kind and lovable to her.

"Who will tell me stories now?"

It was a habit of mine to relate stories to her out of my own fertile imagination. In return for this she kept secret the fact that I sat up and wrote when I should have been in bed. I was obliged to take some means of inducing her to keep silence, as she—even Gertie, who firmly believed in me—on waking once or twice at unearthly hours and discovering me in pursuit of my nightly task, had been so alarmed for my sanity that I had the greatest work to prevent her from yelling to father and mother on the spot. But I bound her to secrecy, and took a strange delight in bringing to her face with my stories the laughter, the wide-eyed wonder, or the tears—just as my humor dictated.

"You'll easily get someone else to tell you stories."

"Not like yours. And who will take my part when Horace bullies me?"

I pressed her to me.

"Gertie, Gertie, promise me you will love me a little always, and never, never forget me. Promise me."

And with a weakly glint of winter sunshine turning her hair to gold, and with her head on my shoulder, Gertie promised—promised with the soluble promise of a butterfly-natured child.

SELF-ANALYSIS

N.B.—This is dull and egotistical. Better skip it. That's my advice—S. P. M.

As a tiny child I was filled with dreams of the great things I was to do when grown up. My ambition was as boundless as the mighty bush in which I have always lived. As I grew it dawned upon me that I was a girl— the makings of a woman! Only a girl!—merely this and nothing more. It came home to me as a great blow that it was only men who could take the world by its ears and conquer their fate, while women, metaphorically speaking, were forced to sit with tied hands and patiently suffer as the waves of fate tossed them hither and thither, battering and bruising without mercy. Familiarity made me used to this yoke; I recovered from the disappointment of being a girl, and was reconciled to that part of my fate. In fact, I found that being a girl was quite pleasant until a hideous truth dawned upon me—I was ugly! That truth has embittered my whole existence. It gives me days and nights of agony. It is a sensitive sore that will never heal, a grim hobgoblin that nought can scare away. In conjunction with this brand of hell I developed a reputation of cleverness. Worse and worse! Girls! girls! Those of you who have hearts, and therefore a wish for happiness, homes, and husbands by and by, never develop a reputation of being clever. It will put you out of the matrimonial running as effectually as though it had been circulated that you had leprosy. So, if you feel that you are afflicted with more than ordinary intelligence, and especially if you are plain with it, hide your brains, cramp your mind, study to appear unintellectual—it is your only chance. Provided a woman is beautiful allowance will be made for all her shortcomings. She can be unchaste, vapid, untruthful, flippant, heartless, and even clever; so long as she is fair to see men will stand by her, and as men, in this world, are "the dog on top," they are the power to truckle to. A plain woman will have nothing forgiven her. Her fate is such that the parents of uncomely female infants should be compelled to put them to death at their birth.

The next unpleasant discovery I made in regard to myself was that I was woefully out of my sphere. I studied the girls of my age around me, and compared myself with them. We had been reared side by side. They had had equal advantages; some, indeed, had had greater. We all moved in the one little, dull world, but they were not only in their world, they were of it; I was not. Their daily tasks and their little pleasures provided sufficient oil for the lamp of their existence— mine demanded more than Possum Gully could supply. They were totally ignorant of the outside world. Patti, Melba, Irving, Terry, Kipling, Caine, Corelli, and even the name of Gladstone, were only names to them. Whether they were islands or racehorses they knew not and cared not. With me it was different. Where I obtained my information, unless it was born in me, I do not know. We took none but the local paper regularly, I saw few books, had the pleasure of conversing with an educated person from the higher walks of life about once in a twelvemonth, yet I knew of every celebrity in literature, art, music, and drama; their world was my world, and in fancy I lived with them. My parents discouraged me in that species of foolishness. They had been fond of literature and the higher arts, but now, having no use for them, had lost interest therein.

I was discontented and restless, and longed unendurably to be out in the stream of life. "Action! Action! Give me action!" was my cry. My mother did her best with me according to her lights. She energetically preached at me. All the old saws and homilies were brought into requisition, but without avail. It was like using common nostrums on a disease which could be treated by none but a special physician.

I was treated to a great deal of harping on that tiresome old string, "Whatsoever your hand findeth to do, do it with all your might." It was daily dinned into my ears that the little things of life were the noblest, and that all the great people I mooned about said the same. I usually retorted to the effect that I was well aware that it was noble, and that I could write as good an essay on it as any philosopher. It was all very well for great people to point out the greatness of the little, empty, humdrum life. Why didn't they adopt it themselves?

> *The toad beneath the harrow knows*
> *Exactly where each tooth-point goes.*
> *The butterfly upon the road*
> *Preaches contentment to the toad.*

I wasn't anxious to patronize the dull kind of tame nobility of the toad; I longed for a few of the triumphs of the butterfly, decried though they are as hollow bubbles. I desired life while young enough to live, and quoted as my motto:

> *Though the pitcher that goes to the sparkling rill*
> *Too oft gets broken at last,*
> *There are scores of others its place to fill*
> *When its earth to the earth is cast.*
> *Keep that pitcher at home, let it never roam,*
> *But lie like a useless clod;*
> *Yet sooner or later the hour will come*
> *When its chips are thrown to the sod.*
>
> *Is it wise, then, say, in the waning day,*
> *When the vessel is crack'd and old,*
> *To cherish the battered potter's clay*
> *As though it were virgin gold?*

Take care of yourself, dull, boorish elf,
 Though prudent and sage you seem;
Your pitcher will break on the musty shelf,
 And mine by the dazzling stream.

I had sense sufficient to see the uselessness of attempting to be other than I was. In these days of fierce competition there was no chance for me—opportunity, not talent, was the main requisite. Fate had thought fit to deny me even one advantage or opportunity, thus I was helpless. I set to work to cut my coat according to my cloth. I manfully endeavored to squeeze my spirit into "that state of life into which it has pleased God to call me." I crushed, compressed, and bruised, but as fast as I managed it on one side it burst out on another, and defied me to cram it into the narrow box of Possum Gully.

The restless throbbings and burnings
 That hope unsatisfied brings,
The weary longings and yearnings
 For the mystical better things,
Are the sands on which is reflected
 The pitiless moving lake,
Where the wanderer falls dejected,
 By a thirst he never can slake.

In a vain endeavor to slake that cruel thirst my soul groped in strange dark places. It went out in quest of a God, and finding one not, grew weary.

By the unknown way that the atmosphere of the higher life penetrated to me, so came a knowledge of the sin and sorrow abroad in the world—the cry of the millions oppressed, down-trodden, God-forsaken! The wheels of social mechanism needed readjusting—things were awry. Oh, that I might find a cure and give it to my fellows! I dizzied my brain with the problem; I was too much for myself. A man with these notions is a curse to himself, but a woman—pity help a woman of that description! She is not merely a creature out of her sphere, she is a creature without a sphere—a lonely being!

Recognizing this, I turned and cursed God for casting upon me a burden greater than I could bear—cursed Him bitterly, and from within came a whisper that there was nothing there to curse. There was no God. I was an unbeliever. It was not that I sought after or desired atheism. I longed to be a Christian, and fought against unbelief. I asked the Christians around me for help. Unsophisticated fool! I might as well have announced that I was a harlot. My respectability vanished in one slap. Some said it was impossible to disbelieve in the existence of God: I was only doing it for notoriety, and they washed their hands of me at once.

Not believe in God! I was mad!

If there really was a God, would they kindly tell me how to find Him!

Pray! pray!

I prayed, often and ardently, but ever came that heart-stilling whisper that there was nothing to pray to.

Ah, the bitter, hopeless heart-hunger of godlessness none but an atheist can understand! Nothing to live for in life—no hope beyond the grave. It plunged me into fits of profound melancholy.

Had my father occupied one of the fat positions of the land, no doubt as his daughter my life would have been so full of pleasant occupation and pleasure that I would not have developed the spirit which torments me now. Or had I a friend—one who knew, who had suffered and understood, one in whom I could lose myself, one on whom I could lean—I might have grown a nicer character. But in all the wide world there was not a soul to hold out a hand to me, and I said bitterly, "There is no good in the world." In softer moods I said, "Ah, the tangle of it! Those who have the heart to help have not the power, and those who have the power have not the heart."

Bad, like a too-strong opponent in a game of chess,

is ever at the elbow of good to checkmate it like a weakly managed king.

I am sadly lacking in self-reliance. I needed some one to help me over the rough spots in life, and finding them not, at the age of sixteen I was as rank a cynic and infidel as could be found in three days' march.

CHAPTER EIGHT

Possum Gully Left Behind. Hurrah! Hurrah!

If a Sydney man has friends residing at Goulburn, he says they are up the country. If a Goulburn man has friends at Yass, he says they are up the country. If a Yass man has friends at Young, he says they are up the country, and so on. Caddagat is "up the country."

Bound thither on the second Wednesday in August 1896, I bought a ticket at the Goulburn railway station, and at some time about 1 a.m. took my seat in a second class carriage of the mail-train on its way to Melbourne. I had three or four hours to travel in this train when I would have to change to a branch line for two hours longer. I was the only one from Goulburn in that carriage; all the other passengers had been in some time and were asleep. One or two opened their eyes strugglingly, stared glumly at the intruder, and then went to sleep again. The motion of the train was a joy to me, and sleep never entered my head. I stood up, and pressing my forehead to the cold window-pane, vainly attempted, through the inky blackness of the foggy night, to discern the objects which flew by.

I was too full of pleasant anticipation of what was ahead of me to think of those I had left behind. I did not regret leaving Possum Gully. Quite the reverse; I felt inclined to wave my arms and yell for joy at being freed from it. Home! God forbid that my experiences at Possum Gully should form the only food for my reminiscences of home. I had practically grown up there, but my heart refused absolutely to regard it as home. I hated it then, I hate it now, with its narrowing, stagnant monotony. It has and had not provided me with one solitary fond remembrance—only with dreary, wing-clipping, mind-starving recollections. No, no; I was not leaving home behind, I was flying homeward now. Home, home to Caddagat, home to ferny gullies, to the sweet sad rush of many mountain waters, to the majesty of rugged Borgongs; home to dear old grannie, and uncle and aunt, to books, to music; refinement, company, pleasure, and the dear old homestead I love so well.

All in good time I arrived at the end of my train journey, and was taken in charge by a big red-bearded man, who informed me he was the driver of the mail-coach, and had received a letter from Mrs. Bossier instructing him to take care of me. He informed me also that he was glad to do what he termed "that same," and I would be as safe under his care as I would be in God's pocket.

My twenty-six miles' coach drive was neither pleasant nor eventful. I was the only passenger, and so had my choice of seats. The weather being cold and wet, I preferred being inside the box, and curled myself up on the seat, to be interrupted every two or three miles by the good-natured driver inquiring if I was "all serene."

At the Halfway House, where a change of the team of five horses was affected, I had a meal and a warm, and so tuned myself up for the remainder of the way. It got colder as we went on, and at 2:30 p.m. I was not at all sorry to see the iron roofs of Gool-Gool township disclosing to my view. We first went to the post office, where the mail-bags were delivered, and then returned and pulled rein in front of the Woolpack Hotel. A tall young gentleman in a mackintosh and cap, who had been standing on the veranda, stepped out on the street as the coach stopped, and lifting his cap and thrusting his head into the coach, inquired, "Which is Miss Melvyn?"

Seeing I was the only occupant, he laughed the pleasantest of laughs, disclosing two wide rows of perfect teeth, and turning to the driver, said, "Is that your only passenger? I suppose it *is* Miss Melvyn?"

"As I wasn't present at her birth, I can't swear, but I believe her to be that same, as sure as eggs is eggs," he replied.

My identity being thus established, the young gentleman with the greatest of courtesy assisted me to alight, ordered the hotel groom to stow my luggage in the Caddagat buggy, and harness the horses with all expedition. He then conducted me to the private parlor, where a friendly little barmaid had some refreshments on a tray awaiting me, and while warming my feet preparatory to eating I read the letter he had given me, which was addressed in my grandmother's handwriting. In it she told me that she and my aunt were only just recovering from bad colds, and on account of the inclemency of the weather thought it unwise to come to town to meet me; but Frank Hawden, the jackeroo, would take every care of me, settle the hotel bill, and tip the coach-driver. Caddagat was twenty-four miles distant from Gool-Gool, and the latter part of the road was very hilly. It was already past three o'clock, and, being rainy, the short winter afternoon would close in earlier; so I swallowed my tea and cake with all expedition, so as not to delay Mr. Hawden, who was waiting to assist me into the buggy, where the groom was in charge of the horses in the yard. He struck up a conversation with me immediately.

"Seeing your name on yer bags, an' knowin' you was belonging to the Bossiers, I ask if yer might be a daughter of Dick Melvyn, of Bruggabrong, out by Timlinbilly."

"Yes, I am."

"Well, miss, please remember me most kindly to yer pa; he was a good boss was Dick Melvyn. I hope he's doin' well. I'm Billy Haizelip, brother to Mary and Jane. You remember Jane, I s'pose, miss?"

I hadn't time to say more than promise to send his remembrances to my father, for Mr. Hawden, saying we would be in the dark, had whipped his horses and was bowling off at a great pace, in less than two minutes covering a rise which put Gool-Gool out of sight. It was raining a little, so I held over us the big umbrella, which grannie had sent, while we discussed the weather, to the effect that rain was badly needed and was a great novelty nowadays, and it was to be hoped it would continue. There had been but little, but the soil here away was of that rich loamy description which little water turns to mud. It clogged the wheels and loaded the break-blocks; and the near side horse had a nasty way of throwing his front feet, so that he deposited soft red lumps of mud in our laps at every step. But, despite these trifling drawbacks, it was delightful to be drawn without effort by a pair of fat horses in splendid harness. It was a great contrast to our poor skinny old horse at home, crawling along in much-broken harness, clumsily and much mended with string and bits of hide.

Mr. Hawden was not at all averse to talking. After emptying our tongues of the weather, there was silence for some time, which he broke with, "So you are Mrs. Bossier's grand-daughter, are you?"

"Not remembering my birth, I can't swear; but I believe myself to be that same, as sure as eggs is eggs," I replied.

He laughed. "Very good imitation of the coach-driver. But Mrs. Bossier's grand-daughter! Well, I should smile!"

"What at?"

"Your being Mrs. Bossier's grand-daughter."

"I fear, Mr. Hawden, there is a suspicion of something the reverse of complimentary in your remark."

"Well, I should smile! Would you like to have my opinion of you?"

"Nothing would please me more. I would value your opinion above all things, and I'm sure—I feel certain—that you have formed a true estimate of me."

At any other time his conceit would have brought upon himself a fine snubbing, but today I was in high feather, and accordingly very pleasant, and resolved to amuse myself by drawing him out.

"Well, you are not a bit like Mrs. Bossier or Mrs. Bell; they are both so good-looking," he continued.

"Indeed!"

"I was disappointed when I saw you had no pretensions to prettiness, as there's not a girl up these parts worth wasting a man's affections on, and I was building great hopes on you. But I'm a great admirer of beauty," he twaddled.

"I am very sorry for you, Mr. Hawden. I'm sure it would take quite a paragon to be worthy of such affection as I'm sure yours would be," I replied sympathetically.

"Never mind. Don't worry about it. You're not a bad sort, and I think a fellow could have great fun with you."

"I'm sure, Mr. Hawden, you do me too much honor. It quite exhilarates me to think that I meet with your approval in the smallest degree," I replied with the utmost deference. "You are so gentlemanly and nice that I was alarmed at first lest you might despise me altogether."

"No fear. You needn't be afraid of me; I'm not a bad sort of fellow," he replied with the greatest encouragement.

By his accent and innocent style I detected he was not a colonial, so I got him to relate his history. He was an Englishman by birth, but had been to America, Spain, New Zealand, Tasmania, etc.; by his own make

out had ever been a man of note, and had played Old
Harry everywhere.

I allowed him to gabble away full tilt for an hour on
this subject, unconscious that I had taken the measure
of him, and was grinning broadly to myself. Then I
diverted him by inquiring how long since the wire fence
on our right had been put up. It bore evidence of recent
erection, and had replaced an old cockatoo fence which
I remembered in my childhood.

"Fine fence, is it not? Eight wires, a top rail, and
very stout posts. Harry Beecham had that put up by
contract this year. Twelve miles of it. It cost him a lot:
couldn't get any very low tenders, the ground being so
hard on account of the drought. Those trees are Five-
Bob Downs—see, away over against the range. But I
suppose you know the places better than I do."

We were now within an hour of our destination.
How familiar were many landmarks to me, although
I had not seen them since I was eight years old.

A river ran on our right, occasionally a glimmer of
its noisy waters visible through the shrubbery which
profusely lined its banks. The short evening was drawing to a close. The white mists brought by the rain
were crawling slowly down the hills, and settling in the
hollows of the ranges on our left. A V-shaped rift in
them, known as Pheasant Gap, came into view. Mr.
Hawden said it was well named, as it swarmed with
lyrebirds. Night was falling. The skreel of a hundred
curlews arose from the gullies—how I love their lonely
wail!—and it was quite dark when we pulled up before
the front gate of Caddagat.

A score of dogs rushed yelping to meet us, the front
door was thrown open, lights and voices came streaming out.

I alighted from the buggy feeling rather nervous. I
was a pauper with a bad character. How would my
grandmother receive me? Dear old soul, I had nothing
to fear. She folded me in a great warm-hearted hug,
saying, "Dear me, child, your face is cold. I'm glad
you've come. It has been a terrible day, but we're glad

to have the rain. You must be frozen. Get in to the
fire, child, as fast as you can. Get in to the fire, get in
to the fire. I hope you forgive me for not going to
meet you." And there was my mother's only sister, my
tall graceful aunt, standing beside her, giving me a kiss
and cordial hand-clasp, and saying, "Welcome, Sybylla.
We will be glad to have a young person to brighten up
the old home once more. I am sorry I was too unwell
to meet you. You must be frozen; come to the fire."

My aunt always spoke very little and very quietly,
but there was something in her high-bred style which
went right home.

I could scarcely believe that they were addressing
me. Surely they were making a mistake. This reception
was meant for some grand relative honoring them with
a visit, and not for the ugly, useless, bad little pauper
come to live upon their bounty.

Their welcome did more than all the sermons I had
ever heard put together toward thawing a little of the
pitiless cynicism which encrusted my heart.

"Take the child inside, Helen, as fast as you can,"
said grannie, "while I see that the boy attends to the
horses. The plaguey fellow can't be trusted any further
than the length of his nose. I told him to tie up these
dogs, and here they are yelp-yelping fit to deafen a
person."

I left my wet umbrella on the veranda, and aunt
Helen led me into the dining-room, where a spruce
maid was making a pleasant clatter in laying the table.
Caddagat was a very old style of house, and all the
front rooms opened onto the veranda without any such
preliminary as a hall, therefore it was necessary to pass
through the dining-room to my bedroom, which was a
skillion at the back. While auntie paused for a moment
to give some orders to the maid, I noticed the heavy
silver serviette rings I remembered so well, and the old-
fashioned dinner-plates, and the big fire roaring in the
broad white fireplace; but more than all, the beautiful
pictures on the walls and a table in a corner strewn
with papers, magazines, and several very new-looking

books. On the back of one of these I saw "Corelli," and on another—great joy!—was *Trilby*. From the adjoining apartment, which was the drawing-room, came the sweet full tones of a beautiful piano. Here were three things for which I had been starving. An impulse to revel in them immediately seized me. I felt like clearing the table at a bound, seizing and beginning to read both books, and rushing into the piano and beginning to play upon it there and then, and examine the pictures—all three things at once. Fortunately for the reputation of my sanity, however, aunt Helen had by this time conducted me to a pretty little bedroom, and saying it was to be mine, helped me to doff my cape and hat.

While warming my fingers at the fire my eyes were arrested by a beautiful portrait hanging above the mantelpiece. It represented a lovely girl in the prime of youth and beauty, and attired in floating white dinner draperies.

"Oh, aunt Helen! isn't she lovely? It's you, isn't it?"

"No. Do you not recognize it as your mother? It was taken just before her marriage. I must leave you now, but come out as soon as you arrange yourself—your grandmother will be anxious to see you."

When aunt Helen left me I plastered my hair down in an instant without even a glance in the mirror. I took not a particle of interest in my attire, and would go about dressed anyhow. This was one symptom which inclined my mother to the belief of my possible insanity, as to most young girls dress is a great delight. I had tried once or twice to make myself look nice by dressing prettily, but, by my own judgment, considering I looked as ugly as ever, I had given it up as a bad job.

The time which I should have spent in arranging my toilet passed in gazing at my mother's portrait. It was one of the loveliest faces imaginable. The features may not have been perfect according to rule of thumb, but the expression was simply angelic—sweet, winning, gentle, and happy. I turned from the contemplation of it to another photograph—one of my father—in a silver frame on the dressing-table. This, too, was a fine countenance, possessed of well-cut features and refined expression. This was the prince who had won Lucy Bossier from her home. I looked around my pretty bedroom—it had been my mother's in the days of her maidenhood. In an exclusive city boarding-school, and amid the pleasant surroundings of this home, her youth had been spent.

I thought of a man and his wife at Possum Gully. The man was blear-eyed, disreputable in appearance, and failed to fulfill his duties as a father and a citizen. The woman was work-roughened and temper-soured by endless care and an unavailing struggle against poverty. Could that pair possibly be identical with this?

This was life as proved by my parents! What right had I to expect any better yield from it? I shut my eyes and shuddered at the possibilities and probabilities of my future. It was for this that my mother had yielded up her youth, freedom, strength; for this she had sacrificed the greatest possession of woman.

Here I made my way to the dining-room, where grannie was waiting for me and gave me another hug.

"Come here, child, and sit beside me near the fire; but first let me have a look at you," and she held me at arm's length.

"Dear, oh, dear, what a little thing you are, and not a bit like any of your relations! I am glad your skin is so nice and clear; all my children had beautiful complexions. Goodness me, I never saw such hair! A plait thicker than my arm and almost to your knees! It is that beautiful bright brown like your aunt's. Your mother's was flaxen. I must see your hair loose when you are going to bed. There is nothing I admire so much as a beautiful head of hair."

The maid announced that dinner was ready, grannie vigorously rang a little bell, aunt Helen, a lady, and a gentleman appeared from the drawing-room, and Mr. Hawden came in from the back. I discovered that the lady and gentleman were a neighboring squatter and a new governess he was taking home. Grannie, seeing them pass that afternoon in the rain, had gone out and prevailed upon them to spend the night at Caddagat.

Mr. Hawden took no notice of me now, but showed off to the others for my benefit. After dinner we had music and singing in the drawing-room. I was enjoying it immensely, but grannie thought I had better go to bed, as I had been traveling since about midnight last night. I was neither tired nor sleepy, but knew it useless to protest, so bade every one good night and marched off. Mr. Hawden acknowledged my salute with great airs and stiffness, and aunt Helen whispered that she would come and see me by and by, if I was awake.

Grannie escorted me to my room, and examined my hair. I shook it out for her inspection. It met with her approval in every way. She pronounced it beautifully fine, silky, and wavy, and the most wonderful head of hair she had seen out of a picture.

A noise arose somewhere out in the back premises. Grannie went out to ascertain the cause of it and did not return to me, so I extinguished my lamp and sat thinking in the glow of the firelight.

For the first time my thoughts reverted to my leave-taking from home. My father had kissed me with no more warmth than if I had been leaving for a day only; my mother had kissed me very coldly, saying shortly, "It is to be hoped, Sybylla, that your behavior to your grandmother will be an improvement upon what it has ever been to me." Gertie was the only one who had felt any sorrow at parting with me, and I knew that she was of such a disposition that I would be forgotten in a day or two. They would never miss me, for I had no place in their affections. True, I was an undutiful child, and deserved none. I possessed no qualities that would win either their pride or love, but my heart cried out in love for them.

Would Gertie miss me tonight, as I would have missed her had our positions been reversed? Not she. Would my absence from the noisy tea-table cause a blank? I feared not.

I thought of poor mother left toiling at home, and my heart grew heavy; I failed to remember my father's faults, but thought of his great patience with me in the years agone, and all my old-time love for him renewed itself. Why, oh, why, would they not love me a little in return! Certainly I had never striven to be lovable. But see the love some have lavished upon them without striving for it! Why was I ugly and nasty and miserable and useless—without a place in the world?

CHAPTER NINE

Aunt Helen's Recipe

"Dear me, Sybylla, not in bed yet, and tears, great big tears! Tell me what is the cause of them."

It was aunt Helen's voice; she had entered and lit the lamp.

There was something beautifully sincere and real about aunt Helen. She never fussed over any one or pretended to sympathize just to make out how nice she was. She was real, and you felt that no matter what wild or awful rubbish you talked to her it would never be retailed for any one's amusement—and, better than all, she never lectured.

She sat down beside me, and I impulsively threw my arms around her neck and sobbed forth my troubles in a string. How there was no good in the world, no use for me there, no one loved me or ever could on account of my hideousness.

She heard me to the end and then said quietly, "When you are fit to listen I will talk to you."

I controlled myself instantly and waited expectantly. What would she say? Surely not that tame old yarn anent this world being merely a place of probation, wherein we were allowed time to fit ourselves for a beautiful world to come. That old tune may be all very well for old codgers tottering on the brink of the grave, but to young persons with youth and romance and good health surging through their veins, it is most boresome. Would she preach that it was flying in the face of providence to moan about my appearance? it being one of the greatest blessings I had, as it would save me from countless temptations to which pretty girls are born. That was another piece of old croaking of the Job's comforter order, of which I was sick unto death, as I am sure there is not an ugly person in the world who thinks her lack of beauty a blessing to her. I need not have feared aunt Helen holding forth in that strain. She always said something brave and comforting which made me ashamed of myself and my selfish conceited egotism.

"I understand you, Sybylla," she said slowly and distinctly, "but you must not be a coward. There is any amount of love and good in the world, but you must search for it. Being misunderstood is one of the trials we all must bear. I think that even the most common-minded person in the land has inner thoughts and feelings which no one can share with him, and the higher one's organization the more one must suffer in that respect. I am acquainted with a great number of young girls, some of them good and true, but you have a character containing more than any three of them put together. With this power, if properly managed, you can gain the almost universal love of your fellows. But you are wild and wayward, you must curb and strain your spirit and bring it into subjection, else you will be worse than a person with the emptiest of characters. You will find that plain looks will not prevent you from gaining the *friendship* love of your fellows—

the only real love there is. As for the hot fleeting passion of the man for the maid, which is wrongfully designated love, I will not tell you not to think of it, knowing that it is human nature to demand it when arriving at a certain age; but take this comfort: it as frequently passes by on the other side of those with well-chiseled features as those with faces of plainer mold."

She turned her face away, sighed, and forgetful of my presence lapsed into silence. I knew she was thinking of herself.

Love, not *friendship* love, for anyone knowing her must give her love and respect, but the other sort of love had passed her by.

Twelve years before I went to Caddagat, when Helen Bossier had been eighteen and one of the most beautiful and lovable girls in Australia, there had come to Caddagat on a visit a dashing colonel of the name of Bell, in the enjoyment of a most extended furlough for the benefit of his health. He married aunt Helen and took her to some part of America where his regiment was stationed. I have heard them say she worshiped Colonel Bell, but in less than a twelvemonth he tired of his lovely bride, and becoming enamored of another woman, he tried to obtain a divorce. On account of his wife's spotless character he was unable to do this; he therefore deserted her and openly lived with the other woman as his mistress. This forced aunt Helen to return to Caddagat, and her mother had induced her to sue for a judicial separation, which was easily obtained.

When a woman is separated from her husband it is the religion of the world at large to cast the whole blame on the wife. By reason of her youth and purity Mrs. Bell had not as much to suffer in this way as some others. But, comparatively speaking, her life was wrecked. She had been humiliated and outraged in the cruelest way by the man whom she loved and trusted. He had turned her adrift, neither a wife, widow, nor maid, and here she was, one of the most estimably lovable and noble women I have ever met.

"Come, Sybylla," she said, starting up brightly, "I have a plan—will you agree to it? Come and take one good long look at yourself in the glass, then I will turn it to the wall, and you must promise me that for three or four weeks you will not look in a mirror. I will put as many as I can out of your way, and you must avoid the remainder. During this time I will take you in hand, and you must follow my directions implicitly. Will you agree? You will be surprised what a nice-looking little girl I will make of you."

Of course I agreed. I took a long and critical survey of myself in the glass. There was reflected a pair of hands, red and coarsened with rough work, a round face, shiny and swollen with crying, and a small round figure enshrouded in masses of hair falling in thick waves to within an inch or two of the knees. A very ugly spectacle, I thought. Aunt Helen turned the face of the large mirror flat against the wall, while I remarked despondently, "If you can make me only middling ugly, you must be a magician."

"Come now, part of my recipe is that you must not think of yourself at all. I'll take you in hand in the morning. I hope you will like your room; I have arranged it on purpose to suit you. And now good night, and happy dreams."

I awoke next morning in very fine spirits, and slithering out of my bed with alacrity, reveled—literally wallowed—in the appointments of my room. My poor old room at Possum Gully was lacking in barest necessaries. We could not afford even a wash-hand basin and jug; Gertie, the boys, and myself had to perform our morning ablutions in a leaky tin dish on a stool outside the kitchen door, which on cold frosty mornings was a pretty peppery performance: but this room contained everything dear to the heart of girlhood. A lovely bed, pretty slippers, dainty white China-matting and many soft skins on the floor, and in one corner a most artistic toilet set, and a wash-stand liberally supplied with a great variety of soap—some of it so exquisitely perfumed that I felt tempted to taste it. There were pretty pictures on the walls, and on a commodious dressing-table a big mirror and large hand-glasses, with their faces to the wall at present. Hairpins, fancy combs, ribbons galore, and a pretty work-basket greeted my sight, and with delight I swooped down upon the most excruciatingly lovely little writing-desk. It was stuffed full with all kinds of paper of good quality— fancy, all colors, sizes, and shapes, plain, foreign note, pens, ink, and a generous supply of stamps. I felt like writing a dozen letters there and then, and was on the point of giving way to my inclination, when my attention was arrested by what I considered the gem of the whole turn-out. I refer to a nice little bookcase containing copies of all our Australian poets, and two or three dozen novels which I had often longed to read. I read the first chapters of four of them, and then lost myself in Gordon, and sat on my dressing-table in my night-gown, regardless of cold, until brought to my senses by the breakfast-bell. I made great pace, scrambled into my clothes helter-skelter, and appeared at table when the others had been seated and unfolded their servi-ettes.

Aunt Helen's treatment for making me presentable was the wearing of gloves and a shady hat every time I went outside; and she insisted upon me spending a proper time over my toilet, and would not allow me to encroach upon it with the contents of my bookshelf.

"Rub off some of your gloomy pessimism and culti-vate a little more healthy girlish vanity, and you will do very well," she would say.

I observed these rites most religiously for three days. Then I contracted a slight attack of influenza, and in poking around the kitchen, doing one of the things I oughtn't at the time I shouldn't, a servant-girl tipped a pot of boiling pot-liquor over my right foot, scalding it rather severely. Aunt Helen and grannie put me to bed, where I yelled with pain for hours like a mad Red Indian, despite their applying every alleviative possible. The combined forces of the burn and influenza made me a trifle dicky, so a decree went forth that I was to stay in bed until recovered from both complaints. This effectually prevented me from running in the way of any looking-glasses.

I was not sufficiently ill to be miserable, and being a pampered invalid was therefore fine fun. Aunt Helen was a wonderful nurse. She dressed my foot splendidly every morning, and put it in a comfortable position many times throughout the day. Grannie brought me every dainty in the house, and sent special messengers to Gool-Gool for more. Had I been a professional glutton I would have been in paradise. Even Mr. Hawden condescended so far as to express his regret concerning the accident, and favored me with visits throughout each day; and one Sunday his gallantry carried him to a gully where he plucked a bouquet of maidenhair fern—the first of the season—and put them in a bowl beside my bed. My uncle Julius, the only other member of the family besides the servants, was away "up the country" on some business or another, and was not expected home for a month or so.

The Bossiers and Beechams were leaders of swell-dom among the squattocracy up the country, and firm and intimate friends. The Beechams resided at Five-Bob Downs, twelve miles from Caddagat, and were a family composed of two maiden ladies and their nephew, Harold. One of these ladies was aunt Helen's particular friend, and the other had stood in the same capacity to my mother in days gone by, but of late years, on account of her poverty, mother had been too proud to keep up communication with her. As for Harold Beecham, he was nearly as much at home at Caddagat as at Five-Bob Downs. He came and went with that pleasant familiarity practiced between congenial spirits among squatterdom. The Bossiers and Beechams were congenial spirits in every way—they lived in the one sphere and held the one set of ideas, the only difference between them, and that an unnoticeable one, being that the Bossiers, though in comfortable circumstances, were not at all rich, while Harold Beecham was immensely wealthy. When my installa-

tion in the role of invalid took place, one Miss Beecham
was away in Melbourne, and the other not well enough
to come and see me, but Harold came regularly to inquire how I was progressing. He always brought me a
number of beautiful apples. This kindness was because
the Caddagat orchard had been too infested with codlin
moth for grannie to save any last season.

Aunt Helen used to mischievously tease me about
this attention.

"Here comes Harry Beecham with some more apples," she would say. "No doubt he is far more calcu-
lating and artful than I thought he was capable of
being. He is taking time by the forelock and wooing
you ere he sees you, and so will take the lead. Young
ladies are in the minority up this way, and every one is
snapped up as soon as she arrives."

"You'd better tell him how ugly I am, auntie, so that
he will carry apples twelve miles on his own responsibility, and when he sees me won't be vexed that all his
work has been for nothing. Perhaps, though, it would
be better not to describe me, or I will get no more
apples," I would reply.

Aunt Helen was a clever needlewoman. She made all
grannie's dresses and her own. Now she was making
some for me, which, however, I was not to see until I
wore them. Aunt Helen had this as a pleasant surprise, and went to the trouble of blindfolding me while
I was being fitted. While in bed, grannie and auntie
being busy, I was often left hours alone, and during
that time devoured the contents of my bookshelf.

The pleasure, so exquisite as to be almost pain, which
I derived from the books, and especially the Australian
poets, is beyond description. In the narrow peasant life
of Possum Gully I had been deprived of companionship with people of refinement and education who
would talk of the things I loved; but, at last! here was
congeniality, here was companionship.

The weird witchery of mighty bush, the breath of
wide sunlit plains, the sound of camp-bells and jingle

of hobble chains, floating on the soft twilight breezes, had come to these men and had written a tale on their hearts as had been written on mine. The glory of the starlit heavens, the mighty wonder of the sea, and the majesty of thunder had come home to them, and the breathless fullness of the sunset hour had whispered of something more than the humor of tomorrow's weather. The wind and rain had a voice which spoke to Kendall, and he too had endured the misery of lack of companionship. Gordon, with his sad, sad humanism and bitter disappointment, held out his hand and took me with him. The regret of it all was I could never meet them—Byron, Thackeray, Dickens, Longfellow, Gordon, Kendall, the men I loved, all were dead; but, blissful thought! Caine, Paterson, and Lawson were still living, breathing human beings—two of them actually countrymen, fellow Australians!

I pored with renewed zeal over the terse realism and pathos of Lawson, and enjoyed Paterson's redolence of the rollicking side of the wholesome life beneath these sunny skies, which he depicted with grand touches of power flashing here and there. I learned them by heart, and in that gloriously blue receptacle, by and by, where many pleasant youthful dreams are stowed, I put the hope that one day I would clasp hands with them, and feel and know the unspeakable comfort and heart-rest of congenial companionship.

CHAPTER TEN

Everard Grey

Uncle Julius had taken a run down to Sydney before returning to Caddagat, and was to be home during the first week in September, bringing with him Everard Grey. This young gentleman always spent Christmas at Caddagat, but as he had just recovered from an illness he was coming up for a change now instead. Having heard much of him, I was curious to see him. He was grandmamma's adopted son, and was the orphan of very aristocratic English parents who had left him to the guardianship of distant relatives. They had proved criminally unscrupulous. By finding a flaw in deeds, or something which none but lawyers understand, they had deprived him of all his property and left him to sink or swim. Grannie had discovered, reared, and educated him. Among professions he had chosen the bar, and was now one of Sydney's most promising young barristers. His foster-mother was no end proud of him, and loved him as her own son.

In due time a telegram arrived from uncle Julius, containing instructions for the buggy to be sent to Gool-Gool to meet him and Everard Grey.

By this time I had quite recovered from influenza and my accident, and as they would not arrive till near nightfall, for their edification I was to be dressed in full-blown dinner costume, also I was to be favored with a look at my reflection in a mirror for the first time since my arrival.

During the afternoon I was dispatched by grannie on a message some miles away, and meeting Mr. Hawden some distance from the house, he took it upon himself to accompany me. Everywhere I went he followed after, much to my annoyance, because grannie gave me many and serious talkings-to about the crime of encouraging young men.

Frank Hawden had changed his tune, and told me now that it mattered not that I was not pretty, as pretty or not I was the greatest brick of a girl he had met. His idea for this opinion was that I was able to talk theaters with him, and was the only girl there, and because he had arrived at that overflowing age when young men have to be partial to some female whether she be ugly or pretty, fat or lean, old or young. That I should be the object of these puerile emotions in a fellow like Frank Hawden, filled me with loathing and disgust.

It was late in the afternoon when Hawden and I returned, and the buggy was to be seen a long way down the road, approaching at the going-for-the-doctor pace at which uncle Julius always drove.

Aunt Helen hustled me off to dress, but I was only half-rigged when they arrived, and so was unable to go out and meet them. Uncle Julius inquired for that youngster of Lucy's, and aunt Helen replied that she would be forthcoming when they were dressed for dinner. The two gentlemen took a nip, to put a little heart in them uncle Julius said, and auntie Helen came to finish my toilet while they were making theirs.

"There now, you have nothing to complain of in the way of looks," she remarked at the completion of the ceremony. "Come and have a good look at yourself."

I was decked in my first evening dress, as it was a great occasion. It was only on the rarest occasion that we donned full war-paint at Caddagat. I think that evening dress is one of the prettiest and most idiotic customs extant. What can be more foolish than to endanger one's health by exposing at night the chest and arms—two of the most vital spots of the body—which have been covered all day? On the other hand, what can be more beautiful than a soft white bosom rising and falling amid a dainty nest of silk and lace? Every woman looks more soft and feminine in a *décolleté* gown. And is there any of the animal lines known pleasanter to the eye than the contour of shapely arms? Some there are who cry down evening dress as being immodest and indecent. These will be found among those whose chest and arms will not admit of being displayed, or among those who, not having been reared to the custom, dislike it with many other things from want of use.

Aunt Helen took me into the wide old drawing-room, now brilliantly lighted. A heavy lamp was on each of the four brackets in the corners, and another swung from the center of the ceiling, and candelabra threw many lights from the piano. Never before had I seen this room in such a blaze of light. During the last week or two aunt Helen and I had occupied it every night, but we never lighted more than a single candle on the piano. This had been ample light for our purpose. Aunt Helen would sing in her sweet sad voice all the beautiful old songs I loved, while I curled myself on a mat at her side and read books—the music often compelling me to forget the reading, and the reading occasionally rendering me deaf to the music; but through both ever came the solemn rush of the stream outside in its weird melancholy, like a wind ceaselessly endeavoring to outstrip a wild vain regret which relentlessly pursued.

"Your uncle Julius always has the drawing-room lighted like this; he does not believe in shadowy half light—calls it sentimental bosh," said aunt Helen in explanation.

"Is uncle like that?" I remarked, but my question remained unanswered. Leaving a hand-mirror with me, aunt Helen had slipped away.

One wall of the drawing-room was monopolized by a door, a big bookcase, and a heavy beveled-edged old-fashioned mirror—the two last-mentioned articles reaching from floor to ceiling. Since my arrival the face of the mirror had been covered, but this evening the blue silken curtains were looped up, and it was before this that I stood.

I looked, and looked again in pleased surprise. I beheld a young girl with eyes and skin of the clearest and brightest, and lips of brilliant scarlet, and a chest and pair of arms which would pass muster with the best. If Nature had been in bad humor when molding my face, she had used her tools craftily in forming my figure. Aunt Helen had proved a clever maid and dressmaker. My pale blue cashmere dress fitted my fully developed yet girlish figure to perfection. Some of my hair fell in cunning little curls on my forehead; the remainder, tied simply with a piece of ribbon, hung in thick waves nearly to my knees. My toilet had altered me almost beyond recognition. It made me look my age—sixteen years and ten months—whereas before, when dressed carelessly and with my hair plastered in a tight coil, people not knowing me would not believe that I was under twenty. Joy and merriment lit up my face, which glowed with youth, health, and happiness, which rippled my lips in smiles, which displayed a splendid set of teeth, and I really believe that on that night I did not look out of the way ugly.

I was still admiring my reflection when aunt Helen returned to say that Everard and uncle Julius were smoking on the veranda and asking for me.

"What do you think of yourself, Sybylla?"

"Oh, aunt Helen, tell me that there is something about me not completely hideous!"

She took my face between her hands, saying:

"Silly child, there are some faces with faultless features, which would receive nothing more than an indifferent glance while beside other faces which might have few if any pretensions to beauty. Yours is one of those last mentioned."

"But that does not say I am not ugly."

"No one would dream of calling you plain, let alone ugly; brilliant is the word which best describes you."

Uncle Julius had the upper part of his ponderous figure arrayed in a frock-coat. He did not take kindly to what he termed "those skittish sparrow-tailed affairs." Frock-coats suited him, but I am not partial to them on every one. They look well enough on a podgy, fat, or broad man, but on a skinny one they hang with such a forlorn, dying-duck expression, that they invariably make me laugh.

Julius John Bossier, better known as J. J. Bossier, and better still as Jay-Jay—big, fat, burly, broad, a jovial bachelor of forty, too fond of all the opposite sex ever to have settled his affections on one in particular—was well known, respected, and liked from Wagga Wagga to Albury, Forbes to Dandaloo, Bourke to Hay, from Tumut to Monaro, and back again to Peak Hill, as a generous man, a straight goer in business matters, and a jolly good fellow all around.

I was very proud to call him uncle.

"So this is yourself, is it!" he exclaimed, giving me a tremendous hug.

"Oh, uncle," I expostulated, "I'll wipe your old kisses off! Your breath smells horribly of whisky and tobacco."

"Gammon, that's what makes my kisses so nice!" he answered; and, after holding me at arm's-length for inspection, "By George, you're a wonderful-looking girl! You're surely not done growing yet, though! You are such a little nipper. I could put you in my pocket with ease. You aren't a scrap like your mother. I'll give the next shearer who passes a shilling to cut that hair off. It would kill a dog in the hot weather."

"Everard, this is my niece, Sybylla" (aunt Helen was introducing us). "You will have to arrange yourselves—what relation you are, and how to address each other."

The admiration expressed in his clear sharp eyes gave me a sensation different to any I had ever experienced previously.

"I suppose I'm a kind of uncle and brother in one, and as either relationship entitles me to a kiss, I'm going to take one," he said in a very gallant manner.

"You may take one if you can," I said with mischievous defiance, springing off the veranda into the flower-garden. He accepted my challenge, and, being lithe as a cat, a tremendous scamper ensued. Round and round the flower-beds we ran. Uncle Jay-Jay's beard opened in a broad smile, which ended in a loud laugh. Everard Grey's coat-tails flew in the breeze he made, and his collar was too high for athletic purposes. I laughed too, and was lost, and we returned to the veranda—Everard in triumph, and I feeling very red and uncomfortable.

Grannie had arrived upon the scene, looking the essence of brisk respectability in a black silk gown and a white lace cap. She cast on me a glance of severe disapproval, and denounced my conduct as shameful; but uncle Jay-Jay's eyes twinkled as he dexterously turned the subject.

"Gammon, mother! I bet you were often kissed when that youngster's age. I bet my boots now that you can't count the times you did the same thing yourself. Now, confess."

Grannie's face melted in a smile as she commenced a little anecdote, with that pathetic beginning, "When I was young."

Aunt Helen sent me inside lest I should catch cold, and I stationed myself immediately inside the window so that I should not miss the conversation. "I should think your niece is very excitable," Mr. Grey was saying to aunt Helen.

"Oh, very."

"Yes; I have never seen any but very highly strung temperaments have that transparent brilliance of expression."

"She is very variable—one moment all joy, and the next the reverse."

"She has a very striking face. I don't know what it is that makes it so."

"It may be her complexion," said aunt Helen; "her skin is whiter than the fairest blonde, and her eyebrows

and lashes very dark. Be very careful you do not say
anything that would let her know you think her not
nice looking. She broods over her appearance in such a
morbid manner. It is a weak point with her, so be careful not to sting her sensitiveness in that respect."

"Plain-looking! Why, I think she has one of the most
fascinating faces I've seen for some time, and her eyes
are simply magnificent. What color are they?"

"The grass is not bad about Sydney. I think I will
send a truck of fat wethers away next week," said uncle
Jay-Jay to grannie.

"It is getting quite dark. Let's get in to dinner at
once," said grannie.

During the meal I took an opportunity of studying
the appearance of Everard Grey. He had a typically
aristocratic English face, even to the cold rather heartless expression, which is as established a point of an
English blue blood as an arched neck is of a thoroughbred horse.

A ringer, whose wife had been unexpectedly con-
fined, came for grannie when dinner was over, and the
rest of us had a delightful musical evening. Uncle Jay-
Jay bawled "The Vicar of Bray" and "Drink, Puppy,
Drink" in a stentorian bass voice, holding me on his
knee, pinching, tickling, pulling my hair, and shaking
me up and down between whiles. Mr. Hawden favored
us by rendering "The Holy City." Everard Grey sang
several new songs, which was a great treat, as he had a
well-trained and musical baritone voice. He was a
veritable carpet knight, and though not a fop, was exquisitely dressed in full evening costume, and showed
his long pedigreed blood in every line of his clean-
shaven face and tall slight figure. He was quite a cham-
pion on the piano, and played aunt Helen's accom-
paniments while he made her sing song after song.
When she was weary uncle Jay-Jay said to me, "Now
it's your turn, me fine lady. We've all done something
to keep things rolling but you. Can you sing?"

"No."

"Can this youngster sing, Helen?"

"She sings very nicely to herself sometimes, but I do not know how she would manage before company. Will you try something, Sybylla?"

Uncle Jay-Jay waited to hear no more, but carrying me to the music-stool, and depositing me thereon, warned me not to attempt to leave it before singing something.

To get away to myself, where I was sure no one could hear me, and sing and sing till I made the echoes ring, was one of the chief joys of my existence, but I had never made a success in singing to company. Besides losing all nerve, I had a very queer voice, which every one remarked. However, tonight I made an effort in my old favorite, "Three Fishers Went Sailing." The beauty of the full-toned Ronisch piano, and Everard's clever and sympathetic accompanying, caused me to forget my audience, and sing as though to myself alone, forgetting that my voice was odd.

When the song ceased Mr. Grey wheeled abruptly on the stool and said, "Do you know that you have one of the most wonderful natural voices I have heard. Why, there is a fortune in such a voice if it were trained! Such chest-notes, such feeling, such rarity of tone!"

"Don't be sarcastic, Mr. Grey," I said shortly.

"Upon my word as a man, I mean every word I say," he returned enthusiastically.

Everard Grey's opinion on artistic matters was considered worth having. He dabbled in all the arts—writing, music, acting, and sketching, and went to every good concert and play in Sydney. Though he was clever at law, it was whispered by some that he would wind up on the stage, as he had a great leaning that way.

I walked away from the piano treading on air. Would I really make a singer? I with the voice which had often been ridiculed; I who had often blasphemously said that I would sell my soul to be able to sing just passably. Everard Grey's opinion gave me an intoxicated sensation of joy.

"Can you recite?" he inquired.

"Yes," I answered firmly.

"Give us something," said uncle Jay-Jay.

I recited Longfellow's "The Slave's Dream." Everard Grey was quite as enthusiastic over this as he had been about my singing.

"Such a voice! Such depth and width! Why, she could fill the Centennial Hall without an effort. All she requires is training."

"By George, she's a regular dab! But I wish she would give us something not quite so glum," said uncle Jay-Jay.

I let myself go. Carried away by I don't know what sort of a spirit, I exclaimed, "Very well, I will, if you will wait till I make up, and will help me."

I disappeared for a few minutes, and returned made up as a fat old Irish woman, with a smudge of dirt on my face. There was a general laugh.

Would Mr. Hawden assist me? Of course he was only too delighted, and flattered that I had called upon him in preference to the others. What would he do?

I sat him on a footstool, so that I might with facility put my hand on his sandy hair, and turning to uncle, commenced:

"Shure, sir, seeing it was a good bhoy yez were afther to run errants, it's meself that has brought this youngsther for yer inspection. It's a jool ye'll have in him. Shure I rared him meself, and he says his prayers every morning. Kape sthill, honey! Faith, ye're not afraid of yer poor old mammy pullin' yer beautiful cur-r-rls?"

Uncle Jay-Jay was laughing like fun; even aunt Helen deigned to smile; and Everard was looking on with critical interest.

"Go on," said uncle. But Mr. Hawden got huffy at the ridicule which he suspected I was calling down upon him, and jumped up looking fit to eat me.

I acted several more impromptu scenes with the other occupants of the drawing-room. Mr. Hawden emitted "Humph!" from the corner where he grumpily sat, but Mr. Grey was full of praise.

"Splendid! splendid!" he exclaimed. "You say you have not had an hour's training, and never saw a play. Such versatility. Your fortune would be made on the stage. It is a sin to have such exceptional talent wasting in the bush. I must take her to Sydney and put her under a good master."

"Indeed, you'll do no such thing," said uncle. "I'll keep her here to liven up the old barracks. You've got enough puppets on the stage without a niece of mine ever being there."

I went to bed that night greatly elated. Flattery is sweet to youth. I felt pleased with myself, and imagined, as I peeped in the looking-glass, that I was not half bad-looking after all.

CHAPTER ELEVEN

Yah!

"Bah, you hideous animal! Ha ha! Your peerless conceit does you credit. So you actually imagined that by one or two out of every hundred you might be considered passable. You are the most uninteresting person in the world. You are small and nasty and bad, and every other thing that's abominable. That's what you are."

This address I delivered to my reflection in the glass next morning. My elation of the previous night was as flat as a pancake. Dear, oh dear, what a fool I had been to softly swallow the flattery of Mr. Grey without

a single snub in return! To make up for my laxity, if
he continued to amuse himself by plastering my vanity
with the ointment of flattery, I determined to serve up
my replies to him red-hot and well seasoned with
pepper.

I finished my toilet, and in a very what's-the-good-
o'-anything mood took a last glance in the glass to say,
"You're ugly, you're ugly and useless; so don't forget
that and make a fool of yourself again."

I was in the habit of doing this; it had long ago
taken the place of a morning prayer. I said this, that by
familiarity it might lose a little of its sting when I
heard it from other lips, but somehow it failed in
efficacy.

I was late for breakfast that morning. All the others
were half through the meal when I sat down.

Grannie had not come home till after twelve, but
was looking as brisk as usual.

"Come, Sybylla, I suppose this comes of sitting up
too late, as I was not here to hunt you to bed. You are
always very lively at night, but it's a different tune in
the morning," she said, when giving me the usual morning hug.

"When I was a nipper of your age, if I didn't turn
out like greased lightning every morning, I was assisted
by a little strap oil," remarked uncle Jay-Jay.

"Sybylla should be excused this morning," interposed Mr. Grey. "She entertained us for hours last
night. Little wonder if she feels languid this morning."

"Entertained you! What did she do?" queried grannie.

"Many things. Do you know, gran, that you are rob-
bing the world of an artist by keeping Sybylla hidden
away in the bush? I must persuade you to let me take
her to Sydney and have her put under the best masters
in Sydney."

"Under masters for what?"

"Elocution and singing."

"I couldn't afford it."

"But I'd bear the expense myself. It would only be returning a trifle of all you have done for me."

"What nonsense! What would you have her do when she was taught?"

"Go on the stage, of course. With her talent and hair she would cause quite a sensation."

Now grannie's notions re the stage were very tightly laced. All actors and actresses, from the lowest circus man up to the most glorious cantatrice, were people defiled in the sight of God, and utterly outside the pale of all respectability, when measured with her code of morals.

She turned energetically in her chair, and her keen eyes flashed with scorn and anger as she spoke.

"Go on the stage! A grand-daughter of mine! Lucy's eldest child! An actress—a vile, low, brazen hussy! Use the gifts God has given her with which to do good in showing off to a crowd of vile bad men! I would rather see her struck dead at my feet this instant! I would rather see her shear off her hair and enter a convent this very hour. Child, promise you will never be a bold bad actress."

"I will never be a *bold bad* actress, grannie," I said, putting great stress on the adjectives, and bringing out the actress very faintly.

"Yes," she continued, calming down, "I'm sure you have not enough bad in you. You may be boisterous, and not behave with sufficient propriety sometimes, but I don't think you are wicked enough to ever make an actress."

Everard attempted to defend his case.

"Look here, gran, that's a very exploded old notion about the stage being a low profession. It might have been once, but it is quite the reverse nowadays. There are, of course, low people on the stage, as there are in all walks of life. I grant you that; but if people are good they can be good on the stage as well as anywhere else. On account of a little prejudice it would be a sin to rob Sybylla of the brilliant career she might have."

"Career!" exclaimed his foster-mother, catching at the word. "Career! That is all girls think of now, instead of being good wives and mothers and attending to their homes and doing what God intended. All they think of is gadding about and being fast, and ruining themselves body and soul. And the men are as bad to encourage them," looking severely at Everard.

"There is a great deal of truth in what you say, gran, I admit. You can apply it to many of our girls, I am sorry to confess, but Sybylla could not be brought under that classification. You must look at her in a different way. If——"

"I look at her as the child of respectable people, and will not have the stage mentioned in connection with her." Here grannie thumped her fist down on the table, and there was silence, complete, profound. Few dared argue with Mrs. Bossier.

Dear old lady, she was never angry long, and in a minute or two she proceeded with her breakfast, saying quite pleasantly:

"Never mention such a subject to me again; but I'll tell you what you can do. Next autumn, some time in March or April, when the fruit-preserving and jam-making are done with, Helen can take the child to Sydney for a month or so, and you can show them around. It will be a great treat for Sybylla as she has never been in Sydney."

"That's right, let's strike a bargain on that, gran," said Everard.

"Yes; it's a bargain, if I hear no more about the stage. God intends His creatures for a better life than that."

After breakfast I was left to entertain Everard for some while. We had a fine time. He was a perfect gentleman and a clever conversationalist.

I was always desirous of enjoying the company of society people who were well bred and lived according to etiquette, and possessed of leisure and culture sufficient to fill their minds with something more than the price of farm produce and a hard struggle for existence.

Hitherto I had only read of such or seen them in pictures, but here was a real live one, and I seized my opportunity with vim. At my questioning and evident interest in his talk he told me of all the latest plays, actors, and actresses with whom he was acquainted, and described the fashionable balls, dinners, and garden-parties he attended. Having exhausted this subject, we fell to discussing books, and I recited snatches of poems dear to me. Everard placed his hands upon my shoulders and said:

"Sybylla, do you know you are a most wonderful girl? Your figure is perfect, your style refreshing, and you have a most interesting face. It is as ever-changing as a kaleidoscope—sometimes merry, then stern, often sympathetic, and always sad when at rest. One would think you had had some sorrow in your life."

Lifting my skirt at either side, I bowed several times very low in what I called my stage bow, and called into requisition my stage smile, which displayed two rows of teeth as white and perfect as any twenty-guinea set turned out on a gold plate by a fashionable dentist.

"The handsome gentleman is very kind to amuse himself at the expense of a little country bumpkin, but he would do well to ascertain if his flattery would go down before administering it next time," I said sarcastically, and I heard him calling to me as I abruptly went off to shut myself in my room.

"How dare anyone ridicule me by paying idle brainless compliments! I knew I was ugly, and did not want any one to perjure his soul pretending they thought differently. What right had I to be small? Why wasn't I possessed of a big aquiline nose and a tall commanding figure?" Thus I sat in burning discontent and ill-humor until soothed by the scent of roses and the gleam of soft spring sunshine which streamed in through my open window. Some of the flower-beds in the garden were completely carpeted with pansy blossoms, all colors, and violets—blue and white, single and double. The scent of mignonette, jonquils, and narcissi filled the air. I reveled in rich perfumes, and these tempted me forth. My ruffled feelings gave way before the delights of the old garden. I collected a number of vases, and, filling them with water, set them on a table in the veranda near one of the drawing-room windows. I gathered lapfuls of the lovely blossoms, and commenced arranging them in the vases.

Part of the old Caddagat house was built of slabs, and one of the wooden walls ran along the veranda side of the drawing-room, so the songs aunt Helen and Everard Grey were trying to the piano came as a sweet accompaniment to my congenial task.

Presently they left off singing and commenced talking. Under the same circumstances a heroine of a story would have slipped away; or, if that were impossible without discovery, she would have put her fingers in her ears, and would have been in a terrible state of agitation lest she should hear something not intended for her. I did not come there with a view to eavesdropping. It is a degradation to which I never stoop. I thought they were aware of my presence on the veranda; but it appears they were not, as they began to discuss me (wonderfully interesting subject to myself), and I stayed there, without one word of disapproval from my conscience, to listen to their conversation.

"My word, didn't gran make a to-do this morning when I proposed to train Sybylla for the stage! Do you know that girl is simply reeking with talent; I must have her trained. I will keep bringing the idea before gran until she gets used to it. I'll work the we-should-use-the-gifts-God-has-given-us racket for all it is worth, and you might use your influence too, Helen."

"No, Everard; there are very few who succeed on the stage. I would not use my influence, as it is a life of which I do not approve."

"But Sybylla *would* succeed. I am a personal friend of the leading managers, and my influence would help her greatly."

"Yes; but what would you do with her? A young gentleman couldn't take charge of a girl and bring her out without ruining her reputation. There would be no end of scandal, as the sister theory would only be non-sense."

"There is another way; I could easily stop scandal."

"Everard, what do you mean!"

"I mean marriage," he replied deliberately.

"Surely, boy, you must be dreaming! You have only seen her for an hour or two. I don't believe in these sudden attachments."

Perhaps she here thought of one (her own) as sudden, which had not ended happily.

"Everard, don't do anything rashly. You know you are very fickle and considered a lady-killer—be merciful to my poor little Sybylla, I pray. It is just one of your passing fancies. Don't wile her passionate young heart away and then leave her to pine and die."

"I don't think she is that sort," he replied laughingly.

"No, she would not die, but would grow into a cynic and skeptic, which is the worst of fates. Let her alone. Flirt as much as you will with society belles who understand the game, but leave my country maiden alone. I hope to mold her into a splendid character yet."

"But, Helen, supposing I am in earnest at last, you don't think I'd make her a bad old hubby, do you?"

"She is not the girl for you. You are not the man who could ever control her. What I say may not be complimentary but it is true. Besides, she is not seventeen yet, and I do not approve of romantic young girls throwing themselves into matrimony. Let them develop their womanhood first."

"Then I expect I had better hide my attractions under a bushel during the remainder of my stay at Caddagat?"

"Yes. Be as nice to the child as you like, but mind, none of those little ladies'-man attentions with which it is so easy to steal——"

I waited to hear no more, but, brimming over with a mixture of emotions, tore through the garden and into the old orchard. Bees were busy, and countless bright-colored butterflies flitted hither and thither, sipping from hundreds of trees, white or pink with bloom

—their beauty was lost upon me. I stood ankle-deep in violets, where they had run wild under a gnarled old appletree, and gave way to my wounded vanity.

"Little country maiden, indeed! There's no need for him to bag his attractions up. If he exerted himself to the utmost of his ability, he could not make me love him. I'm not a child. I saw through him in the first hour. There's not enough in him to win my love. I'll show him I think no more of him than of the caterpillars on the old tree there. I'm not a booby that will fall in love with every gussie I see. Bah, there's no fear of that! I hate and detest men!"

"I suppose you are rehearsing some more airs to show off with tonight," sneered a voice behind me.

"No, I'm realisticing; and how *dare* you thrust your obnoxious presence before me when I wish to be alone! Haven't I often shown——"

"While a girl is disengaged, any man who is her equal has the right to pay his addresses to her if he is in earnest," interrupted Mr. Hawden. It was he who stood before me.

"I am well aware of that," I replied. "But it is a woman's privilege to repel those attentions if distasteful to her. You seem disinclined to accord me that privilege."

Having delivered this retort, I returned to the house, leaving him standing there looking the fool he was.

I do not believe in spurning the love of a blackfellow if he behaves in a manly way; but Frank Hawden was such a driveling mawkish style of sweetheart that I had no patience with him.

Aunt Helen and Everard had vacated the drawing-room, so I plumped down on the piano-stool and dashed into Kowalski's galop, from that into "Gaîté de Coeur" until I made the piano dance and tremble like a thing possessed. My annoyance faded, and I slowly played that saddest of waltzes, "Weber's Last." I became aware of a presence in the room, and, facing about, confronted Everard Grey.

"How long have you been here?" I demanded sharply.

"Since you began to play. Where on earth did you learn to play? Your execution is splendid. Do sing 'Three Fishers,' please."

"Excuse me; I haven't time now. Besides I am not competent to sing to you," I said brusquely, and made my exit.

"Mr. Hawden wants you, Sybylla," called aunt Helen. "See what he wants and let him get away to his work, or your grannie will be vexed to see him loitering about all the morning."

"Miss Sybylla," he began, when we were left alone, "I want to apologize to you. I had no right to plague you, but it all comes of the way I love you. A fellow gets jealous at the least little thing, you know."

"Bore me with no more such trash," I said, turning away in disgust.

"But, Miss Sybylla, what am I to do with it?"

"Do with what?"

"My love."

"Love!" I retorted scornfully. "There is no such thing."

"But there is, and I have found it."

"Well, you stick to it—that's my advice to you. It will be a treasure. If you send it to my father he will get it bottled up and put it in the Goulburn museum. He has sent several things there already."

"Don't make such a game of a poor devil. You know I can't do that."

"Bag it up, then; put a big stone to make it sink, and pitch it in the river."

"You'll rue this," he said savagely.

"I may or may not," I sang over my shoulder as I departed.

CHAPTER TWELVE

One Grand Passion

I had not the opportunity of any more private interviews with Everard Grey till one morning near his departure, when we happened to be alone on the veranda.

"Well, Miss Sybylla," he began, "when I arrived I thought you and I would have been great friends; but we have not progressed at all. How do you account for that?"

As he spoke he laid his slender shapely hand kindly upon my head. He was very handsome and winning, and moved in literary, musical, and artistic society—a man from my world, a world away.

Oh, what pleasure I might have derived from companionship with him! I bit my lip to keep back the tears. Why did not social arrangements allow a man and a maid to be chums—chums as two men or two maids may be to each other, enjoying each other without thought beyond pure platonic friendship? But no; it could not be. I understood the conceit of men. Should I be very affable, I feared Everard Grey would imagine he had made a conquest of me. On the other hand, were I glum he would think the same, and that I was trying to hide my feelings behind a mask of brusquerie. I therefore steered in a bee-line between the two manners, and remarked with the greatest of indifference:

"I was not aware that you expected us to be such

cronies—in fact, I have never given the matter a thought."

He turned away in a piqued style. Such a beau of beaux, no doubt he was annoyed that an insignificant little country bumpkin should not be flattered by his patronage, or probably he thought me rude or ill-humored.

Two mornings later uncle Jay-Jay took him to Gool-Gool *en route* for Sydney. When departing he bade me a kindly good-bye, made me promise to write to him, and announced his intention of obtaining the opinion of some good masters re my dramatic talent and voice, when I came to Sydney as promised by my grand-mother. I stood on the garden fence waving my hand-kerchief until the buggy passed out of sight among the messmate-trees about half a mile from the house.

"Well I hope, as that dandified ape has gone—and good riddance to him—that you will pay more heed to my attentions now," said Mr. Hawden's voice, as I was in the act of descending from the fence.

"What do you mean by your attentions?" I demanded.

"What do I mean! That is something like coming to business. I'll soon explain. You know what my intentions are very well. When I am twenty-four, I will come into my property in England. It is considerable, and at the end of that time I want to marry you and take you home. By Jove! I would just like to take you home. You'd surprise some English girls I know."

"There would be more than one person surprised if I married you," I thought to myself, and laughed till I ached with the motion.

"You infernal little vixen! What are you laughing at? You've got no more sense than a bat if such a solemn thing only provokes your mirth."

"Solemn—why, it's a screaming farce!" I laughed more and more.

"What's a farce?" he demanded fiercely.

"The bare idea of you proposing to me."

"Why? Have I not as much right to propose as any other man?"

"Man!" I laughed. "That's where the absurdity arises. My child, if you were a man, certainly you could propose, but do you think I'd look at a boy, a child! If ever I perpetrate matrimony the participant in my degradation will be a fully developed man—not a hobbledehoy who falls in love, as he terms it, on an average about twice a week. Love! Ho!"

I moved in the direction of the house. He barred my path.

"You are not going to escape me like that, my fine lady. I will make you listen to me this time or you will hear more about it," and he seized me angrily by the wrist.

I cannot bear the touch of any one—it is one of my idiosyncrasies. With my disengaged hand I struck him a vigorous blow on the nose, and wrenching myself free sprang away, saying, "How dare you lay a finger on me! If you attempt such a thing again I'll make short work of you. Mark my words, or you'll get something more than a bleeding nose next time, I promise you."

"You'll hear more of this! You'll hear more of this! You fierce, wild, touch-me-not thing," he roared.

"Yes; my motto with men is touch-me-not, and it is your own fault if I'm fierce. If children attempt to act the role of a man with adult tools, they are sure to cut themselves. Hold hard a bit, honey, till your whiskers grow," I retorted as I departed, taking flying leaps over the blossom-burdened flower-beds.

At tea that night, after gazing interestedly at Mr. Hawden's nose for some time, uncle Julius inquired, "In the name of all that's mysterious, what the devil have you been doing to your nose? You look as though you had been on the spree."

I was quaking lest he would get me into a fine scrape, but he only muttered, "By Jove!" with great energy, and glowered menacingly across the table at me.

After tea he requested an interview with grannie,

which aroused my curiosity greatly. I was destined to hear all about it next morning. When breakfast was over grannie called me into her room and interviewed me about Mr. Hawden's interview. She began without any preliminaries:

"Mr. Hawden has complained of your conduct. It grieves me that any young man should have to speak to me of the behavior of my own grand-daughter. He says you have been flirting with him. Sybylla, I scarcely thought you would be so immodest and unwomanly."

On hearing this my thoughts of Frank Hawden were the reverse of flattering. He had persecuted me beyond measure, yet I had not deigned to complain of him to either uncle, grannie, or auntie, as I might reasonably have done, and have obtained immediate redress. He had been the one to blame in the case, yet for the rebuffs he had brought upon himself, went tattling to my grandmother.

"Is that all you have to say, grannie?"

"No. He wants to marry you, and has asked my consent. I told him it all rested with yourself and parents. What do you say?"

"Say," I exclaimed, "grannie, you are only joking, are you not?"

"No, my child, this is not a matter to joke about."

"Marry that creature! A boy!" I uttered in consternation.

"He is no boy. He has attained his majority some months. He is as old as your grandfather was when we married. In three years you will be almost twenty, and by that time he will be in possession of his property which is very good—in fact, he will be quite rich. If you care for him there is nothing against him as I can see. He is healthy, has a good character, and comes of a high family. Being a bit wild won't matter. Very often, after they sow their wild oats, some of these scampy young fellows settle down and marry a nice young girl and turn out very good husbands."

"It is disgusting, and you ought to be downright ashamed of yourself, grannie! A man can live a life of bestiality and then be considered a fit husband for the youngest and purest girl! It is shameful! Frank Hawden is not wild, he hasn't got enough in him to be so. I hate him. No, he hasn't enough in him to hate. I loathe and despise him. I would not marry him or any one like him though he were King of England. The idea of marriage even with the best man in the world seems to me a lowering thing," I raged; "but with him it would be pollution—the lowest degradation that could be heaped upon me! I will never come down to marry any one——" here I fell a victim to a flood of excited tears.

I felt there was no good in the world, especially in men—the hateful creatures!—and never would be while it was not expected of them, even by rigidly pure, true Christians such as my grandmother. Grannie, dear old grannie, thought I should marry any man who, from a financial point of view, was a good match for me. That is where the sting came in. No, I would never marry. I would procure some occupation in which I could tread my life out, independent of the degradation of marriage.

"Dear me, child," said grannie, concernedly, "there is no need to distress yourself so. I remember you were always fearfully passionate. When I had you with me as a tiny toddler, you would fret a whole day about a thing an ordinary child would forget inside an hour. I will tell Hawden to go about his business. I would not want you to consider marriage for an instant with any-one distasteful to you. But tell me truly, have you ever flirted with him? I will take your word, for I thank God you have never yet told me a falsehood!"

"Grannie," I exclaimed emphatically, "I have dis-couraged him all I could. I would scorn to flirt with any man."

"Well, well, that is all I want to hear about it. Wash your eyes, and we will get our horses and go over to see Mrs. Hickey and her baby, and take her something good to eat."

I did not encounter Frank Hawden again till the

afternoon, when he leered at me in a very triumphant manner. I stiffened myself and drew out of his way as though he had been some vile animal. At this treatment he whined, so I agreed to talk the matter over with him and have done with it once and for all.

He was on his way to water some dogs, so I accompanied him out to the stables near the kennels, to be out of hearing of the household.

I opened fire without any beating about the bush.

"I ask you, Mr. Hawden, if you have any sense of manliness, from this hour to cease persecuting me with your idiotic professions of love. I have two sentiments regarding it, and in either you disgust me. Sometimes I don't believe there is such a thing as love at all—that is, love between men and women. While in this frame of mind I would not listen to professions of love from an angel. Other times I believe in love, and look upon it as a sacred and solemn thing. When in that humor, it seems to me a desecration to hear you twaddling about the holy theme, for you are only a boy, and don't know how to feel. I would not have spoken thus harshly to you, but by your unmanly conduct you have brought it upon yourself. I have told you straight all that I will ever deign to tell you on the subject, and take much pleasure in wishing you good afternoon."

I walked away quickly, heedless of his expostulations.

My appeal to his manliness had no effect. Did I go for a ride, or a walk in the afternoon to enjoy the glory of the sunset, or a stroll to drink in the pleasures of the old garden, there would I find Frank Hawden by my side, yah, yah, yahing about the way I treated him, until I wished him at the bottom of the Red Sea.

However, in those glorious spring days the sense of life was too pleasant to be much clouded by the trifling annoyance Frank Hawden occasioned me. The graceful wild clematis festooned the shrubbery along the creeks with great wreaths of magnificent white bloom, which loaded every breeze with perfume; the pretty bright green senna shrubs along the river-banks were decked

in blossoms which rivaled the deep blue of the sky in
brilliance; the magpies built their nests in the tall gum-
trees, and savagely attacked unwary travelers who ventured too near their domain; the horses were rolling
fat, and invited one to get on their satin backs and have
a gallop; the cry of the leather-heads was heard in the
orchard as the cherry season approached. Oh, it was
good to be alive!

At Caddagat I was as much out of the full flood of
life for which I craved as at Possum Gully, but here
there were sufficient pleasant little ripples on the stream
of existence to act as a stop-gap for the present.

CHAPTER THIRTEEN

He

Here goes for a full account of my first, my last, my
only *real* sweetheart, for I considered the professions
of that pestiferous jackeroo as merely a grotesque cari-
cature on the genuine article.

On making my first appearance before my lover, I
looked quite the reverse of a heroine. My lovely hair
was not conveniently escaping from the comb at the
right moment to catch him hard in the eye, neither
was my thrillingly low sweet voice floating out on the
scented air in a manner which went straight to his
heart, like the girls I had read of. On the contrary, I
much resembled a female clown. It was on a day
toward the end of September, and I had been up the

creek making a collection of ferns. I had on a pair of men's boots with which to walk in the water, and was garbed in a most dilapidated old dress, which I had borrowed from one of the servants for the purpose. A pair of gloves made of basil, and a big hat, much torn in struggling through the undergrowth, completed my make-up. My hair was most unbecomingly screwed up, the short ends sticking out like a hurrah's nest.

It was late in the day when, returning from my ramble, I was met on the doorstep by aunt Helen.

"While you are in that trim, I wish you would pluck some lemons for me. I'm sure there is no danger of you ruining your turn-out. A sketch of you would make a good item for the *Bulletin*," she said.

I went readily to do her bidding, and fetching a ladder with rungs about two feet six apart, placed it against a lemon-tree at the back of the house, and climbed up.

Holding a number of lemons in my skirt, I was making a most ungraceful descent, when I heard an unknown footstep approaching toward my back.

People came to Caddagat at all hours of the day, so I was not in the least disconcerted. Only a tramp, an agent, or a hawker, I bet, I thought, as I reached my big boot down for another rung of the ladder without turning my head to see whom it might be.

A pair of strong brown hands encircled my waist, I was tossed up a foot or so and then deposited lightly on the ground, a masculine voice saying, "You're a mighty well-shaped young filly—'a waist rather small, but a quarter superb.'"

"How dare anyone speak to me like that," I thought, as I faced about to see who was parodying Gordon. There stood a man I had never before set eyes on, smiling mischievously at me. He was a young man—a very young man, a bushman—tremendously tall and big and sunburnt, with an open pleasant face and chestnut moustache—not at all an awe-inspiring fellow, in spite of his unusual, though well-proportioned and carried, height. I knew it must be Harold Beecham, of

Five-Bob Downs, as I had heard he stood six feet three and a half in his socks.

I hurriedly let down my dress, the lemons rolling in a dozen directions, and turned to flee, but that well-formed figure bounded before me with the agility of a cat and barred my way.

"Now, not a step do you go, my fine young blood, until you pick up every jolly lemon and put them away tidily, or I'll tell the missus on you as sure as eggs."

It dawned on me that he had mistaken me for one of the servant-girls. That wasn't bad fun. I determined not to undeceive but to have a lark with him. I summed him up as conceited, but not with the disgusting conceit with which some are afflicted, or perhaps blessed. It was rather an air of I-have-always-got-what-I-desire-and-believe,-if-people-fail-it-is-all-their-own-fault, which surrounded him.

"If you please, sir," I said humbly, "I've gathered them all up, will you let me go now."

"Yes, when you've given me a kiss."

"Oh, sir, I couldn't do that!"

"Go on, I won't poison you. Come now, I'll make you."

"Oh, the missus might catch me."

"No jolly fear; I'll take all the blame if she does."

"Oh don't, sir; let me go, please," I said in such unfeigned distress, for I feared he was going to execute his threat, that he laughed and said:

"Don't be frightened, sissy, I never kiss girls, and I'm not going to start at this time of day, and against their will to boot. You haven't been long here, have you? I haven't seen you before. Stand out there till I see if you've got any grit in you, and then I am done with you."

I stood in the middle of the yard, the spot he indicated, while he uncurled his long heavy stock-whip with its big lash and scented myall handle. He cracked it round and round my head and arms, but I did not feel the least afraid, as I saw at a glance that he was exceedingly dexterous in the bushman's art of handling a stock-whip, and knew, if I kept perfectly still, I was quite safe. It was thanks to uncle Jay-Jay that I was able to bear the operation with unruffled equanimity, as he was in the habit of testing my nerves in this way.

"Well, I never! Not so much as blinked an eyelash! Thoroughbred!" He said after a minute or so, "Where's the boss?"

"In Gool-Gool. He won't be home till late."

"Is Mrs. Bossier in?"

"No, she's not, but Mrs. Bell is somewhere around in front."

"Thanks."

I watched him as he walked away with an easy swinging stride, which spoke of many long, long days in the saddle. I felt certain as I watched him that he had quite forgotten the incident of the little girl with the lemons.

"Sybylla, hurry up and get dressed. Put on your best bib and tucker, and I will leave Harry Beecham in your charge, as I want to superintend the making of some of the dishes myself this evening."

"It's too early to put on my evening dress, isn't it, auntie?"

"It is rather early; but you can't spare time to change twice. Dress yourself completely; you don't know what minute your uncle and his worship will arrive."

I had taken a dip in the creek, so had not to bathe, and it took me but a short time to don full war-paint— blue evening dress, satin slippers, and all. I wore my hair flowing, simply tied with a ribbon. I slipped out into the passage and called aunt Helen. She came.

"I'm ready, auntie. Where is he?"

"In the dining-room."

"Come into the drawing-room and call him. I will take charge of him till you are at leisure. But, auntie, it will be a long time till dinner—how on earth will I manage him?"

"Manage him!" she laughed; "he is not at all an obstreperous character."

We had reached the drawing-room by this, and I looked at myself in the looking-glass while aunt Helen went to summon Harold Augustus Beecham, bachelor, owner of Five-Bob Downs, Wyambeet, Wallerawang West, Quat-Quatta, and a couple more stations in New South Wales, besides an extensive one in Queensland.

I noticed as he entered the door that since I had seen him he had washed, combed his stiff black hair, and divested himself of his hat, spurs, and whip—his leggings had perforce to remain, as his nether garment was a pair of closely fitting gray cloth riding-breeches, which clearly defined the shapely contour of his lower limbs.

"Harry, this is Sybylla. I'm sure you need no further introduction. Excuse me, I have something on the fire which is likely to burn." And aunt Helen hurried off leaving us facing each other.

He stared down at me with undisguised surprise. I looked up at him and laughed merrily. The fun was all on my side. He was a great big man—rich and important. I was a chit—an insignificant nonentity—yet, despite his sex, size, and importance, I was complete master of that situation, and knew it: thus I laughed.

I saw that he recognized me again by the dusky red he flushed beneath his sun-darkened skin. No doubt he regretted having called me a filly above all things. He bowed stiffly, but I held out my hand, saying:

"Do shake hands. When introduced I always shake hands with anyone I think I'll like. Besides, I seem to know you well. Just think of all the apples you brought me!"

He acceded to my request, holding my hand a deal longer than necessary, and looking at me helplessly. It amused me greatly, for I saw that it was he who did not know how to manage me, and not I that couldn't manage him.

" 'Pon my honor, Miss Melvyn, I had no idea it was you, when I said——" Here he boggled completely, which had the effect of reviving my laughter.

"You had no right to be dressed like that—deceiving a fellow. It wasn't fair."

"That's the best of it. It shows what a larrikin Don Juan sort of character you are. You can't deceive me now if you pretend to be a virtuous well-behaved member of society."

"That is the first time I've ever meddled with any of the kitchen fry, and, by Jove, it will be the last!" he said energetically. "I've got myself into a pretty mess."

"What nonsense you talk," I replied. "If you say another word about it, I'll write a full account of it and paste it in my scrapbook. But if you don't worry about it, neither will I. You said nothing very uncomplimentary; in fact, I was quite flattered."

I was perched on the high end of a couch, and he was leaning with big careless ease on the piano. Had grannie seen me, I would have been lectured about unladylike behavior.

"What is your uncle at today?" he inquired.

"He's not at anything. He went to Gool-Gool yesterday on the jury. Court finishes up today, and he is going to bring the judge home tonight. That's why I am dressed so carefully," I answered.

"Good gracious! I never thought of court this time as I wasn't called on the jury, and for a wonder hadn't so much as a case against a Chinaman. I was going to stay tonight, but can't if his worship is going to dine here."

"Why? You're surely not afraid of Judge Fossilt? He's a very simple old customer."

"Imagine dining with a judge in this toggery!" and he glanced down his great figure at his riding gear.

"That doesn't matter; he's near-sighted. I'll get you put at the far end of the table under my wing. Men don't notice dress. If you weren't so big uncle or Frank Hawden could oblige you."

"Do you think I could pass muster?"

"Yes; after I brush you down you'll look as spruce as a brass penny."

"I did brush myself," he answered.

"You brush yourself!" I retorted. "There's a big splash of mud on your shoulder. You couldn't expect to do anything decently, for you're only a man, and men are the uselessest, good-for-nothingest, clumsiest animals in the world. All they're good for is to smoke and swear."

I fetched a clothes brush.

"You'll have to stand on the table to reach me," he said, looking down with amused indulgence.

"As you are so impertinent you can go dusty," and I tossed the brush away.

The evening was balmy, so I invited him into the garden. He threw his handkerchief over my chest, saying I might catch cold, but I scouted the idea.

We wandered into an arbor covered with wistaria, banksia, and Maréchal Niel roses, and I made him a buttonhole.

A traveler pulled rein in the roadway, and, dismounting, threw his bridle over a paling of the garden fence while he went inside to try and buy a loaf of bread.

I jumped up, frightening the horse so that it broke away, pulling off the paling in the bridle-rein. I ran to bring a hammer to repair the damage. Mr. Beecham caught the horse while I attempted to drive the nail into the fence. It was a futile attempt. I bruised my fingers. He took the hammer from me, and fixing the paling in its place with a couple of well-aimed blows, said laughingly:

"You drive a nail! You couldn't expect to do anything. You're only a girl. Girls are the helplessest, uselessest, troublesomest little creatures in the world. All they're good for is to torment and pester a fellow."

I had to laugh.

At this juncture we heard uncle Jay-Jay's voice, so Mr. Beecham went toward the back, whence it proceeded, after he left me at the front door.

"Oh, auntie, we got on splendidly! He's not a bit of trouble. We're as chummy as though we had been reared together," I exclaimed.

"Did you get him to talk?"

"Oh yes."

"Did you really?" in surprise.

When I came to review the matter I was forced to confess that I had done all the talking, and young Beecham the listening; moreover I described him as the quietest man I had ever seen or heard of.

The judge did not come home with uncle Jay-Jay as expected so it was not necessary for me to shelter Harold Beecham under my wing. Grannie greeted him cordially as "Harold, my boy"—he was a great favorite with her. She and uncle Julius monopolized him for the evening. There was great talk of trucking sheep, the bad outlook as regarded the season, the state of the grass in the triangle, the Leigh Spring, the Bimbalong, and several other paddocks, and of the condition of the London wool market. It did not interest me, so I dived into a book, only occasionally emerging therefrom to smile at Mr. Beecham.

He had come to Caddagat for a pair of bullocks which had been fattening in grannie's home paddock. Uncle gave him a start with them next morning. When they came out on the road I was standing in a bed of violets in a tangled corner of the garden, where roses climbed to kiss the lilacs, and spiraea stooped to rest upon the wallflowers, and where two tall kurrajongs stood like sentries over all. Harold Beecham dismounted, and, leaning over the fence, lingered with me, leaving the bullocks to uncle Jay-Jay. Uncle raved vigorously. Women, he asserted, were the bane of society and the ruination of all men; but he had always considered Harold as too sensible to neglect his business to stand grinning at a pesky youngster in short skirts and a pigtail. Which was the greatest idiot of the two he didn't know.

His grumbling did not affect Harold in the least.

"Complimentary to both of us," he remarked as he leisurely threw himself across his great horse, and smiled his pleasant quiet smile, disclosing two rows of magnificent teeth, untainted by contamination with beer or tobacco. Raising his panama hat with the green fly-

veil around it, he cantered off. I wondered as I watched
him if anything ever disturbed his serenity, and desired
to try. He looked too big and quiet to be ruffled by
such emotions as rage, worry, jealousy, or even love.
Returning to the house, I put aunt Helen through an
exhaustive catechism concerning him.

Question. Auntie, what age is Harold Beecham?
Answer. Twenty-five last December.

Q. Did he ever have any brothers or sisters?
A. No. His birth caused his mother's death.

Q. How long has his father been dead?
A. Since Harold could crawl.

Q. Who reared him?
A. His aunts.

Q. Does he ever talk any more than that?
A. Often a great deal less.

Q. Is he really very rich?
A. If he manages to pull through these seasons he
     will be second to none but Tyson in point of
     wealth.

Q. Is Five-Bob a very pretty place?
A. Yes; one of the show places of the district.

Q. Does he often come to Caddagat?
A. Yes, he often drops in.

Q. What makes his hair so black and his moustache
     that light color?
A. You'll have to study science to find that out.
     I'm sure I can't tell you.

Q. Does he——?

"Now, Sybylla," said auntie, laughing, "you are taking a suspicious interest in my sunburnt young giant.
Did I not tell you he was taking time by the forelock
when he brought the apples?"

"Oh, auntie, I am only asking questions because——"

"Yes, because, because, I understand perfectly. Because you are a girl, and all the girls fall a victim to
Harry's charms at once. If you don't want to succumb
meekly to your fate, 'Heed the spark or you may dread
the fire.' That is the only advice I can tender you."

This was a Thursday, and on the following Sunday Harold Beecham reappeared at Caddagat and remained from three in the afternoon until nine at night. Uncle Julius and Frank Hawden were absent. The weather had taken a sudden backward lurch into winter again, so we had a fire. Harold sat beside it all the time, and interposed yes and no at the proper intervals in grannie's brisk business conversation, but he never addressed one word to me beyond "Good afternoon, Miss Melvyn," on his arrival, and "Good night, Miss Melvyn," when leaving.

I studied him attentively all the while. What were his ideas and sentiments it were hard to tell: he never expressed any. He was fearfully and wonderfully quiet. Yet his was an intelligent silence, not of that wooden brainless description which casts a damper on company, neither was it of the morose or dreaming order.

CHAPTER FOURTEEN

Principally Letters

Caddagat, 29th *Sept.*, 1896

My dearest Gertie,

I have started to write no less than seven letters to you, but something always interrupted me and I did not finish them. However, I'll finish this one in the teeth of Father Peter himself. I will parenthesize all the interruptions. (A traveler just asked me for a rose. I had to get up and give him one.) Living here is lovely. (Another man inquired the way to Somingley Gap, and I've just finished directing him.) Grannie is terribly nice. You could not believe. She is always giving me something, and takes me wherever she goes. Auntie is an angel. I wish you could hear the piano. It is a beauty. There are dozens of papers and books to read. Uncle is a dear old fellow. You should hear him rave and swear sometimes when he gets in a rage. It is great fun. He brings me lollies, gloves, ribbons, or something every time he comes from town. (Two Indian hawkers have arrived, and I am going out to see their goods. There were nineteen hawkers here last week. I am sitting on a squatter's chair and writing on a table in the veranda, and the road goes right by the flower-garden. That is how I see everyone.) Have you had rain down there this week? They have great squawking about the drought up here. I wish they could see Goulburn, and then they'd know what drought means. I don't know what sort of a bob-berie they would kick up. It's pretty dry out on the run, but everyone calls the paddocks about the house an oasis. You see there are such splendid facilities for irrigation here. Uncle has put on a lot of men. They have cut races between the two creeks between which the house is situated. Every now and again they let the water from these over the orchard gardens and about a hundred acres of paddock land around the house. The grass therein is up to the horses' fetlocks. There is any amount of rhubarb and early vegetables in the garden. Grannie says there is a splendid promise of fruit in the orchard, and the flower-garden is a perfect dream. This is the dearest old place in the world. Dozens of people plague grannie to be let put their horses in the grass—especially shearers, there are droves of them going home now—but she won't let them; wants all the grass for her own stock. Uncle has had to put another man on to mind it, or at night all the wires are cut and the horses put in. (An agent, I think by the cut of him, is asking for grannie. I'll have to run and find her.) It is very lively here. Never a night but we have the house full of agents or travelers of one sort or another, and there are often a dozen swaggies in the one day.

Harold Beecham is my favorite of all the men hereaway. He is delightfully big and quiet. He isn't good-looking, but I like his face. (Been attending to the demands of a couple of impudent swaggies. Being off the road at Possum Gully, you escape them.) For the love of life, next time you write, fire into the news at once and don't half-fill your letter telling me about the pen and your bad writing. I am scribbling at the rate of 365 miles an hour, and don't care a jot whether it is good writing or not.

Auntie, uncle, Frank Hawden and I, are going to ride to Yabtree church next Sunday. It is four miles beyond Five-Bob Downs, so that is sixteen miles. It is the nearest church. I expect it will be rare fun. There will be such a crowd coming home, and that always makes the horses delight-fully frisky. (A man wants to put his horses in the paddock for the night, so I will have to find uncle.) I never saw such a place for men. It is all men, men, men. You cannot go anywhere outside the house but you see men coming and going in all directions. It wouldn't do to undress without bothering to drop the window-blind like we used at Possum Gully. Grannie and uncle say it is a curse to be living beside the road, as it costs them a tremendous lot a year. There are seven lemon-trees here, loaded (another hawker). I hope you think of me sometimes. I am just as ugly as ever. (A traveler wants to buy a loaf of bread.)

With stacks of love to all at home, and a whole dray-load for yourself, from your loving sister,

Sybylla.

Remember me to Goulburn, drowsing lazily in its dreamy graceful hollow in the blue distance.

Caddagat, 29th *Sept.,* 1896

Dear Everard,

Thank you very much for the magazines and "An Australian Bush Track." I suppose you have quite forgotten us and Caddagat by this time. The sun has sunk behind the gum-trees, and the blue evening mists are hanging lazily in the hollows of the hills. I expect you are donning your "swallow-tail" preparatory to leading some be-satined "faire ladye" in to a gorgeous dinner, thence to the play, then to a dance probably. No doubt all around you is bustle, glare of lights, noise, and fun. It is such a different scene here. From down the road comes the tinkle of camp-bells and jingle of hobble-chains. From down in that sheltered angle where the creek meets the river comes the gleam of camp-fires through the gathering twilight, and I can see several tents rigged for the night, looking like white specks in the distance.

I long for the time to come when I shall get to Sydney. I'm going to lead you and aunt Helen a pretty dance. You'll have to keep going night and day. It will be great. I must get up and dance a jig on the veranda when I think of it. You'll have to show me everything—slums and all. I want to find out the truth of heaps of things for myself.

Save for the weird rush of the stream and the kookaburras' good-night, all is still, with a mighty far-reaching stillness which can be felt. Now the curlews are beginning their wild moaning cry. From the rifts in the dark lone ranges, far down the river, it comes like a hunted spirit until it makes me feel——

At this point I said, "Bah! I'm mad to write to Everard Grey like this. He would laugh and call me a poor little fool." I tore the half-finished letter to shreds, and consigned it to the kitchen fire. I substituted a prim formal note, merely thanking him for the books and magazine he had sent me. To this I never received an answer. I heard through his letters to grannie that he was much occupied. Had been to Brisbane and Melbourne on important cases, so very likely had not time to be bothered with me; or, he might have been like the majority of his fellows who make a great parade of friendship while with one, then go away and forget one's existence in an hour.

While at Caddagat there were a few duties allotted to me. One of these was to attend to the drawing-room; another was to find uncle Jay-Jay's hat when he mislaid it—often ten times per day. I assisted my grandmother to make up her accounts and write business letters, and I attended to tramps. A man was never refused a bit to eat at Caddagat. This necessitated the purchase of an extra ton of flour per year, also nearly a ton of sugar, to say nothing of tea, potatoes, beef, and all broken meats which went thus. This was not reckoning the consumption of victuals by the other class of travelers with which the house was generally full year in and year out. Had there been any charge for their board and lodging, the Bossiers would surely have made a fortune. I interviewed on an average fifty tramps a week, and seldom saw the same man twice. What a great army they were! Hopeless, homeless, aimless, shameless souls, tramping on from north to south, and east to west, never relinquishing their heart-sickening, futile quest for work—some of them so long on the tramp that the ambitions of manhood had been ground out of them, and they wished for nothing more than this.

There were all shapes, sizes, ages, kinds, and conditions of men—the shamefaced boy in the bud of his youth, showing by the way he begged that the humiliation of the situation had not yet worn off, and poor old creatures tottering on the brink of the grave, with nothing left in life but the enjoyment of beer and tobacco. There were strong men in their prime who really desired work when they asked for it, and skulking cowards who hoped they would not get it. There were the diseased, the educated, the ignorant, the deformed, the blind, the evil, the honest, the mad, and the sane. Some in real professional beggars' style called down blessings on me; others were morose and glum, while some were impudent and thankless, and said to supply them with food was just what I should do, for the swagmen kept the squatters—as, had the squatters not monopolized the land, the swagmen would have had plenty. A moiety of the last-mentioned—dirty, besotted, ragged creatures—had a glare in their eyes which made one shudder to look at them, and, while spasmodically twirling their billies or clenching their fists, talked wildly of making one to "bust up the damn banks," or to drive all the present squatters out of the country and put the people on the land—clearly showing that, because they had failed for one reason or another, it had maddened them to see others succeed.

In a wide young country of boundless resources, why is this thing? This question worried me. Our legislators are unable or unwilling to cope with it. They trouble not to be patriots and statesmen. Australia can bring forth writers, orators, financiers, singers, musicians, actors, and athletes which are second to none of any nation under the sun. Why can she not bear sons, men! of soul, mind, truth, godliness, and patriotism sufficient to rise and cast off the grim shackles which widen around us day by day?

I was the only one at Caddagat who held these silly ideas. Harold Beecham, uncle Julius, grannie, and Frank Hawden did not worry about the cause of tramps. They simply termed them a lazy lot of sneaking creatures, fed them, and thought no more of the matter.

I broached the subject to uncle Jay-Jay once, simply to discover his ideas thereon.

I was sitting on a chair in the veranda sewing; he, with his head on a cushion, was comfortably stretched on a rug on the floor.

"Uncle Boss, why can't something be done for tramps?"

"How done for 'em?"

"Couldn't some means of employing them be arrived at?"

"Work!" he ejaculated. "That's the very thing the crawling divils are terrified they might get."

"Yes; but couldn't some law be made to help them?"

"A law to make me cut up Caddagat and give ten of 'em each a piece, and go on the wallaby myself, I suppose?"

"No, uncle; but there was a poor young fellow here this morning who, I feel sure, was in earnest when he asked for work."

"Helen!" bawled uncle Jay-Jay.

"Well, what is it?" she inquired, appearing in the doorway.

"Next time Sybylla is giving a tramp some tucker, you keep a sharp eye on her or she will be sloping one of these days. There was a young fellow here today with a scarlet moustache and green eyes, and she's clean gone on him, and has been bullying me to give him half Caddagat."

"What a disgusting thing to say! Uncle, you ought to be ashamed of yourself," I exclaimed.

"Very well, I'll be careful," said aunt Helen, departing.

"What with the damned flies, and the tramps, and a pesky thing called Sybylla, a man's life ain't worth a penny to him," said uncle.

We fell into silence, which was broken presently by a dirty red-bearded face appearing over the garden gate, and a man's voice:

"Good day, boss! Give us a chew of tobaccer?"

"I'm not the boss," said uncle with assumed fierceness.

"Then who is?" inquired the man.

Uncle pointed his thumb at me, and, rolling out on the floor again as though very sleepy, began to snore. The tramp grinned, and made his request of me. I took him around to the back, served him with flour, beef, and an inch or two of rank tobacco out of a keg which had been bought for the purpose. Refusing a drink of

milk which I offered, he resumed his endless tramp with
a "So long, little missy. God bless your pleasant face."

I watched him out of sight. One of my brothers—
one of God's children under the Southern Cross. Did
these old fellows really believe in the God whose name
they mentioned so glibly? I wondered. But I am thankful that while at Caddagat it was only rarely that my
old top-heavy thoughts troubled me. Life was so pleasant that I was content merely to be young—a chit in
the first flush of teens, health, hope, happiness, youth—
a heedless creature recking not for the morrow.

CHAPTER FIFTEEN

When the Heart is Young

About a week or so after I first met Harold Beecham,
aunt Helen allowed me to read a letter she had received
from the elder of the two Misses Beecham. It ran as
follows:

My dearest Helen,
    This is a begging letter, and I am writing an-
other to your mother at the same time. I am asking her to allow her grand-daughter to spend a few
weeks with me, and I want you to use your influence in the matter. Sarah has not been well lately,
and is going to Melbourne for a change, and as I
will be lonely while she is away Harold insists upon me having someone to keep me company—
you know how considerate the dear boy is. I
hardly like to ask you to spare your little girl to
me. It must be a great comfort to have her. I could

have got Miss Benson to stay with me, but Harold will not hear of her. He says she is too slow, and would give us both the mopes. But he says your little niece will keep us all alive. Julius was telling me the other day that he could not part with her, as she makes "the old barracks," as he always calls Caddagat, echo with fun and noise. I am so looking forward to seeing her, as she is dear Lucy's child. Give her my love, &c., &c.

and as a postscript the letter had—"Harold will go up for Sybylla on Wednesday afternoon. I do hope you will be able to spare her to me for a while."

"Oh, auntie, how lovely!" I exclaimed. "What are you laughing at?"

"For whom do you think Harry wants the companion? It is nice to have an old auntie, as a blind, is it not? Well, all is fair in love and war. You have permission to use me in any way you like."

I pretended to miss her meaning.

Grannie consented to Miss Beecham's proposal, and ere the day arrived I had a trunk packed with some lovely new dresses, and was looking forward with great glee to my visit to Five-Bob Downs.

One o'clock on Wednesday afternoon arrived; two o'clock struck, and I was beginning to fear no one was coming for me, when, turning to look out the window for the eighteenth time, I saw the straight blunt nose of Harold Beecham passing. Grannie was serving afternoon tea on the veranda. I did not want any, so got ready while my escort was having his.

It was rather late when we bowled away at a tremendous pace in a red sulky, my portmanteau strapped on at the back, and a thoroughbred American trotter, which had taken prizes at Sydney shows, harnessed to the front. We just whizzed! It was splendid! The stones and dust rose in a thick cloud from the whirling wheels and flying hoofs, and the posts of the wire fence on our left passed like magic as we went. Mr. Beecham allowed me to drive after a time while he sat ready to take the reins should an emergency arise.

It was sunset—most majestic hour of the twenty-four —when we drove up to the great white gates which opened into the avenue leading to the main homestead of Five-Bob Downs station—beautiful far-reaching Five-Bob Downs! Dreamy blue hills rose behind, and wide rich flats stretched before, through which the Yarrangung river, glazed with sunset, could be seen like a silver snake winding between shrubberied banks. The odor from the six-acred flower-garden was overpowering and delightful. A breeze gently swayed the crowd of trees amid the houses, and swept over the great orchard which sloped down from the south side of the houses. In the fading sunlight thirty iron roofs gleamed and glared, and seemed like a little town; and the yelp of many dogs went up at the sound of our wheels. Ah! beautiful, beautiful Five-Bob Downs!

It seemed as though a hundred dogs leapt forth to greet us when that gate flew open, but I subsequently discovered there were but twenty-three.

Two female figures came out to meet us—one nearly six feet high, the other, a tiny creature, seemed about eighteen inches, though, of course, was more than that.

"I've brought her, aunt Gussie," said Harold, jumping out of the sulky, though not relinquishing the reins, while he kissed the taller figure, and the small one attached itself to his leg saying, "Dimme wide."

"Hullo! Possum, why wasn't old Spanker let go? I see he's not among the dogs," and my host picked the tiny individual up in his arms and got into the sulky to give her the desired ride, while after being embraced by Miss Beecham and lifted to the ground by her nephew, I went with the former over an asphalted tennis-court, through the wide garden, then across a broad veranda into the great, spreading, one-storied house from which gleamed many lights.

"I am so glad you have come, my dear. I must have a good look at you when we get into the light. I hope you are like your mother."

This prospect discomfited me. I knew she would find a very ugly girl with not the least resemblance to her pretty mother, and I cursed my appearance under my breath.

"Your name is Sybylla," Miss Beecham continued, "Sybylla Penelope. Your mother used to be very dear to me, but I don't know why she doesn't write to me now. I have never seen her since her marriage. It seems strange to think of her as the mother of eight— five boys and three girls, is it not?"

Miss Beecham had piloted me through a wide hall and along an extended passage out of which a row of bedrooms opened, into one of which we went.

"I hope you will be comfortable here, child. You need not dress for dinner while you are here; we never do, only on very special occasions."

"Neither do we at Caddagat," I replied.

"Now, child, let me have a good look at you without your hat."

"Oh, please don't!" I exclaimed, covering my face with my hands. "I am so dreadfully ugly that I cannot bear to have anyone look at me."

"What a silly little girl! You are not like your mother, but you are not at all plain-looking. Harold says you are the best style of girl he has seen yet, and sing beautifully. He got a tuner up from Sydney last week, so we will expect you to entertain us every night."

I learned that what Harold pronounced good no one dared gainsay at Five-Bob Downs.

We proceeded direct to the dining-room, and had not been there long when Mr. Beecham entered with the little girl on his shoulder. Miss Beecham had told me she was Minnie Benson, daughter of Harold's married overseer on Wyambeet, his adjoining station. Miss Beecham considered it would have been more seemly for her nephew to have selected a little boy as a plaything, but his sentiments regarding boys were that they were machines invented for the torment of adults.

"Well, O'Doolan, what sort of a day has it been?"

Harold inquired, setting his human toy upon the floor.

"Fine wezzer for yim duts," she promptly replied.

"Harold, it is shameful to teach a little innocent child such abominable slang; and you might give her a decent nickname," said Miss Beecham.

"O'Doolan, this is Miss Melvyn, and you have to do the same to her as you do to me."

The little thing held out her arms to me. I took her up, and she hugged and kissed me, saying:

"I luz oo, I luz oo," and turning to Mr. Beecham, "zat anuff?"

"Yes, that will do," he said; and she struggled to be put down.

Three jackeroos, an overseer, and two other young men came in, were introduced to me, and then we began dinner.

O'Doolan sat on a high chair beside Mr. Beecham, and he attended to all her wants. She did everything he did, even taking mustard, and was very brave at quelling the tears that rose to the doll-like blue eyes. When Mr. Beecham wiped his moustache, it was amusing to see her also wipe an imaginary one.

After dinner the jackeroos and the three other men repaired to a sitting-room in the backyard, which was specially set apart for them, and where they amused themselves as they liked. My host and hostess, myself, and the child, spent the evening in a tiny sitting-room adjoining the dining-room. Miss Beecham entertained me with conversation and the family albums, and Harold amused himself entirely with the child.

Once when they were absent for a few minutes, Miss Beecham told me it was ridiculous the way he fussed with the child, and that he had her with him more than half his time. She also asked me what I thought of her nephew. I evaded the question by querying if he was always so quiet and good-tempered.

"Oh dear, no. He is considered a particularly bad-tempered man. Not one of the snarling nasty tempers, but——"

Here the re-entry of the owner of the temper put a stop to this conversation.

Harold gave O'Doolan rides on his back, going on all-fours. She shouted in childish glee, and wound up by curling her small proportions on his broad chest, and going to sleep there.

Mrs. Benson had sent for little O'Doolan, and Harold took her home next day. He invited me to accompany him, so we set out in the sulky with O'Doolan on my lap. It was a pleasant drive of twelve miles to and from Wyambeet. O'Doolan was much distressed at parting from Mr. Beecham, but he promised to come for her again shortly.

"One little girl at a time is enough for me to care for properly," he said to me in the winning manner with which, and his wealth, unintentionally and unconsciously made slaughter among the hearts of the fair sex.

CHAPTER SIXTEEN

When Fortune Smiles

"Now, Harold, you have compelled Sybylla to come here, you must not let the time drag with her," said Miss Beecham.

It was the second day after my arrival at Five-Bob. Lunch was over, and we had adjourned to the veranda. Miss Beecham was busy at her work-table; I was ensconced on a mat on the floor reading a book; Harold was stretched in a squatter's chair some distance away. His big brown hands were clasped behind his head, his chin rested on his broad chest, his eyes were closed, he

occasionally thrust his lower lip forward and sent a puff
of breath upwards to scatter the flies from his face; he
looked a big monument of comfort, and answered his
aunt's remarks lazily:

"Yes, aunt, I'll do my best"; and to me, "Miss
Melvyn, while here, please bear in mind that it will be
no end of pleasure to me to do anything for your enjoyment. Don't fail to command me in any way."

"Thank you, Mr. Beecham. I will not fail to avail
myself of your offer."

"The absurdity of you two children addressing each
other so formally," said Miss Beecham. "Why, you are
a sort of cousins almost, by right of old friendship between the families. You must call me aunt."

After this Mr. Beecham and I called each other
nothing when in Miss Beecham's hearing, but adhered
to formality on other occasions.

Harold looked so comfortable and lazy that I longed
to test how far he meant the offer he had made me.

"I'm just dying for a row on the river. Would you
oblige me?" I said.

"Just look at the thermometer!" exclaimed Miss Augusta. "Wait till it gets cooler, child."

"Oh, I love the heat!" I replied. "And I am sure it
won't hurt his lordship. He's used to the sun, to judge
from all appearances."

"Yes, I don't think it can destroy my complexion,"
he said good-humoredly, rubbing his finger and thumb
along his stubble-covered chin. The bushmen up-coun-
try shaved regularly every Sunday morning, but never
during the week for anything less than a ball. They did
this to obviate the blue—what they termed "scraped
pig"—appearance of the faces of city men in the habit
of using the razor daily, and to which they preferred
the stubble of a seven-days' beard. "I'll take you to the
river in half an hour," he said, rising from his seat.
"First I must stick on one of Warrigal's shoes that he's
flung. I want him tomorrow, and must do it at once, as
he always goes lame if ridden immediately after shoeing."

"Shall I blow the bellows?" I volunteered.

"Oh no, thanks. I can manage myself. It would be better though if I had some one. But I can get one of the girls."

"Can't you get one of the boys?" said his aunt.

"There's not one in. I sent every one off to the Triangle paddock today to do some drafting. They all took their quart pots and a snack in their saddle-bags, and won't be home till dark."

"Let me go," I persisted; "I often blow the bellows for uncle Jay-Jay, and think it great fun."

The offer of my services being accepted, we set out.

Harold took his favorite horse, Warrigal, from the stable, and led him to the blacksmith's forge under an open, stringybark-roofed shed, nearly covered with creepers. He lit a fire and put a shoe in it. Doffing his coat and hat, rolling up his shirt-sleeves, and donning a leather apron, he began preparing the horse's hoof.

When an emergency arose that necessitated uncle Jay-Jay shoeing his horses himself, I always manipulated the bellows, and did so with great decorum, as he was very exacting and I feared his displeasure. In this case it was different. I worked the pole with such energy that it almost blew the whole fire out of the pan, and sent the ashes and sparks in a whirlwind around Harold. The horse—a touchy beast—snorted and dragged his foot from his master's grasp.

"That the way to blow?" I inquired demurely.

"Take things a little easier," he replied.

I took them so very easily that the fire was on the last gasp and the shoe nearly cold when it was required.

"This won't do," said Beecham.

I recommended blowing with such force that he had to retreat.

"Steady! steady!" he shouted.

"Sure O'i can't plaze yez anyhows," I replied.

"If you don't try to plaze me directly I'll punish you in a way you won't relish," he said laughingly. But I knew he was thinking of a punishment which I would have secretly enjoyed.

"If you don't let me finish this work I'll make one of the men do it tonight by candle-light when they come home tired. I know you wouldn't like them to do that," he continued.

" 'Arrah, go on, ye're only tazin'!" I retorted. "Don't you remember telling me that Warrigal was such a nasty-tempered brute that he allowed no one but yourself to touch him?"

"Oh well, then, I'm floored, and will have to put up with the consequences," he good-humoredly made answer.

Seeing that my efforts to annoy him failed, I gave in, and we were soon done, and then started for the river— Mr. Beecham clad in a khaki suit and I in a dainty white wrapper and fly-away sort of hat. In one hand my host held a big white umbrella, with which he shaded me from the hot rays of the October sun, and in the other was a small basket containing cake and lollies for our delectation.

Having traversed the half-mile between the house and river, we pushed off from the bank in a tiny boat just big enough for two. In the teeth of Harold's remonstrance I persisted in dangling over the boat-side to dabble in the clear, deep, running water. In a few minutes we were in it. Being unable to swim, but for my companion it would have been all up with me. When I rose to the surface he promptly seized me, and without much effort, clothes and all, swam with me to the bank, where we landed—a pair of sorry figures. Harold had mud all over his nose, and in general looked very ludicrous. As soon as I could stand I laughed.

"Oh, for a snapshot of you!" I said.

"We might have both been drowned," he said sternly.

"Mights don't fly," I returned. "And it was worth the dip to see you looking such a comical article." We were both minus our hats.

His expression relaxed.

"I believe you would laugh at your own funeral. If I look queer, you look forty times worse. Run for your life and get a hot bath and a drop of spirits or you'll catch your death of cold. Aunt Augusta will take a fit and tie you up for the rest of the time in case something more will happen to you."

"Catch a death of cold!" I ejaculated. "It is only good, pretty little girls, who are a blessing to everyone, who die for such trifles; girls like I am always live till nearly ninety, to plague themselves and everybody else. I'll sneak home so that your aunt won't see me, and no one need be a bit the wiser."

"You'll be sun-struck!" he said in dismay.

"Take care you don't get daughter-struck," I said perkily, turning to flee, for it had suddenly dawned upon me that my thin wet clothing was outlining my figure rather too clearly for propriety.

By a circuitous way I managed to reach my bedroom unseen. It did not take me long to change my clothes, hang them to dry, and appear on the main veranda where Miss Augusta was still sewing. I picked up the book I had left on the mat, and, taking up a position in a hammock near her, I commenced to read.

"You did not stay long at the river," she remarked. "Have you been washing your head? I never saw the like of it. Such a mass of it. It will take all day to dry."

Half an hour later Harold appeared dressed in a warm suit of tweed. He was looking pale and languid, as though he had caught a chill, and shivered as he threw himself on a lounge. I was feeling none the worse for my immersion.

"Why did you change your clothes, Harold? You surely weren't cold on a day like this. Sybylla has changed hers too, when I come to notice it, and her hair is wet. Have you had an accident?" said Miss Augusta, rising from her chair in a startled manner.

"Rubbish!" ejaculated Harold in a tone which forbade further questioning, and the matter dropped.

She presently left the veranda, and I took the opportunity to say, "It is yourself that requires the hot bath and a drop of spirits, Mr. Beecham."

"Yes; I think I'll take a good stiff nobbler. I feel a

trifle squeamish. It gave me a bit of a turn when I rose
to the top and could not see you. I was afraid the boat
might have stunned you in capsizing, and you would be
drowned before I could find you."

"Yes; I would have been such a loss to the world in
general if I had been drowned," I said satirically.

Several jackeroos, a neighboring squatter, and a couple
of bicycle tourists turned up at Five-Bob that evening,
and we had a jovial night. The great, richly furnished
drawing-room was brilliantly lighted, and the magnificent Erard grand piano sang and rang again with music,
now martial and loud, now soft and solemn, now gay
and sparkling. I made the very pleasant discovery that
Harold Beecham was an excellent pianist, a gifted
player on the violin, and sang with a strong, clear, well-
trained tenor, which penetrated far into the night. How
many, many times I have lived those nights over again!
The great room with its rich appointments, the superb
piano, the lights, the merriment, the breeze from the
east, rich with the heavy intoxicating perfume of countless flowers; the tall perfect figure, holding the violin
with a master hand, making it speak the same language
as I read in the dark eyes of the musician, while above
and around was the soft warmth of an Australian summer night.

Ah, health and wealth, happiness and youth, joy and
light, life and *love!* What a warm-hearted place is the
world, how full of pleasure, good, and beauty, when
fortune smiles! *When fortune smiles!*

Fortune did smile, and broadly, in those days. We
played tricks on one another, and had a deal of innocent fun and frolic. I was a little startled one night on
retiring to find a huge goanna near the head of my bed.
I called Harold to dislodge the creature, when it came
to light that it was roped to the bedpost. Great was the
laughter at my expense. Who tethered the goanna I
never discovered, but I suspected Harold. In return for
this joke, I collected all the portable clocks in the

house—about twenty—and arrayed them on his bed-room table. The majority of them were Waterburys for common use, so I set each alarm for a different hour. Inscribing a placard "Hospital for Insane," I erected it above his door. Next morning I was awakened at three o'clock by fifteen alarms in concert outside my door. When an hour or two later I emerged I found a notice on my door, "This way to the Zoo."

It was a very busy time for the men at Five-Bob. Wagons were arriving with shearing supplies, for it was drawing nigh unto the great event of the year. In another week's time the bleat of thousands of sheep, and the incense of much tar and wool, would be ascending to the heavens from the vicinity of Five-Bob Downs. I was looking forward to the shearing. There never was any at Caddagat. Uncle did not keep many sheep, and always sold them long-wooled and rebought after shearing.

I had not much opportunity of persecuting Harold during the daytime. He and all his subordinates were away all day, busy drafting, sorting, and otherwise pottering with sheep. But I always, and Miss Augusta sometimes, went to meet them coming home in the evening. It was great fun. The dogs yelped and jumped about. The men were dirty with much dust, and smelled powerfully of sheep, and had worked hard all day in the blazing sun, but they were never too tired for fun, or at night to dance, after they had bathed and dressed. We all had splendid horses. They reared and pranced; we galloped and jumped every log which came in our path. Jokes, repartee, and nonsense rattled off our tongues. We did not worry about thousands of our fellows—starving and reeking with disease in city slums. We were selfish. We were heedless. We were happy. We were young.

Harold Beecham was a splendid host. Anyone possessed of the least talent for enjoyment had a pleasant time as his guest. He was hospitable in a quiet unostentatious manner. His overseer, jackeroos, and other em-

ployees were all allowed the freedom of home, and
could invite whom they pleased to Five-Bob Downs. It
is all very well to talk of good hosts. Bah, I could be a
good hostess myself if I had Harold Beecham's superior
implements of the art! With an immense station, plenty
of house-room, tennis courts, musical instruments; a
river wherein to fish, swim, and boat; any number of
horses, vehicles, orchards, gardens, guns, and ammu-
nition no object, it is easy to be a good host.

I had been just a week at Five-Bob when uncle Julius
came to take me home, so I missed the shearing. Caddagat had been a dull hole without me, he averred, and
I must return with him that very day. Mr. and Miss
Beecham remonstrated. Could I not be spared at least
a fortnight longer? It would be lonely without me.
Thereupon uncle Jay-Jay volunteered to procure Miss
Benson from Wyambeet as a substitute. Harold de-
clined the offer with thanks.

"The schemes of youngsters are very transparent,"
said uncle Jay-Jay and Miss Augusta, smiling signifi-
cantly at us. I feigned to be dense, but Harold smiled
as though the insinuation was not only known, but also
agreeable to him.

Uncle was inexorable, so home I had to go. It was
sweet to me to hear from the lips of my grandmother
and aunt that my absence had been felt.

As a confidante aunt Helen was the pink of perfection—tactful and sympathetic. My feather-brained chatter must often have bored her, but she apparently was
ever interested in it.

I told her long yarns of how I had spent my time at
the Beechams; of the deafening duets Harold and I
had played on the piano; and how he would persist in
dancing with me, and he being so tall and broad, and I
so small, it was like being stretched on a hay-rack, and
very fatiguing. I gave a graphic account of the arguments—tough ones they were too—that Miss Augusta
had with the overseer on religion, and many other subjects; of one jackeroo who gabbed never-endingly about
his great relations at home; another who incessantly

clattered about spurs, whips, horses, and sport; and the third one—Joe Archer—who talked literature and trash with me.

"What was Harry doing all this time?" asked auntie. "What did he say?"

Harold had been present all the while, yet I could not call to mind one thing he had said. I cannot remember him ever holding forth on a subject or cause, as most people do at one time or another.

CHAPTER SEVENTEEN

Idylls of Youth

In pursuance of his duty a government mail-contractor passed Caddagat every Monday, dropping the Bossier mail as he went. On Thursday we also got the post, but had to depend partly on our own exertions.

A selector at Dogtrap, on the Wyambeet run, at a point of the compass ten miles down the road from Caddagat, kept a hooded van. Every Thursday he ran this to and from Gool-Gool for the purpose of taking to market vegetables and other farm produce. He also took parcels and passengers, both ways, if called upon to do so. Caddagat and Five-Bob gave him a great deal of carrying, and he brought the mail for these and two or three other places. It was one of my duties, or rather privileges, to ride thither on Thursday afternoon for the post, a leather bag slung around my shoulders for the purpose. I always had a splendid mount, and the weather being beautifully hot, it was a jaunt which I never failed to enjoy. Frank Hawden went with me once or twice—not because grannie or I thought his escort necessary. The idea was his own; but I gave him such a time that he was forced to relinquish accompanying me as a bad job.

Harold Beecham kept a sniveling little Queensland black boy as a sort of black-your-boots, odd-jobs slavey or factotum, and he came to Dogtrap for the mail, but after I started to ride for it Harold came regularly for his mail himself. Our homeward way lay together for two miles, but he always came with me till nearly in sight of home. Some days we raced till our horses were white with lather; and once or twice mine was in such a state that we dismounted, and Harold unsaddled him and wiped the sweat off with his towel saddle-cloth, to remove the evidence of hard riding, so that I would not get into a scrape with uncle Jay-Jay. Other times we dawdled, so that when we parted the last rays of sunset would be laughing at us between the white trunks of the tall gum-trees, the kookaburras would be making the echoes ring with their mocking good-night, and scores of wild duck would be flying quickly roostward. As I passed through the angle formed by the creek and the river, about half a mile from home, there came to my ears the cheery clink-clink of hobble-chains, the jangle of horse-bells, and the gleam of a dozen campfires. The shearing was done out in Riverina now, and the men were all going home. Day after day dozens of them passed along the long white road, bound for Monaro and the cool country beyond the blue peaks to the southeast, where the shearing was about to begin. When I had come to Caddagat the last of them had gone "down" with horses poor; now they were traveling "up" with their horses—some of them thoroughbreds —rolling fat, and a check for their weeks of back-bending labor in their pockets. But whether coming or going they always made to Caddagat to camp. That camping-ground was renowned as the best from Monaro to Riverina. It was a well-watered and sheltered nook, and the ground was so rich that there was always a mouthful of grass to be had there. It was a rare thing to see it without a fire; and the empty jam-tins, bottles, bits of bag, paper, tent-pegs, and fish-tins to be found there would have loaded a dozen wagons.

Thursday evening was always spent in going to Dog-trap, and all the other days had their pleasant tasks and were full of wholesome enjoyment. The blue senna flowers along the river gave place to the white bloom of the tea-tree. Grannie, uncle, and aunt Helen filled the house with girl visitors for my pleasure. In the late afternoon, as the weather got hot, we went for bogeys in a part of the river two miles distant. Some of the girls from neighboring runs brought their saddles, others from town had to be provided therewith, which produced a dearth in side-saddles, and it was necessary for me to take a man's. With a rollicking gallop and a bogey ahead, that did not trouble me. Aunt Helen always accompanied us on our bathing expeditions to keep us in check. She was the only one who bothered with a bathing-dress. The rest of us reefed off our clothing, in our hurry sending buttons in all directions, and plunged into the pleasant water. Then—such water-fights, frolic, laughter, shouting and roaring fun as a dozen strong healthy girls can make when enjoying themselves. Aunt Helen generally called time before we were half inclined to leave. We would linger too long, then there would be a great scramble for clothes, next for horses, and with wet hair streaming on our towels, we would go home full belt, twelve sets of galloping hoofs making a royal clatter on the hard dusty road. Grannie made a rule that when we arrived late we had to unsaddle our horses ourselves, and not disturb the working men from their meal for our pleasure. We mostly were late, and so there would be a tight race to see who would arrive at table first. A dozen heated horses were turned out unceremoniously, a dozen saddles and bridles dumped down anywhere anyhow, and their occupants, with wet disheveled hair and cloth-ing in glorious disarray, would appear at table averring that they were starving.

The Caddagat folk were enthusiastic anglers. Fishing was a favorite and often enjoyed amusement of the household. In the afternoon a tinful of worms would be dug out of one of the water-races, tackle collected, horses saddled, and grannie, uncle, aunt, Frank Hawden, myself, and any one else who had happened to drop in, would repair to the fish-holes three miles distant. I hate fishing. Ugh! The hideous barbarity of shoving a hook through a living worm, and the cruelty of taking the fish off the hook! Uncle allowed no idlers at the river—all had to manipulate a rod and line. Indulging in pleasant air-castles, I generally forgot my cork till the rod would be jerked in my hand, when I would pull—too late! the fish would be gone. Uncle would lecture me for being a jackdaw, so next time I would glare at the cork unwinkingly, and pull at the first signs of it bobbing—too soon! the fish would escape again, and I would again be in disgrace. After a little experience I found it was a good plan to be civil to Frank Hawden when the prospect of fishing hung around, and then he would attend to my line as well as his own, while I read a book which I smuggled with me. The fish-hole was such a shrub-hidden nook that, though the main road passed within two hundred yards, neither we nor our horses could be seen by the travelers thereon. I lay on the soft moss and leaves and drank deeply of the beauties of nature. The soft rush of the river, the scent of the shrubs, the golden sunset, occasionally the musical clatter of hoofs on the road, the gentle noises of the fishers fishing, the plop, plop of a platypus disporting itself midstream, came to me as sweetest elixir in my ideal, dream-of-a-poet nook among the pink-based, gray-topped, moss-carpeted rocks.

I was a creature of joy in those days. Life is made up of little things. It was a small thing to have a little pocket-money to spend on anything that took my fancy —a very small thing, and yet how much pleasure it gave me. Though eating is not one of the great aims of my life, yet it was nice to have enough of any delicacy one fancied. Not that we ever went hungry at home, but when one has nothing to eat in the hot weather but bread and beef it gives them tendency to dream of fruit and cool dainties. When one thinks of the countless army of one's fellows who are daily selling their very souls for the barest necessaries of life, I suppose we—irresponsible beings—should be thankful to God for allowing us, by scratching and scraping all our lives, to keep a crust in our mouth and a rag on our back. I am not thankful. I have been guilty of what Pat would term a "digresshion"—I started about going for the mail at Dogtrap. Harold Beecham never once missed taking me home on Thursdays, even when his shearing was in full swing and he must have been very busy. He never once uttered a word of love to me—not so much as one of the soft nothings in which young people of opposite sexes often deal without any particular significance. Whether he went to all the bother and waste of time accruing from escorting me home out of gentlemanliness alone, was a mystery to me. I desired to find out, and resolved to drive instead of ride to Dogtrap one day to see what he would say.

Grannie assented to the project. Of course I could drive for once if I didn't feel able to ride, but the horses had been spelling for a long time and were very frisky. I must take Frank with me or I might get my neck broken.

I flatly opposed the idea of Frank Hawden going with me. He would make a mull of the whole thing. It was no use arguing with grannie and impressing upon her the fact that I was not the least nervous concerning the horses. I could take Frank with me in the buggy, ride, or stay at home. I preferred driving. Accordingly the fat horses were harnessed to the buggy, and with many injunctions to be careful and not forget the parcels, we set out. Frank Hawden's presence spoiled it all, but I determined to soon make short work of him.

There was one gate to go through, about four miles from the house. Frank Hawden got out to open it. I drove through, and while he was pushing it to, laid the whip on the horses and went off full tilt. He ran after me shouting all manner of things that I could not hear on account of the rattle of the buggy. One horse began kicking up, so, to give him no time for further pranks, I drove at a good round gallop, which quickly left the lovable jackeroo a speck in the distance. The dust rose in thick clouds, the stones rattled from the whirling wheels, the chirr! chirr! of a myriad cicadas filled the air, and the white road glistened in the dazzling sunlight. I was enjoying myself tip-top, and chuckled to think of the way I had euchred Frank Hawden. It was such a good joke that I considered it worth two of the blowings-up I was sure of getting from grannie for my conduct.

It was not long before I fetched up at Dogtrap homestead, where, tethered to the "six-foot" paling fence which surrounded the flower-garden, was Harold Beecham's favorite, great, black, saddle-horse Warrigal. The vicious brute turned his beautiful head, displaying a white star on the forehead, and snorted as I approached. His master appeared on the veranda raising his soft panama hat, and remarking, "Well I never! You're not by yourself, are you?"

"I am. Would you please tell Mrs. Butler to bring out grannie's parcels and post at once. I'm afraid to dawdle, it's getting late."

He disappeared to execute my request and reappeared in less than a minute.

"Mr. Beecham, please would you examine Barney's harness. Something must be hurting him. He has been kicking up all the way."

Examining the harness and noticing the sweat that was dripping from the animals, panting from their run, he said:

"It looks as though you've been making the pace a cracker. There is nothing that is irritating Barney in the least. If he's putting on any airs it is because he is frisky and not safe for you to drive. How did Julius happen to let you away by yourself?"

"I'm not frightened," I replied.

"I see you're not. You'd be game to tackle a pair of wild elephants, I know, but you must remember you're not much bigger than a sparrow sitting up there, and I won't let you go back by yourself."

"You cannot stop me."

"I can."

"You can't."

"I can."

"You can't."

"I can."

"How?"

"I'm going with you," he said.

"You're not."

"I am."

"You're not."

"I am."

"You ar-r-re not."

"I am."

"You are, ar-r-re not."

"We'll see whether I will or not in a minute or two," he said with amusement.

"But, Mr. Beecham, I object to your company. I am quite capable of taking care of myself; besides, if you come home with me I will not be allowed out alone again—it will be altogether unpleasant for me."

Mrs. Butler now appeared with the mail and some parcels, and Harold stowed them in the buggy.

"You'd better come in an' 'ave a drop of tay-warter, miss, the kittle's bilin'; and I have the table laid out for both of yez."

"No, thank you, Mrs. Butler. I can't possibly stay today, it's getting late. I must hurry off. Good-bye! Good afternoon, Mr. Beecham."

I turned my buggy and pair smartly around and was swooping off. Without a word Harold was at their heads and seized the reins. He seized his horse's bridle, where it was over the paling, and in a moment had him tied on the off-side of Barney, then stepping quietly into the buggy he put me away from the driver's seat as though I were a baby, quietly took the reins and whip, raised his hat to Mrs. Butler, who was smiling knowingly, and drove off.

I was highly delighted with his action, as I would have despised him as a booby had he given in to me, but I did not let my satisfaction appear. I sat as far away from him as possible, and pretended to be in a great huff. For a while he was too fully occupied in making Barney "sit up" to notice me, but after a few minutes he looked around, smiling a most annoying and pleasant smile.

"I'd advise you to straighten out your chin. It is too round and soft to look well screwed up that way," he said provokingly.

I tried to extinguish him with a look, but it had not the desired effect.

"Now you had better be civil, for I have got the big end of the whip," he said.

"I reserve to myself the right of behaving as I think fit in my own uncle's buggy. You are an intruder; it is yourself that should be civil."

I erected my parasol and held it so as to tease Harold. I put it down so that he could not see the horses. He quietly seized my wrist and held it out of his way for a time, and then loosing me said, "Now, behave."

I flouted it now, so that his ears and eyes were endangered, and he was forced to hold his hat on.

"I'll give you three minutes to behave, or I'll put you out," he said with mock severity.

"Shure it's me wot's behavin' beautiful," I replied, continuing my nonsense.

He pulled rein, seized me in one arm, and lifted me lightly to the ground.

"Now, you can walk till you promise to conduct yourself like a Christian!" he said, driving at a walk.

"If you wait till I promise anything, you'll wait till the end of the century. I'm quite capable of walking home."

"You'll soon get tired of walking in this heat, and your feet will be blistered in a mile with those bits of paper."

The bits of paper to which he alluded were a pair of

thin-soled white canvas slippers—not at all fitted for walking the eight miles on the hard hot road ahead of me. I walked resolutely on, without deigning a glance at Harold, who had slowed down to a crawling walk.

"Aren't you ready to get up now?" he inquired presently.

I did not reply. At the end of a quarter of a mile he jumped out of the buggy, seized upon me, lifted me in, and laughed, saying, "You're a very slashing little concern, but you are not big enough to do much damage."

We were about half-way home when Barney gave a tremendous lurch, breaking a trace and some other straps. Mr. Beecham was at the head of the plunging horse in a twinkling. The harness seemed to be scattered everywhere.

"I expect I had better walk on now," I remarked.

"Walk, be grannied! With two fat lazy horses to draw you?" returned Mr. Beecham.

Men are clumsy, stupid creatures regarding little things, but in their right place they are wonderful animals. If a buggy was smashed to smithereens, from one of their many mysterious pockets they would produce a knife and some string, and put the wreck into working order in no time.

Harold was as clever in this way as any other man with as much bushman ability as he had, so it was not long ere we were bowling along as merrily as ever.

Just before we came in sight of Caddagat he came to a standstill, jumped to the ground, untied Warrigal, and put the reins in my hand, saying—

"I think you can get home safely from here. Don't be in such a huff—I was afraid something might happen to you if alone. You needn't mention that I came with you unless you like. Good-bye."

"Good-bye, Mr. Beecham. Thank you for being so officious," I said by way of a parting shot.

"Old Nick will run away with you for being so ungrateful," he returned.

"Old Nick will have me anyhow," I thought to my-

self as I drove home amid the shadows. The hum of
the cicadas was still, and dozens of rabbits, tempted
out by the cool of the twilight, scuttled across my path
and hid in the ferns.

I wished the harness had not broken, as I feared it
would put a clincher on my being allowed out driving
alone in future.

Joe Slocombe, the man who acted as groom and
rouseabout, was waiting for me at the entrance gate.

"I'm glad you come at last, Miss Sybyller. The missus
has been in a dreadful stoo for fear something had
happened yuz. She's been runnin' in an' out like a
gurrl on the look-out fer her lover, and was torkin'
of sendin' me after yuz, but she went to her tea soon as
she see the buggy come in sight. I'll put all the parcels
on the back veranda, and yuz can go in at woncest or
yuz'll be late for yer tea."

"Joe, the harness broke and had to be tied up. That
is what kept me so late," I explained.

"The harness broke!" he exclaimed. "How the doose
is that! Broke here in the trace, and that strap! Well,
I'll be hanged! I thought them straps couldn't break
only onder a tremenjous strain. The boss is so dashed
partickler too. I believe he'll sool me off the place;
and I looked at that harness only yesterday. I can't
make out how it come to break so simple. The boss
will rise the devil of a shine, and say you might have
been killed."

This put a different complexion on things. I knew Joe
Slocombe could mend the harness with little trouble,
as it was because he was what uncle Jay-Jay termed a
"handy divil" at saddlery that he was retained at Caddagat. I said carelessly:

"If you mend the harness at once, Joe, uncle Julius
need not be bothered about it. As it happened, there
is no harm done, and I won't mention the matter."

"Thank you, miss," he said eagerly. "I'll mend it
at once."

Now that I had that piece of business so luckily disposed of, I did not feel the least nervous about meeting grannie. I took the mail in my arms and entered the dining-room, chirping pleasantly:

"Grannie, I'm such a good mail-boy. I have heaps of letters, and did not forget one of your commissions."

"I don't want to hear that now," she said, drawing her dear old mouth into a straight line, which told me I was not going to palm things off as easily as I thought. "I want a reason for your conduct this afternoon."

"Explain what, grannie?" I inquired.

"None of that pretence! Not only have you been most outrageously insulting to Mr. Hawden when I sent him with you, but you also deliberately and willfully disobeyed me."

Uncle Julius listened attentively, and Hawden looked at me with such a leer of triumph that my fingers tingled to smack his ears. Turning to my grandmother, I said distinctly and cuttingly:

"Grannie, I did not intentionally disobey you. Disobedience never entered my head. I hate that thing. His presence was detestable to me. When he got out at the gate I could not resist the impulse to drive off and leave him there. He looked such a complete jackdaw that you would have laughed yourself to see him."

"Dear, oh dear! You wicked hussy, what will become of you!" And grannie shook her head, trying to look stern, and hiding a smile in her serviette.

"Your manners are not improving, Sybylla. I fear you must be incorrigible," said aunt Helen.

When uncle Jay-Jay heard the whole particulars of the affair, he lay back in his chair and laughed fit to kill himself.

"You ought to be ashamed to always encourage her in her tomboyish ways, Julius. It grieves me to see she makes no effort to acquire a ladylike demeanor," said grannie.

Mr. Hawden had come off second-best, so he arose from his half-finished meal and stamped out, banging the door after him, and muttering something about "a disgustingly spoiled and petted tomboy," "a hideous barbarian," and so forth.

Uncle Jay-Jay related that story to everyone, dwelling with great delight upon the fact that Frank Hawden was forced to walk four miles in the heat and dust.

CHAPTER EIGHTEEN

As Short as I Wish had been the Majority of Sermons to which I have been Forced to give Ear

When alone I confessed to aunt Helen that Harold had accompanied me to within a short distance of home. She did not smile as usual, but looked very grave, and, drawing me in front of her, said:

"Sybylla, do you know what you are doing? Do you love Harry Beecham? Do you mean to marry him?"

"Aunt Helen, what a question to ask! I never dreamt of such a thing. He has never spoken a word of love to me. Marriage! I am sure he does not for an instant think of me in that light. I'm not seventeen."

"Yes, you are young, but some people's age cannot be reckoned by years. I am glad to see you have developed a certain amount of half-real and half-assumed youthfulness lately, but when the novelty of your present life wears away, your old mature nature will be there, so it is of no use feigning childishness. Harold Beecham is not given to speech—action with him is the same thing. Can you look at me straight, Sybylla, and say that Harold has not extended you something more than common politeness?"

Had aunt Helen put that question to me a day before, I would have blushed and felt guilty. But today not so. The words of the jackeroo the night before had struck home. "A hideous barbarian," he had called me, and it seemed to me he had told the truth. My life had been so pleasant lately that I had overlooked this fact, but now it returned to sting with redoubled bitterness. I had no lovable qualities to win for me the love of my fellows, which I so much desired.

I returned aunt Helen a gaze as steady as her own, and said bitterly:

"Aunt Helen, I can truly say he has never, and will never extend to me more than common politeness. Neither will any other man. Surely you know enough of masculine human nature to see there is no danger of a man losing his heart to a plain woman like me. Love in fancy and song is a pretty myth, embracing unity of souls, congeniality of tastes, and such like commodities. In workaday reality it is the lowest of passions, which is set alight by the most artistic nose and mouth, and it matters not if its object is vile, low, or brainless to idiocy, so long as it has these attributes."

"Sybylla, Sybylla," said auntie sadly, as if to herself. "In the first flush of girlhood, and so bitter. Why is this?"

"Because I have been cursed with the power of seeing, thinking, and, worse than all, feeling, and branded with the stinging affliction of ugliness," I replied.

"Now, Sybylla, you are going to think of yourself again. Something has put you out. Be sensible for once in a way. What you have said of men's love may be true in a sense, but it is not always so, and Harry is not that kind of man. I have known him all his life, and understand him, and feel sure he loves you truly. Tell me plainly, do you intend to accept him?"

"Intend to accept him!" I echoed. "I haven't once thought of such a possibility. I never mean to marry anyone."

"Don't you care for Harold? Just a little? Think."

"How could I care for him?"

"For many, many reasons. He is young, and very kind and gentle. He is one of the biggest and finest-looking men you could find. He is a man whom no one could despise, for he has nothing despicable about him. But, best of all, he is true, and that, I think, is the bedrock of all virtues."

"But he is so conceited," I remarked.

"That does not make him any the less lovable. I know another young person very conceited, and it does not prevent me from loving her dearly," here aunt Helen smiled affectionately at me. "What you complain of in Harold will wear off presently—life has been very easy for him so far, you see."

"But, auntie, I'm sure he thinks he could have any girl for the asking."

"Well, he has a great number to choose from, for they all like him."

"Yes, just for his money," I said scornfully. "But I'll surprise him if he thinks he can get me for the asking."

"Sybylla, never flirt. To play with a man's heart, I think, is one of the most horribly unwomanly actions our sex can be guilty of."

"I would scorn to flirt with any man," I returned with vigor. "Play with a man's heart! You'd really think they had such a thing, aunt Helen, to hear you talk. Hurt their vanity for a few days is the most a woman could do with any of them. I am sick of this preach, preach about playing with men's hearts. It is an old fable which should have been abolished long ago. It does not matter how a woman is played with."

"Sybylla, you talk at random. The shortcomings of men are no excuse for you to be unwomanly," said aunt Helen.

CHAPTER NINETEEN

The 9th of November 1896

The Prince of Wales's birthday up the country was celebrated as usual thereaway by the annual horse-races on the Wyambeet course, about fifteen miles from Caddagat.

The holding of these races was an elderly institution, and was followed at night by a servants' ball given by one of the squatters. Last year it had been Beecham's ball, the year before Bossier's, and this year it was to take place in the woolshed of James Grant of Yabtree. Our two girls, the gardener, and Joe Slocombe the groom, were to be present, as also were all the other employees about. Nearly every one in the district —masters and men—attended the races. We were going, Frank Hawden volunteering to stay and mind the house.

We started at nine o'clock. Grannie and uncle Boss sat in the front seat of the buggy, and aunt Helen and I occupied the back. Uncle always drove at a good round gallop. His idea was to have good horses, not donkeys, and not to spare them, as there were plenty more to be had any day. On this morning he went off at his usual pace. Grannie urged as remonstrance that the dust was fearful when going at that rate. I clapped my hands and exclaimed, "Go it, Mr. Bossier! Well done, uncle Jay-Jay! Hurrah for Clancy!"

Uncle first said he was glad to see I had the spirit of an Australian, and then threatened to put my nose above my chin if I failed to behave properly. Grannie remarked that I might have the spirit of an Australian, but I had by no means the manners of a lady; while aunt Helen ventured a wish that I might expend all my superfluous spirits on the way, so that I would be enabled to deport myself with a little decorum when arrived at the racecourse.

We went at a great pace; lizards and goannas scampered out of the way in dozens, and, clambering trees, eyed us unblinkingly as we passed. Did we see a person or vehicle a tiny speck ahead of us—in a short time they were as far away in the background.

"Please, uncle, let me drive," I requested.

"Couldn't now. Your grannie can't sit in the back-seat—neither could I—and look like a tame cuckatoo while you sat in front. You ask Harry to let you drive him. I bet he'll consent; he's sure to be in a sulky with a spare seat on spec. We're sure to overtake him in a few minutes."

There was a vehicle in the distance which proved to be from Five-Bob Downs, but as we overhauled it, it was the drag, and not a sulky. Harold occupied the driver's seat, and the other occupants were all ladies. I noticed the one beside him was wearing a very big hat, all ruffles, flowers, and plumes.

"Shall I pull up and get you a seat?" inquired uncle Jay-Jay.

"No, no, no."

The boss of Five-Bob drew to his side of the road, and when we had passed uncle began to tease:

"Got faint-hearted, did you? The flower-garden on that woman's hat corked your chances altogether. Never mind, don't you funk; I'll see that you have a fair show. I'll get you a regular cart-wheel next time I go to town, and we'll trim it up with some of old Barney's tail. If that won't fetch him, I'm sure nothing will."

Before we got to the racecourse Barney went lame through getting a stone in his hoof; this caused a delay which enabled the Five-Bob trap to catch us, and we pulled rein a little distance apart at the same time, to alight.

Mr. Beecham's groom went to his horses' heads while Harold himself assisted his carriageful of ladies to set foot on the ground. Aunt Helen and grannie went to talk to them, but I stayed with uncle Jay-Jay while he took the horses out. Somehow I was feeling very disappointed. I had expected Harold Beecham to be alone. He had attended on me so absolutely everywhere I had met him lately, that I had unconsciously grown to look upon him as mine exclusively; and now, seeing he would belong to his own party of ladies for the day, things promised to be somewhat flat without him.

"I told that devil of a Joe to be sure and turn up as soon as I arrived. I wanted him to water the horses, but I can't see him anywhere—the infernal, crawling, doosed idiot!" ejaculated uncle Julius.

"Never mind, uncle, let him have his holiday. I suppose he'd like to have time to spoon with his girl. I can easily water the horses."

"That would suit Joe, I have no doubt; but I don't pay him to let you water the horses. I'll water 'em myself."

He led one animal, I took the other, and we went in the direction of water a few hundred yards away.

"You run along to your grannie and the rest of them, and I'll go by myself," said uncle, but I kept on with the horse.

"You mustn't let a five-guinea hat destroy your hopes altogether," he continued, with a mischievous twinkle in his eyes. "If you stick to your guns you have a better show than anyone to bag the boss of Five-Bob."

"I am at a loss to interpret your innuendo, Mr. Bossier," I said stiffly.

"Now, little woman, you think you are very smart, but you can't deceive me. I've seen the game you and Harry have been up to this last month. If it had been

any other man, I would have restricted your capers
long ago."

"Uncle——" I began.

"Now, Sybylla, none of your crammers. There is no
harm in being a bit gone on Harry. It's only natural,
and just what I'd expect. I've known him since he was
born, and he's a good all-round fellow. His head is
screwed on the right way, his heart is in the right place,
and his principles are tip-top. He could give you fal-de-
rals and rubbish to no end, and wouldn't be stingy
either. You'll never get a better man. Don't you be
put out of the running so cheaply: hold your own and
win, that's my advice to you. There is nothing against
him, only temper—old Nick himself isn't a patch on
him for temper."

"Temper!" I exclaimed. "He is always so quiet and
pleasant."

"Yes, he controls it well. He's a fellow with a will
like iron, and that is what you want, as I find you have
none of your own. But be careful of Harry Beecham
in a temper. He is like a raging lion, and when his
temper dies away is a sulking brute, which is the vilest
of all tempers. But he is not vindictive, and is easy
managed, if you don't mind giving in and coaxing a
little."

"Now, uncle, you have had your say, I will have
mine. You seem to think I have more than a friendly
regard for Mr. Beecham, but I have not. I would not
marry him even if I could. I am so sick of every one
thinking I would marry any man for his possessions.
I would not stoop to marry a king if I did not love
him. As for trying to win a man, I would scorn any
action that way; I never intend to marry. Instead of
wasting so much money on me in presents and other
ways, I wish you would get me something to do, a profession that will last me all my life, so that I may be
independent."

"No mistake, you're a rum youngster. You can be
my companion till further orders. That's a profession
that will last you a goodish while."

With this I had to be contented, as I saw he considered what I had said as a joke.

I left uncle and went in quest of grannie, who, by this, was beyond the other side of the course, fully a quarter of a mile away. Going in her direction I met Joe Archer, one of the Five-Bob jackeroos, and a great chum of mine. He had a taste for literature, and we got on together like one o'clock. We sat on a log under a stringybark-tree and discussed the books we had read since last we met, and enjoyed ourselves so much that we quite forgot about the races or the flight of time until recalled from book-land by Harold Beecham's voice.

"Excuse me, Miss Melvyn, but your grannie has commissioned me to find you as we want to have lunch, and it appears you are the only one who knows the run of some of the tucker bags."

"How do you do, Mr. Beecham? Where are they going to have lunch?"

"Over in that clump of box-trees," he replied, pointing in the direction of a little rise at a good distance.

"How are you enjoying yourself?" he asked, looking straight at me.

"Treminjous intoirely, sor," I replied.

"I suppose you know the winner of every race," he remarked, quizzically watching Joe Archer, who was blushing and as uneasy as a schoolgirl when nabbed in the enjoyment of an illicit love-letter.

"Really, Mr. Beecham, Mr. Archer and I have been so interested in ourselves that we quite forgot there was such a thing as a race at all," I returned.

"You'd better see where old Boxer is. He might kick some of the other horses if you don't keep a sharp look-out," he said, turning to his jackeroo.

"Ladies before gentlemen," I interposed. "I want Mr. Archer to take me to grannie, then he can go and look after old Boxer."

"I'll escort you," said Beecham.

"Thank you, but I have requested Mr. Archer to do so."

"In that case, I beg your pardon, and will attend to Boxer while Joe does as you request."

Raising his hat he walked swiftly away with a curious expression on his usually pleasant face.

"By Jove, I'm in for it!" ejaculated my escort. "The boss doesn't get that expression on his face for nothing. You take my tip for it, he felt inclined to seize me by the scruff of the neck and kick me from here to Yabtree."

"Go on!"

"It's a fact. He did not believe in me not going to do his bidding immediately. He has a roaring derry on disobedience. Everyone has to obey him like winkie or they can take their beds up and trot off quick and lively."

"Mr. Beecham has sufficient sense to see I was the cause of your disobedience," I replied.

"That's where it is. He would not have cared had it been some other lady, but he gets mad if any one dares to monopolize you. I don't know how you are going to manage him. He is a pretty hot member sometimes."

"Mr. Archer, you presume! But throwing such empty banter aside, is Mr. Beecham really bad-tempered?"

"Bad-tempered is a tame name for it. You should have seen the dust he raised the other day with old Benson. He just did perform."

I was always hearing of Harold Beecham's temper, and wished I could see a little of it. He was always so imperturbably calm, and unfailingly good-tempered under the most trying circumstances, that I feared he had no emotions in him, and longed to stir him up.

Grannie greeted me with, "Sybylla, you are such a tiresome girl. I don't know how you have packed these hampers, and we want to have lunch. Where on earth have you been?"

Miss Augusta Beecham saluted me warmly with a kiss, and presented me to her sister Sarah, who also embraced me. I went through an introduction to several ladies and gentlemen, greeted my acquaintances, and then set to work in dead earnest to get our provisions laid out—the Five-Bob Downs party had theirs in readiness. Needless to say, we were combining forces. I had my work completed when Mr. Beecham appeared upon the scene with two young ladies. One was a bright-faced little brunette, and the other a tall light blonde, whom, on account of her much trimmed hat, I recognized as the lady who had been sitting on the box-seat of the Beecham drag that morning.

Joe Archer informed me in a whisper that she was Miss Blanche Derrick from Melbourne, and was considered one of the greatest beauties of that city.

This made me anxious to examine her carefully, but I did not get an opportunity of doing so. In the hurry to attend on the party, I missed the honor of an introduction, and when I was at leisure she was sitting at some distance on a log, Harold Beecham shading her in a most religious manner with a dainty parasol. In the afternoon she strolled away with him, and after I had attended to the remains of the feast, I took Joe Archer in tow. He informed me that Miss Derrick had arrived at Five-Bob three days before, and was setting her cap determinedly at his boss.

"Was she really very handsome?" I inquired.

"By Jove, yes!" he replied. "But one of your disdainful haughty beauties, who wouldn't deign to say good-day to a chap with less than six or seven thousand a year."

I don't know why I took no interest in the races. I knew nearly all the horses running. Some of them were uncle's; though he never raced horses himself, he kept some swift stock which he lent to his men for the occasion.

Of more interest to me than the races was the pair strolling at a distance. They were fit for an artist's models. The tall, broad, independent figure of the bushman with his easy gentlemanliness, his jockey costume enhancing his size. The equally tall majestic form of the city belle, whose self-confident fashionable style spoke of nothing appertaining to girlhood, but of the full-blown rose—indeed, a splendid pair physically!

Then I thought of my lack of beauty, my miserable five-feet-one-inch stature, and I looked at the man beside me, small and round-shouldered, and we were both dependent children of indigence. The contrast we presented to the other pair struck me hard, and I laughed a short bitter laugh.

I excused myself to my companion, and acceded to the request of several children to go on a flower- and gum-hunting expedition. We were a long time absent, and returning, the little ones scampered ahead and left me alone. Harold Beecham came to meet me, looking as pleasant as ever.

"Am I keeping grannie and uncle waiting?" I inquired.

"No. They have gone over an hour," he replied.

"Gone! How am I to get home? She must have been very angry to go and leave me. What did she say?"

"On the contrary, she was in great fiddle. She said to tell you not to kill yourself with fun, and as you are not going home, she left me to say good night. I suppose she kisses you when performing that ceremony," he said mischievously.

"Where am I going tonight?"

"To Five-Bob Downs, the camp of yours truly," he replied.

"I haven't got a dinner dress, and am not prepared. I will go home."

"We have plenty dinner dresses at Five-Bob without any more. It is Miss Melvyn we want," he said.

"Oh, bother you!" I retorted. "Men are such stupid creatures, and never understand about dress or anything. They think you could go to a ball in a wrapper."

"At all events, they are cute enough to know when they want a young lady at their place, no matter how she's dressed," he said good-humoredly.

On reaching the racecourse I was surprised to see aunt Helen there. From her I learned that grannie and uncle Jay-Jay had really gone home, but Mr. Beecham had persuaded them to allow aunt Helen and me to spend the night at Five-Bob Downs, our host promising to send or take us home on the morrow. Now that I was to have aunt Helen with me I was delighted at the prospect, otherwise I would have felt a little out of it. With aunt Helen, however, I was content anywhere, and built a castle in the air, wherein one day she and I were always to live together—for ever! Till death!

Going home aunt Helen occupied a front seat with Harold and Miss Derrick, and I was crammed in at the back beside Miss Augusta, who patted my hand and said she was delighted to see me.

A great concourse of young men and women in vehicles and on horseback, and in expectation of great fun, were wending their way to Yabtree—nearly every trap containing a fiddle, concertina, flute, or accordion in readiness for the fray.

CHAPTER TWENTY

Same Yarn—continued

Every station hand from Five-Bob, male and female, had gone to the ball at Yabtree. Harold and his overseer had to attend to the horses, while the jackeroos started a fire in the kitchen, opened windows and doors which had been locked all day, and saw to the comfort of the gentlemen guests.

Aunt Helen and I shared the one bedroom. As we

had not fresh dresses to put on we had to make the best of our present toilet.

I unplaited my hair (shook the dust out of it) and wore it flowing. We washed and dusted ourselves, and wore as adornment—roses. Crimson and cream roses paid the penalty of peeping in the window. Aunt Helen plucked some of them, which she put in my hair and belt, and pinned carefully at my throat, and then we were ready. Miss Beecham assured us there was nothing to be done, as the maids had set the table and prepared the viands for a cold meal before leaving in the morning, so we proceeded to the drawing-room to await the arrival of the other visitors. They soon made their appearance. First, two stout old squatters with big laughs and bigger corporations, then Miss Augusta Beecham, next Joe Archer the overseer, and the two other jackeroos. After these appeared a couple of governesses, Mr., Mrs., and Miss Benson, a clergyman, an auctioneer, a young friend of Harold's from Cootamundra, a horse-buyer, a wool-classer, Miss Sarah Beecham, and then Miss Derrick brought herself and her dress in with great style and airs. She was garbed in a sea-green silk, and had jewelry on her neck, arms, and hair. Her self-confident mien was suggestive of the conquest of many masculine hearts. She was a big handsome woman. Beside her, I in my crushed white muslin dress was as overshadowed as a little white handkerchief would be in comparison to a gorgeous shawl heavily wrought in silks and velvet. She was given the best seat as though she were a princess. She sat down with great indifference, twirled a bracelet around her wrist, languidly opened her fan, and closed her eyes as she wafted it slowly to and fro.

"By Jove, isn't she a splendid creature!" enthusiastically whispered a gentleman sitting beside me.

I looked at her critically. She was very big, and in a bony stiff way was much developed in figure. She had a nice big nose, and a long well-shaped face, a thin straight mouth, and empty light eyes. If my attention had not been called to her I would not have noticed her one way or the other, but being pointed to as a beauty, I weighed her according to my idea of facial charm, and pronounced her one of the most insipid-looking people I had set eyes upon.

She was the kind of woman with whom men become much infatuated. She would never make a fool of herself by letting her emotions run away with her, because she had no emotions, but lived in a sea of unruffled self-consciousness and self-confidence. Any man would be proud to introduce her as his wife to his friends whom he had brought home to dinner. She would adorn the head of his table. She would never worry him with silly ideas. She would never act with impropriety. She would never become a companion to her husband. Bah, a man does not want his wife to be a companion! There were myths and fables in the old day; so there are now. The story that men like a companion as well as a wife is an up-to-date one.

This train of thought was interrupted by our host, who appeared in the doorway, clad from sole to neck in white. We steered for the dining-room—twenty-two all told—thirteen men and nine representatives of the other sex.

Aunt Helen got one seat of honor near the head of the table and Miss Derrick another. I drifted to the foot among the unimportant younger fry, where we had no end of fun and idle chatter. We had to wait on ourselves, and as all formality was dispensed with, it was something like a picnic.

The heat was excessive. Every window and door were open, and the balmy, almost imperceptible, zephyrs which faintly rustled the curtains and kissed our perspiration-beaded brows were rich with many scents from the wide old flower-garden, which, despite the drought, brought forth a wealth of blossom.

When done eating we had to wash the dishes. Such a scamper ensued back and forward to the kitchen, which rang with noise and merriment. Everyone was helping, hindering, laughing, joking, teasing, and brimming over with fun and enjoyment. When we had completed this task, dancing was proposed. Some of the elderly and more sensible people said it was too hot, but all the young folks did not care a rap for the temperature. Harold had no objections, Miss Derrick was agreeable, Miss Benson announced herself ready and willing, and Joe Archer said he was "leppin'" to begin, so we adjourned to the dancing-room and commenced operations.

I played the piano for the first quadrille, and aunt Helen for the second dance. It was most enjoyable. There was a table at one end of the room on which was any amount of cherries, lollies, cake, dainties, beers, syrups, and glasses, where all could regale themselves without ceremony or bother every time the inclination seized them. Several doors and windows of the long room opened into the garden, and, provided one had no fear of snakes, it was delightful to walk amid the flowers and cool oneself between dances.

A little exertion on such a night made us very hot. After the third dance the two old squatters, the horse-buyer, the clergyman, and Mr. Benson disappeared. Judging from the hilarity of their demeanor and the killing odor of their breaths when they returned an hour or so later, during their absence they must have conscientiously sampled the contents of every whisky decanter on the dining-room sideboard.

I could not dance, but had no lack of partners, as, ladies being in the minority, the gentlemen had to occasionally put up with their own sex in a dance.

"Let's take a breeze now and have a song or two, but no more dancing for a while," said some of them; but Harold Beecham said, "One more turn, and then we will have a long spell and a change of program."

He ordered Joe Archer to play a waltz, and the floor soon held several whirling couples. Harold "requested the pleasure" of me—the first time that night. I demurred. He would not take a refusal.

"Believe me, if I felt competent, Mr. Beecham, I would not refuse. I cannot dance. It will be no pleasure to you."

"Allow me to be the best judge of what is a pleasure to me," he said, quietly placing me in position.

He swung me once around the room, and then through an open window into the garden.

"I am sorry that I haven't had more time to look after you today. Come around into my room. I want to strike a bargain with you," were his words.

I followed him in the direction of a detached building in the garden. This was Harold's particular domain. It contained three rooms—one a library and office, another an arsenal and deed-room, and the third, into which he led me, was a sort of sitting-room, containing a piano, facilities for washing, a table, easy-chairs, and other things. As we entered I noticed the lamp, burning brightly on the table, gleamed on the face of a clock on the wall, which pointed to half past ten.

We stood beside the table, some distance apart, and, facing me, he said:

"It is no use of me making a long yarn about nothing. I'm sure you know what I want to say better than I do myself. You always are wonderfully smart at seeing through a fellow. Tell me, will it be yes or no?"

This was an experience in love. He did not turn red or white, or yellow or green, nor did he tremble or stammer, or cry or laugh, or become fierce or passionate, or tender or anything but just himself, as I had always known him. He displayed no more emotion than had he been inviting me to a picnic. This was not as I had pictured a man would tell his love, or as I had read of it, heard of it, or wished it should be. A curious feeling—disappointment, perhaps—stole over me. His matter-of-fact coolness flabbergasted me.

"Is this not rather sudden? You have given me no intimation of your intentions," I stammered.

"I didn't think it wise to dawdle any longer," he replied. "Surely you have known what I've been driving at ever since I first clapped eyes on you. There's plenty of time. I don't want to hurry you, only I want you to be engaged to me for safety."

He spoke as usual in his slow twangy drawl, which

would have proclaimed his Colonial nationality anywhere. No word of love was uttered to me and none requested from me.

I put it down to his conceit. I thought that he fancied he could win any woman, and me without the least palaver or trouble. I felt annoyed. I said aloud, "I will become engaged to you"; to myself I added, "Just for a little while, the more to surprise and take the conceit out of you when the time comes."

Now that I understand his character I know that it was not conceit, but just his quiet unpretending way. He had meant all his actions toward me, and had taken mine in return.

"Thank you, Sybylla, that is all I want. We will talk about the matter more some other time. I will go up to Caddagat next Sunday. You have surprised me nearly out of my wits," here he laughed. "I never dreamt you would say yes so easily, just like any other girl. I thought I would have a lot of trouble with you."

He approached me and was stooping to kiss me. I cannot account for my action or condemn it sufficiently. It was hysterical—the outcome of an overstrung, highly excitable, and nervous temperament. Perhaps my vanity was wounded, and my tendency to strike when touched was up in arms. The calm air of ownership with which Harold drew near annoyed me, or, as Sunday-school teachers would explain it, Satan got hold of me. He certainly placed a long strong riding-whip on the table beneath my hand. As Harold stooped with the intention of pressing his lips to mine, I quickly raised the whip and brought it with all my strength right across his face. The instant the whip had descended I would have smashed my arm on the door-post to recall that blow. But that was impossible. It had left a great weal on the healthy sun-tanned skin. His moustache had saved his lips, but it had caught his nose, the left cheek, had blinded the left eye, and had left a cut on the temple from which drops of blood were rolling down his cheek and staining his white coat. A momentary gleam of anger shot into his eyes and he gave a gasp, whether of surprise, pain, or annoyance, I know not. He made a gesture toward me. I half expected and fervently wished he would strike. The enormity of what I had done paralyzed me. The whip fell from my fingers and I dropped on to a low lounge behind me, and placing my elbows on my knees crouchingly buried my face in my hands; my hair tumbled softly over my shoulders and reached the floor, as though to sympathetically curtain my humiliation. Oh, that Harold would thrash me severely! It would have infinitely relieved me. I had done a mean unwomanly thing in thus striking a man, who by his great strength and sex was debarred retaliation. I had committed a violation of self-respect and common decency; I had given a man an ignominious blow in the face with a riding-whip. And that man was Harold Beecham, who with all his strength and great stature was so wondrously gentle—who had always treated my whims and nonsense with something like the amused tolerance held by a great Newfoundland for the pranks of a kitten.

The clock struck eleven.

"A less stinging rebuke would have served your purpose. I had no idea that a simple caress from the man whose proposal of marriage you had just accepted would be considered such an unpardonable familiarity."

Harold's voice fell clearly, calmly, cuttingly on the silence. He moved away to the other end of the room and I heard the sound of water.

A desire filled me to tell him that I did not think he had attempted a familiarity, but that I had been mad. I wished to say I could not account for my action, but I was dumb. My tongue refused to work, and I felt as though I would choke. The splash of the water came from the other end of the room. I knew he must be suffering acute pain in his eye. A far lighter blow had kept me sleepless a whole night. A fear possessed me that I might have permanently injured his sight. The splash of water ceased. His footfall stopped beside me. I could feel he was within touching distance, but I did not move.

Oh, the horrible stillness! Why did he not speak? He placed his hand lightly on my head.

"It doesn't matter, Syb. I know you didn't mean to hurt me. I suppose you thought you couldn't affect my dark, old, saddle-flap-looking phiz. That is one of the disadvantages of being a big lumbering concern like I am. Jump up. That's the girl."

I arose. I was giddy, and would have fallen but for Harold steadying me by the shoulder. I looked up at him nervously and tried to ask his forgiveness, but I failed.

"Good heavens, child, you are as white as a sheet! I was a beast to speak harshly to you." He held a glass of water to my lips and I drank.

"Great Jupiter, there's nothing to worry about! I know you hadn't the slightest intention of hurting me. It's nothing—I'll be right in a few moments. I've often been amused at and have admired your touch-me-not style. You only forgot you had something in your hand."

He had taken it quite as a matter of fact, and was excusing me in the kindest possible terms.

"Good gracious, you mustn't stew over such a trifling accident! It's nothing. Just tie this handkerchief on for me, please, and then we'll go back to the others or there will be a search-party after us."

He could have tied the handkerchief just as well himself—it was only out of kindly tact he requested my services. I accepted his kindness gratefully. He sank on his knee so that I could reach him, and I tied a large white handkerchief across the injured part. He could not open his eye, and hot water poured from it, but he made light of the idea of it paining. I was feeling better now, so we returned to the ballroom. The clock struck the half-hour after eleven as we left the room. Harold entered by one door and I by another, and I slipped into a seat as though I had been there some time.

There were only a few people in the room. The majority were absent—some love-making, others playing cards. Miss Beecham was one who was not thus engaged. She exclaimed at once:

"Good gracious, boy, what have you done to yourself?"

"Looks as if he had been interviewing a belligerent tramp," said aunt Helen, smilingly.

"He's run into the clothes-line, that's what he's done," said Miss Augusta confidently, after she had peeped beneath the bandage.

"You ought to get a bun for guessing, aunt Gus," said Harold laughing.

"I told them to put the clothes-lines up when they had done with them. I knew there would be an accident."

"Perhaps they were put up high enough for ordinary purposes," remarked her nephew.

"Let me do something for you, dear."

"No, thank you, aunt Gus. It is nothing," he said carelessly, and the matter dropped.

Harold Beecham was not a man to invite inquiry concerning himself.

Seeing I was unobserved by the company, I slipped away to indulge in my foolish habit of asking the why and the wherefore of things. Why had Harold Beecham (who was a sort of young sultan who could throw the handkerchief where he liked) chosen me of all women? I had no charms to recommend me—none of the virtues which men demand of the woman they wish to make their wife. To begin with, I was small, I was erratic and unorthodox, I was nothing but a tomboy—and, cardinal disqualification, I was ugly. Why, then, had he proposed matrimony to me? Was it merely a whim? Was he really in earnest?

The night was soft and dark; after being out in it for a time I could discern the shrubs dimly silhouetted against the light. The music struck up inside again. A step approached me on the graveled walk among the flowers, and Harold called me softly by name. I answered him.

"Come," he said, "we are going to dance; will you be my partner?"

We danced, and then followed songs and parlor games, and it was in the small hours when the merry goodnights were all said and we had retired to rest. Aunt Helen dropped to sleep in a short time; but I lay awake listening to the soft distant call of the mopokes in the scrub beyond the stables.

CHAPTER TWENTY-ONE

My Unladylike Behavior Again

Joe Archer was appointed to take us home on the morrow. When our host was seeing us off—still with his eye covered—he took opportunity of whispering to me his intention of coming to Caddagat on the following Sunday.

Early in the afternoon of that day I took a book, and, going down the road some distance, climbed up a broad-branched willow-tree to wait for him.

It was not long before he appeared at a smart canter. He did not see me in the tree, but his horse did, and propping, snorted wildly, and gave a backward run. Harold spurred him, he bucked spiritedly. Harold now saw me and sang out:

"I say, don't frighten him any more or he'll fling me, saddle and all. I haven't got a crupper or a breast-plate."

"Why haven't you, then? Hang on to him. I do like the look of you while the horse is going on like that."

He had dismounted, and had thrown the bridle rein over a post of the fence.

"I came with nothing but a girth, and that loose, as it was so hot; and I was as near as twopence to being off, saddle and all. You might have been the death of me," he said good-humoredly.

"Had I been, my fortune would have been made," I replied.

"How do you make that out? You're as complimentary as ever."

"Everyone would be wanting to engage me as the great noxious weed-killer and poisonous insect exterminator if I made away with you," I answered. I gave him an invitation to take a seat with me, and accepting, he swung up with easy grace. There was any amount of accommodation for the two of us on the good-natured branches of the old willow-tree.

When he had settled himself, my companion said, "Now, Syb, I'm ready for you. Fire away. But wait a minute, I've got something here for you which I hope you'll like."

As he searched in his pockets, I noticed that his eye had quite recovered, though there was still a slight mark on his cheek. He handed me a tiny morocco case, which on being opened disclosed a costly ring. I have about as much idea of the prices of things as a turkey would have. Perhaps that ring cost thirty pounds or possibly fifty guineas, for all I know. It was very heavy, and had a big diamond supported on either side by a large sapphire, and had many small gems surrounding it.

"Let me see if it fits," he said, taking my hand; but I drew it away.

"No; don't you put it on. That would make us irrevocably engaged."

"Isn't that what we intend to be?" he said in a tone of surprise.

"Not just yet; that is what I want to say to you. We

will have three months' probation to see how we get on. At the end of that time, if we manage to sail along smoothly, we'll have the real thing; until then we will not be any more than we have been to each other."

"But what am I to do in the meantime?" he asked, with amusement curving the corners of his mouth.

"Do! Do the usual thing, of course; but don't pay me any special attentions, or I'll be done with you at once."

"What's your idea for this?"

"It is no use making fools of ourselves; we might change our minds."

"Very well; so be it," he said laughing. "I might have known you would have things arranged different from any other girl. But you'll take the ring and wear it, won't you? Let me put it on."

"No; I won't let you put a finger on me till the three months are up. Then, if we definitely make up our minds, you can put it on; but till then, don't for the life of you hint by word or sign that we have any sort of an arrangement between us. Give me the ring and I'll wear it sometimes."

He handed it to me again, and I tried it on. It was a little large. Harold took it, and tried to put it on one of his fingers. It would fit on none but the very top of his little finger. We laughed heartily at the disparity in the size of our hands.

"I'll agree to your bargain," he said. "But you'll be really engaged to me all the same."

"Yes; under those conditions. Then it will not matter if we have a tiff. We can part, and no one will be the wiser."

On my suggesting that it was now time to go to the house, he swung himself down by a branch and turned to assist me. Descending from that tree was a feat which presented no difficulties to me when no one was by, but now it seemed an awkward performance.

"Just lead your horse underneath, so that I can get on to his back, thence to the ground quite easily," I said.

"No fear! Warrigal wouldn't stand that kind of

dodge. Won't I do? I don't think your weight will quite squash me," he returned, placing himself in leap-frog position, and I stepped on to his back and slid from there to the ground quite easily.

That afternoon, when leaving the house, I had been followed by one of the dogs, which, when I went up the willow-tree, amused himself chasing water lizards along the bank of the creek. He treed one, and kept up a furious barking at the base of its refuge. The yelping had disturbed grannie where she was reading on the veranda, and coming down the road under a big umbrella to see what the noise was about, as luck would have it she was in the nick of time to catch me standing on Harold Beecham's back. Grannie frequently showed marked displeasure regarding what she termed my larrikinism, but never before had I seen her so thoroughly angry. Shutting her umbrella, she thrust at me with it, saying, "Shame! shame! You'll come to some harm yet, you immodest, bold, bad hussy! I will write to your mother about you. Go home at once, miss, and confine yourself in your room for the remainder of the day, and don't dare eat anything until tomorrow. Spend the time in fasting, and pray to God to make you better. I don't know what makes you so forward with men. Your mother and aunt never gave me the slightest trouble in that way."

She pushed me from her in anger, and I turned and strode housewards without a word or glancing behind. I could hear grannie deprecating my conduct as I departed, and Harold quietly and decidedly differing from her.

From the time of my infancy punishment of any description never had a beneficial effect upon me. But dear old grannie was acting according to her principles in putting me through a term of penance, so I shut myself in my room as directed, with good-will toward her at my heart. I was burning with shame. Was I bold and immodest with men, as accused of being? It was the last indiscretion I would intentionally have been guilty of. In associating with men I never realize that the

trifling difference of sex is sufficient to be a great wall
between us. The fact of sex never for an instant enters
my head, and I find it as easy to be chummy with men
as with girls: men in return have always been very good,
and have treated me in the same way.

On returning from her walk grannie came to my
room, brought me some preachy books to read, and
held out to me the privilege of saying I was sorry, and
being restored to my usual place in the society of the
household.

"Grannie, I cannot say I am sorry and promise to
reform, for my conscience does not reproach me in the
least. I had no evil—not even a violation of manners—
in my intentions; but I am sorry that I vexed you,"
I said.

"Vexing me is not the sinful part of it. It is your un-
repentant heart that fills me with fears for your future.
I will leave you here to think by yourself. The only
redeeming point about you is, you do not pretend to be
sorry when you are not."

The dear old lady shook her head sorrowfully as she
departed.

The afternoon soon ran away, as I turned to my
bookcase for entertainment and had that beautiful ring
to admire.

I heard them come in to tea, and I thought Harold
had gone till I heard uncle Jay-Jay address him:

"Joe Archer told me you ran into a clothes-line on
race-night, and ever since then mother has kept up a
daddy of a fuss about ours. We've got props about a
hundred feet long, and if you weren't in the know you'd
think we had a telegraph wire to old St. Peter up
above."

I wondered what Harold thought of the woman he
had selected as his future wife being shut up for being
a "naughty girl." The situation amused me exceedingly.

About nine o'clock he knocked at my window and
said:

"Never mind, Syb. I tried to get you off, but it was

no go. Old people often have troublesome straitlaced ideas. It will blow over by tomorrow."

I did not answer; so he passed on with firm regular footfall, and presently I heard his horse's hoof-beats dying away in the darkness, and the closing and locking of doors around me as the household retired for the night.

During the following fortnight I saw Harold a good many times at cricket-matches, hare-drives, and so forth, but he did not take any particular notice of me. I flirted and frolicked with my other young men friends, but he did not care. I did not find him an ardent or a jealous lover. He was so irritatingly cool and matter-of-fact that I wished for the three months to pass so that I might be done with him, as I had come to the conclusion that he was barren of emotion or passion of any kind.

CHAPTER TWENTY-TWO

Sweet Seventeen

Monday arrived—last day of November and seventeenth anniversary of my birth—and I celebrated it in a manner which I capitally enjoyed.

It was the time of the annual muster at Cummabella —a cattle-station seventeen miles eastward from Caddagat—and all our men were there assisting. Word had been sent that a considerable number of beasts among those yarded bore the impress of the Bossier brand on their hides; so on Sunday afternoon uncle Jay-Jay had also proceeded thither to be in readiness for the final drafting early on Monday morning. This left us man-less, as Frank Hawden, being incapacitated with a dis-located wrist, was spending a few weeks in Gool-Gool until he should be fit for work again.

Uncle had not been gone an hour when a drover appeared to report that twenty thousand sheep would pass through on the morrow. Grass was precious. It would not do to let the sheep spread and dawdle at their drovers' pleasure. There was not a man on the place; grannie was in a great stew; so I volunteered my services. At first she would not hear of such a thing, but eventually consented. With many injunctions to conduct myself with proper stiffness, I started early on Monday morning. I was clad in a cool blouse, a holland riding-skirt, and a big straw hat; was seated on a big bay horse, was accompanied by a wonderful sheep-dog, and carried a long heavy stock-whip. I sang and cracked my stock-whip as I cantered along, quite forgetting to be reserved and proper. Presently I came upon the sheep just setting out for their day's tramp, with a black boy ahead of them, of whom I inquired which was the boss. He pointed toward a man at the rear wearing a donkey-supper hat. I made my way through the sheep in his direction, and asked if he were in charge of them. On being answered in the affirmative, I informed him that I was Mr. Bossier's niece, and, as the men were otherwise engaged, I would see the sheep through.

"That's all right, miss. I will look out that you don't have much trouble," he replied, politely raising his hat, while a look of amusement played on his face.

He rode away, and shouted to his men to keep the flock strictly within bounds and make good traveling.

"Right you are, boss," they answered; and returning to my side he told me his name was George Ledwood, and made some remarks about the great drought and so on, while we rode in the best places to keep out of the dust and in the shade. I asked questions such as whence came the sheep? whither were they bound? and how long had they been on the road? And having exhausted these orthodox remarks, we fell a-talking in dead earnest without the least restraint. I listened with interest to stories of weeks and weeks spent beneath the sun and stars while crossing widths of saltbush country, mulga and myall scrubs, of encounters with blacks in Queensland, and was favored with a graphic description of a big strike among the shearers when the narrator had been boss-of-the-board out beyond Bourke. He spoke as though well educated, and a gentleman— as drovers often are. Why, then, was he on the road? I put him down as a scapegrace, for he had all the winning pleasant manner of a ne'er-do-well.

At noon—a nice, blazing, dusty noon—we halted within a mile of Caddagat for lunch. I could have easily ridden home for mine, but preferred to have it with the drovers for fun. The men boiled the billy and made the tea, which we drank out of tin pots, with tinned fish and damper off tin plates as the completion of the *menu,* Mr. Ledwood and I at a little distance from the men. Tea boiled in a billy at a bush fire has a deliciously aromatic flavor, and I enjoyed my birthday lunch immensely. Leaving the cook to collect the things and put them in the spring-cart, we continued on our way, lazily lolling on our horses and chewing gumleaves as we went.

When the last of the sheep got off the Caddagat run it was nearing two o'clock.

Mr. Ledwood and I shook hands at parting, each expressing a wish that we might meet again some day.

I turned and rode homewards. I looked back and saw the drover gazing after me. I waved my hand; he raised his hat and smiled, displaying his teeth, a gleam of white in his sunbrowned face. I kissed my hand to him; he bowed low; I whistled to my dog; he resumed his way behind the crawling sheep; I cantered home quickly and dismounted at the front gate at 2:30 p.m., a dusty, heated, tired girl.

Grannie came out to question me regarding the sex,

age, condition, and species of the sheep, what was their destination, whether they were in search of grass or were for sale, had they spread or eaten much grass, and had the men been civil?

When I had satisfactorily informed her on all these points, she bade me have something to eat, to bathe and dress, and gave me a holiday for the remainder of the day.

My hair was gray with dust, so I washed all over, arrayed myself in a cool white dress, and throwing myself in a squatter's chair in the veranda, spread my hair over the back of it to dry. Copies of Gordon, Kendall, and Lawson were on my lap, but I was too physically content and comfortable to indulge in even these, my sworn friends and companions. I surrendered myself to the mere joy of being alive. How the sunlight blazed and danced in the roadway—the leaves of the gum-trees gleaming in it like a myriad gems! A cloud of white, which I knew to be cockatoos, circled over the distant hilltop. Nearer they wheeled until I could hear their discordant screech. The thermometer on the wall rested at 104 degrees despite the dense shade thrown on the broad old veranda by the foliage of creepers, shrubs, and trees. The gurgling rush of the creek, the scent of the flower-laden garden, and the stamp, stamp of a horse in the orchard as he attempted to rid himself of tormenting flies, filled my senses. The warmth was delightful. Summer is heavenly, I said—life is a joy.

Aunt Helen's slender fingers looked artistic among some pretty fancy-work upon which she was engaged. Bright butterflies flitted around the garden, and thousands of bees droned lazily among the flowers. I closed my eyes—my being filled with the beauty of it all.

I could hear grannie's pen fly over the paper as she made out a list of Christmas supplies on a table near me.

"Helen, I suppose a hundredweight of currants will be sufficient?"

"Yes; I should think so."

"Seven dozen yards of unbleached calico be enough?"

"Yes; plenty."

"Which tea-service did you order?"

"Number two."

"Do you or Sybylla want anything extra?"

"Yes; parasols, gloves, and some books."

"Books! Can I get them at Hordern's?"

"Yes."

Grannie's voice faded on my ears, my thoughts ran on uncle Jay-Jay. He had promised to be home in time for my birthday spread, and I was sure he had a present for me. What would it be?—something nice. He would be nearly sure to bring someone home with him from Cummabella, and we would have games and fun to no end. I was just seventeen, only seventeen, and had a long, long life before me wherein to enjoy myself. Oh, it was good to be alive! What a delightful place the world was!—so accommodating, I felt complete mistress of it. It was like an orange—I merely had to squeeze it and it gave forth sweets plenteously. The stream sounded far away, the sunlight blazed and danced, grannie's voice was a pleasant murmur in my ear, the cockatoos screamed over the house and passed away to the west. Summer is heavenly and life is a joy, I reiterated. Joy! Joy! There was joy in the quit! quit! of the green-and-crimson parrots, which swung for a moment in the rose-bush over the gate, and then whizzed on into the summer day. There was joy in the gleam of the sun and in the hum of the bees, and it throbbed in my heart. Joy! Joy! A jackass laughed his joy as he perched on the telegraph wire out in the road. Joy! Joy! Summer is a dream of delight and life is a joy, I said in my heart. I was repeating the one thing over and over—but ah! it was a measure of happiness which allowed of much repetition. The cool murmur of the creek grew far away, I felt my poetry books slip off my knees and fall to the floor, but I was too content to bother about them—too happy to need their consola-

tion, which I had previously so often and so hungrily
sought. Youth! Joy! Warmth!

The clack of the garden gate, as it swung to, awoke me
from a pleasant sleep. Grannie had left the veranda,
and on the table where she had been writing aunt Helen
was filling many vases with maidenhair fern and La
France roses. A pleasant clatter from the dining-room
announced that my birthday tea was in active prepara-
tion. The position of the yellow sunbeams at the far
end of the wide veranda told that the dense shadows
were lengthening, and that the last of the afternoon
was wheeling westward. Taking this in, in an instant I
straightened the piece of mosquito-netting, which, to
protect me from the flies, someone—auntie probably—
had spread across my face, and feigned to be yet asleep.
By the footsteps which sounded on the stoned garden
walk, I knew that Harold Beecham was one of the individuals approaching.

"How do you do, Mrs. Bell? Allow me to introduce my
friend, Archie Goodchum. Mrs. Bell, Mr. Goodchum.
Hasn't it been a roaster today? Considerably over 100
degrees in the shade. Terribly hot!"

Aunt Helen acknowledged the introduction, and
seated her guests, saying:

"Harry, have you got an artistic eye? If so, you can
assist me with these flowers. So might Mr. Goodchum,
if he feels disposed."

Harold accepted the proposal, and remarked:

"What is the matter with your niece? It is the first
time I ever saw her quiet."

"Yes; she is a noisy little article—a perfect whirlwind in the house—but she is a little tired this afternoon; she has been seeing those sheep through today."

"Don't you think it would be a good lark if I get
something and tickle her?" said Goodchum.

"Yes, do," said Harold; "but look out for squalls.
She is a great little fizzer."

"Then she might be insulted."

"Not she," interposed auntie. "No one will enjoy the fun more than herself."

I had my eyes half open beneath the net, so saw him cautiously approach with a rose-stem between his fingers. Being extremely sensitive to tickling, so soon as touched under the ear I took a flying leap from the chair, somewhat disconcerting my tormentor.

He was a pleasant-looking young fellow somewhere about twenty, whose face was quite familiar to me.

He smiled so good-humoredly at me that I widely did the same in return, and he came forward with extended hand, exclaiming, "At last!"

The others looked on in surprise, Harold remarking suspiciously, "You said you were unacquainted with Miss Melvyn, but an introduction does not seem necessary."

"Oh, yes it is," chirped Mr. Goodchum. "I haven't the slightest idea of the young lady's name."

"Don't know each other!" ejaculated Harold; and grannie, who had appeared upon the scene, inquired stiffly what we meant by such capers if unacquainted.

Mr. Goodchum hastened to explain.

"I have seen the young lady on several occasions in the bank where I am employed, and I had the good fortune to be of a little service to her one day when I was out biking. Her harness, or at least the harness on the horse she was driving, broke, and I came to the rescue with my pocket-knife and some string, thereby proving, if not ornamental, I was useful. After that I tried hard to find out who she was, but my inquiries always came to nothing. I little dreamt who Miss Melvyn was when Harry, telling me she was a Goulburn girl, asked if I knew her."

"Quite romantic," said aunt Helen, smiling; and a great thankfulness overcame me that Mr. Goodchum had been unable to discover my identity until now. It was right enough to be unearthed as Miss Melvyn, grand-daughter of Mrs. Bossier of Caddagat, and great friend and intimate of the swell Beechams of Five-Bob Downs station. At Goulburn I was only the daughter of old Dick Melvyn, broken-down farmer-cockatoo, well known by reason of his sprees about the commonest pubs in town.

Mr. Goodchum told us it was his first experience of the country, and therefore he was enjoying himself immensely. He also mentioned that he was anxious to see some of the gullies around Caddagat, which, he had heard, were renowned for the beauty of their ferns. Aunt Helen, accordingly, proposed a walk in the direction of one of them, and hurried off to attend to a little matter before starting. While waiting for her, Harold happened to say it was my birthday, and Mr. Goodchum tendered me the orthodox wishes, remarking, "It is surely pardonable at your time of life to ask what age you have attained today?"

"Seventeen."

"Oh! oh! 'sweet seventeen, and never been kissed'; but I suppose you cannot truthfully say that, Miss Melvyn?"

"Oh yes, I can."

"Well, you won't be able to say it much longer," he said, making a suggestive move in my direction. I ran, and he followed, grannie reappearing from the dining-room just in time to see me bang the garden gate with great force on my pursuer.

"What on earth is the girl doing now?" I heard her inquire.

However, Mr. Goodchum did not execute his threat; instead we walked along decorously in the direction of the nearest ferns, while Harold and aunt Helen followed, the latter carrying a sunbonnet for me.

After we had climbed some distance up a gully aunt Helen called out that she and Harold would rest while I did the honors of the fern grots to my companion.

We went on and on, soon getting out of sight of the others.

"What do you say to my carving our names on a gum-tree, the bark is so nice and soft?" said the bank clerk; and I seconded the proposal.

"I will make it allegorical," he remarked, setting to work.

He was very deft with his penknife, and in a few minutes had carved S. P. M. and A. S. G., encircling the initials by a ring and two hearts interlaced.

"That'll do nicely," he remarked, and turning round, "Why, you'll get a sunstroke; do take my hat."

I demurred, he pressed the matter, and I agreed on condition he allowed me to tie his handkerchief over his head. I was wearing his hat and tying the ends of a big silk handkerchief beneath his chin when the cracking of a twig caused me to look up and see Harold Beecham with an expression on his face that startled me.

"Your aunt sent me on with your hood," he said jerkily.

"You can wear it—I've been promoted," I said flippantly, raising my head-gear to him and bowing. He did not laugh as he usually did at my tricks, but frowned darkly instead.

"We've been carving our names—at least, I have," remarked Goodchum.

Harold tossed my sun-bonnet on the ground, and said shortly, "Come on, Goodchum, we must be going."

"Oh, don't go, Mr. Beecham. I thought you came on purpose for my birthday tea. Auntie has made me a tremendous cake. You must stay. We never dreamt of you doing anything else."

"I've changed my mind," he replied, striding on at such a pace that we had difficulty in keeping near him. As we resumed our own head-wear, Goodchum whispered, "A bulldog ant must have stung the boss. Let's ask him."

On reaching the house we found other company had arrived in the persons of young Mr. Goodjay from Cummabella, his sister, her governess, and a couple of jackeroos. They were seated on the veranda, and uncle Jay-Jay, attired in his shirt-sleeves, was appearing through the dining-room door with half a dozen bottles of home-made ginger ale in his arms. Dumping them down on the floor, he produced a couple of tots from his shirt-pockets, saying, "Who votes for a draw of beer? Everyone must feel inclined for a swig. Harry, you want some; you don't look as though the heat was good for your temper. Hullo, Archie! Got up this far. Take a draw out of one of these bottles. If there had been a dozen pubs on the road, I'd have drunk every one of 'em dry today. I never felt such a daddy of a thirst on me before."

"Good gracious, Julius!" exclaimed grannie, as he offered the governess a pot full of beer, "Miss Craddock can't drink out of that pint."

"Those who don't approve of my pints, let 'em bring their own," said that mischievous uncle Jay-Jay, who was a great hand at acting the clown when he felt that way inclined.

I was dispatched for glasses, and after emptying the bottles uncle proposed a game of tennis first, while the light lasted, and tea afterward. This proposition being carried with acclamation, we proceeded to the tennis court. Harold came too—he had apparently altered his intention of going home immediately.

There were strawberries to be had in the orchard, also some late cherries, so uncle ordered me to go and get some. I procured a basket, and willingly agreed to obey him. Mr. Goodchum offered to accompany me, but Harold stepped forward saying he would go, in such a resolute tragic manner that Goodchum winked audaciously, saying waggishly, "Behold, the hero descends into the burning mine!"

CHAPTER TWENTY-THREE

Ah, For One Hour of Burning Love, 'tis Worth an Age of Cold Respect!

We walked in perfect silence, Harold not offering to carry my little basket. I did not dare lift my eyes, as something told me the face of the big man would not be pleasant to look upon just then. I twirled the ring he had given me round and round my finger. I occasionally put it on, wearing the stones on the palm-side of my finger, so that it would not be taken for other than one of two or three aunt Helen had lent me, saying I was at liberty to use them while at Caddagat, if it gave me any pleasure.

The Caddagat orchard contained six acres, and being a narrow enclosure, and the cherries growing at the extreme end from the house, it took us some time to reach them. I led the way to our destination—a secluded nook where grape-vines clambered up fig-trees, and where the top of gooseberry bushes met the lower limbs of cherry-trees. Blue and yellow lupins stood knee-high, and strawberries grew wild among them. We had not uttered a sound, and I had not glanced at my companion. I stopped; he wheeled abruptly and grasped my wrist in a manner which sent the basket whirling from my hand. I looked up at his face, which was blazing with passion, and dark with a darker tinge than Nature and the sun had given it, from the shapely swelling neck, in its soft well-turned-down collar, to where the stiff black hair, wet with perspiration, hung on the wide forehead.

"Unhand me, sir!" I said shortly, attempting to wrench myself free, but I might as well have tried to pull away from a lion.

"Unhand me!" I repeated.

For answer he took a firmer hold, in one hand seizing my arm above the elbow, and gripping my shoulder with the other so tightly that, through my flimsy covering, his strong fingers bruised me so severely that in a calmer moment I would have squirmed and cried out with pain.

"How dare you touch me!" He drew me so closely to him that, through his thin shirt—the only garment on the upper part of his figure—I could feel the heat of his body, and his big heart beating wildly.

At last! at last! I had waked this calm silent giant into life. After many an ineffectual struggle I had got at a little real love or passion, or call it by any name—something wild and warm and splendidly alive that one could feel, the most thrilling, electric, and exquisite sensation known.

I thoroughly enjoyed the situation, but did not let this appear. A minute or two passed and he did not speak.

"Mr. Beecham, I'll trouble you to explain yourself. How dare you lay your hands upon me?"

"Explain!" he breathed rather than spoke, in a tone of concentrated fury. "I'll make *you* explain, and I'll do what I like with you. I'll touch you as much as I think fit. I'll throw you over the fence if *you* don't explain to *my* satisfaction."

"What is there that I can explain?"

"Explain your conduct with other men. How dare you receive their attentions and be so friendly with them!"

"How dare you speak to me like that! I reserve the right of behaving as I please without your permission."

"I won't have a girl with my engagement ring on her finger going on as you do. I think I have a right to complain, for I could get any amount of splendid women in every way to wear it for me, and behave themselves properly too," he said fiercely.

I tossed my head defiantly, saying, "Loose your hold of me, and I'll quickly explain matters to my own satisfaction and yours, Harold Beecham."

He let me go, I stepped a pace or two away from him, drew the costly ring from my finger, and, with indifference and contempt, tossed it to his feet, where the juice of crushed strawberries was staining the ground, and facing him, said mockingly:

"Now, speak to the girl who wears your engagement ring, for I'll degrade myself by wearing it no more. If you think I think you as great a catch as you think yourself, just because you have a little money, you are a trifle mistaken, Mr. Beecham, that is all. Ha ha ha! So you thought you had a right to lecture me as your future slave! Just fancy! I never had the slightest intention of marrying you. You were so disgustingly conceited that I have been attempting to rub a little of it out of you. Marry you! Ha ha! Because the social laws are so arranged that a woman's only sphere is marriage, and because they endeavor to secure a man who can give them a little more ease, you must not run away with the idea that it is yourself they are angling for, when you are only the bothersome appendage with which they would have to put up, for the sake of your property. And you must not think that because some women will marry for a home they all will. I trust I have explained to your satisfaction, Mr. Beecham. Ha ha ha!"

The jealous rage had died out of his face and was succeeded by trembling and a pallor so ghastly, that I began to have a little faith in descriptions of love which I had hitherto ridiculed.

"Are you in earnest?" he asked in a deadly calm voice.

"Most emphatically I am."

"Then all I can say is that I haven't much respect for you, Miss Melvyn. I always considered that there were three classes of women—one, that would marry a blackfellow if he had money; another, that were shameless flirts, and who amuse themselves by flirting and disgracing the name of woman; and a third class that were pure and true, on whom a man could stake his life and whom he could worship. I thought you belonged to this class, but I have been mistaken. I know you always try to appear heartless and worthless, but I fancied it was only your youth and mischief, and imagined you were good underneath; but I have been mistaken," he repeated with quiet contempt.

His face had regained its natural color, and the well-cut pleasant mouth, clearly seen beneath the soft drooping moustache, had hardened into a sullen line which told me he would never be first to seek reconciliation—not even to save his life.

"Bah!" I exclaimed sarcastically. "It appears that we all labor under delusions. Go and get a beautiful woman to wear your ring and your name. One that will be able to say yes and no at the right time; one who will know how to dress properly; one who wouldn't for the world do anything that other women did not also; one who will know where to buy the best groceries and who will readily sell herself to you for your wealth. That's the sort of woman that suits men, and there are plenty of them; procure one, and don't bother with me. I am too small and silly, and have nothing to recommend me. I fear it speaks little for your sense or taste that you ever thought of me. Ta-ta, Mr. Beecham," I said over my shoulder with a mocking smile, and walked away.

When about half-way down the orchard reflection pulled me up shortly under an apple-tree.

I had said what I had said because, feeling bitter for the want of love, and because full of pain myself, I rejoiced with a sort of revenge to see the same feeling flash across another's face. But now I was cool, and, forgetting myself, thought of Harold.

I had led him on because his perpetually calm demeanor had excited in me a desire to test if it were possible to disturb him. I had thought him incapable of emotion, but he had proved himself a man of strong and deep emotion; might he not also be capable of feeling—of love? He had not been mean or nasty in his rage, and his anger had been righteous. By accepting his proposal of marriage, I had given him the right of expressing his objection to any of my actions of which he disapproved. I on my part had the liberty of trying to please him or of dissolving our engagement. Perhaps in some cases there was actually something more than wounded vanity when a man's alleged love was rejected or spurned. Harold had seemed to suffer, to really experience keen disappointment. I was clearly in the wrong, and had been unwomanly beyond a doubt, as, granting that Harold Beecham was conceited, what right had I to constitute myself his judge or to take into my own hands the responsibility of correcting him? I felt ashamed of my conduct; I was sorry to have hurt any one's feelings. Moreover, I cannot bear to be at ill-will with my fellows, and am ever the first to give in after having quarreled. It is easier than sulking, and it always makes the other party so self-complacent that it is amusing as well as convenient, and—and—and—I found I was very, very fond of Harold Beecham.

I crept noiselessly up the orchard. He had his back to me, and had moved to where a post of the fence was peeping out among the greenery. He had his elbow placed thereon, and his forehead resting on his hand. His attitude expressed dejection. Maybe he was suffering the torture of a broken ideal.

His right hand hung limply by his side. I do not think he heard me approach.

My heart beat quickly, and a fear that he would snub me caused me to pause. Then I nerved myself with the thought that it would be only fair if he did. I had been rude to him, and he had a right to play tit-for-tat if he felt so disposed. I expected my action to be spurned or ignored, so very timidly slipped my fingers into his palm. I need not have been nervous, for the strong brown hand, which had never been known to strike a cowardly blow, completely enfolded mine in a gentle caressing clasp.

"Mr. Beecham, Harold, I am so sorry I was so unwomanly, and said such horrible things. Will you forgive me, and let us start afresh?" I murmured. All flippancy, bitterness, and amusement had died out of me; I was serious and in earnest. This must have expressed itself in my eyes, for Harold, after gazing searchingly right there for a time, seemed satisfied, and his mouth relaxed to its habitually lovable expression as he said:

"Are you in earnest? Well, that is something more like the little woman."

"Yes, I'm in earnest. Can you forgive me?"

"There is nothing to forgive, as I'm sure you didn't mean and don't remember the blood curdling sentiments you aired."

"But I did mean them in one sort of a way, and didn't in another. Let us start afresh."

"How do you mean to start afresh?"

"I mean for us to be chums again."

"Oh, chums!" he said impatiently; "I want to be something more."

"Well, I will be something more if you will try to make me," I replied.

"How? What do you mean?"

"I mean you never try to make me fond of you. You have never uttered one word of love to me."

"Why, bless me!" he ejaculated in surprise.

"It's a fact. I have only flirted to try and see if you cared, but you didn't care a pin."

"Why, bless me, didn't you say I was not to show any affection yet awhile? And talk about not caring—why, I have felt fit to kill you and myself many a time the last fortnight, you have tormented me so; but I have managed to keep myself within bounds till now. Will you wear my ring again?"

"Oh no; and you must not say I am flirting if I cannot manage to love you enough to marry you, but I will try my best."

"Don't you love me, Syb? I have thought of nothing

else but you night and day since I saw you first. Can it be possible that you don't care a straw for me?" and a pained expression came upon his face.

"Oh, Harold, I'm afraid I very nearly love you, but don't hurry me too much! You can think me sort of secretly engaged to you if you like, but I won't take your ring. Keep it till we see how we get on." I looked for it, and finding it a few steps away, gave it to him.

"Can you really trust me again after seeing me get in such a vile beast of a rage? I often do that, you know," he said.

"Believe me, Hal, I liked it so much I wish you would get in a rage again. I can't bear people who never let themselves go, or rather, who have nothing in them to carry them away—they cramp and bore me."

"But I have a frightful temper. Satan only knows what I will do in it yet. Would you not be frightened of me?"

"No fear," I laughed; "I would defy you."

"A tomtit might as well defy me," he said with amusement.

"Well, big as you are, a tomtit having such superior facilities for getting about could easily defy you," I replied.

"Yes, unless it was caged," he said.

"But supposing you never got it caged," I returned.

"Syb, what do you mean?"

"What could I mean?"

"I don't know. There are always about four or five meanings in what you say."

"Oh, thanks, Mr. Beecham! You must be very astute. I am always thankful when I am able to dish one meaning out of my idle gabble."

The glorious summer day had fallen asleep on the bosom of the horizon, and twilight had merged into dusk, as, picking up the basket, Harold and I returned cherry- and strawberry-less to the tennis court. The players had just ceased action, and the gentlemen were putting on their coats. Harold procured his, and thrust his arms into it, while we were attacked on all sides by a flood of banter.

My birthday tea was a great success, and after it was done we enjoyed ourselves in the drawing-room. Uncle Jay-Jay handed me a large box, saying it contained a present. Everyone looked on with interest while I hurriedly opened it, when they were much amused to see —nothing but a doll and materials to make it clothes! I was much disappointed, but uncle said it would be more in my line to play with that than to worry about tramps and politics.

I took care to behave properly during the evening, and when the good-byes were in full swing had an opportunity of a last word with Harold, he stooping to hear me whisper:

"Now that I know you care, I will not annoy you any more by flirting."

"Don't talk like that. I was only mad for the moment. Enjoy yourself as much as you like. I don't want you to be like a nun. I'm not quite so selfish as that. When I look at you and see how tiny you are, and how young, I feel it is brutal to worry you at all, and you don't detest me altogether for getting in such an infernal rage?"

"No. That is the very thing I liked. Good night!"

"Good night," he replied, taking both my hands in his. "You are the best little woman in the world, and I hope we will spend all your other birthdays together."

"It's to be hoped you've said something to make Harry a trifle sweeter than he was this afternoon," said Goodchum. Then it was:

"Good night, Mrs. Bossier! Good night, Harry! Good night, Archie! Good night, Mr. Goodchum! Good-bye, Miss Craddock! Ta-ta, Miss Melvyn! So long, Jay-Jay! Good-bye, Mrs. Bell! Good-bye, Miss Goodjay! Good night, Miss Melvyn! Good night, Mr. Goodjay! Good night, Mrs. Bossier! Good-bye, Miss Melvyn! Good night all!"

*   *   *

I sat long by my writing-table that night—thinking long, long thoughts, foolish thoughts, sad ones, merry ones, old-headed thoughts, and the sweet, sweet thoughts of youth and love. It seemed to me that men were not so invincible and invulnerable as I had imagined them— it appeared they had feeling and affections after all.

I laughed a joyous little laugh, saying, "Hal, we are quits," when, on disrobing for the night, I discovered on my soft white shoulders and arms—so susceptible to bruises—many marks, and black.

It had been a very happy day for me.

CHAPTER TWENTY-FOUR

Thou Knowest Not What a Day May Bring Forth

The next time I saw Harold Beecham was on Sunday the 13th of December. There was a hammock swinging under a couple of trees in an enclosure, half shrubbery, partly orchard and vegetable garden, skirting the road. In this I was gently swinging to and fro, and very much enjoying an interesting book and some delicious gooseberries, and seeing Harold approaching pretended to be asleep, to see if he would kiss me. But no, he was not that style of man. After tethering his horse to the fence and vaulting himself over it, he shook me and informed me I was as sound asleep as a log, and had required no end of waking.

My hair tumbled down. I accused him of disarranging it, and ordered him to repair the damage. He couldn't make out what was the matter with it, only that "It looks a bit dotty."

"Men are queer creatures," I returned. "They have the most wonderful brains in some ways, but in little things they are as stupid as owls. It is no trouble to them to master geology, mineralogy, anatomy, and other things, the very name of which gives me a headache. They can see through politics, mature mighty water reservoir schemes, and manage five stations at once, but they couldn't sew on a button or fix one's hair to save their life."

I cannot imagine how the news had escaped me, for the story with which Harold Beecham surprised and startled me on that long hot afternoon had been common talk for some time.

He had come to Caddagat purposely to explain his affairs to me, and stated as his reason for not having done so earlier that he had waited until the last moment thinking he might pull himself up.

Business to me is a great mystery, into which I haven't the slightest desire to penetrate. I have no brains in that direction, so will not attempt to correctly reproduce all that Harold Beecham told me on that afternoon while leaning against a tree at my feet and looking down at me as I reclined in the hammock.

There was great mention of bogus bonds, bad investments, liabilities and assets and personal estates, and of a thing called an official assignee—whatever that is—voluntary sequestration, and a jargon of such terms that were enough to mither a Barcoo lawyer.

The gist of the matter, as I gathered it, was that Harold Beecham, looked upon as such a "lucky beggar," and envied as a pet of fortune, had been visited by an unprecedented run of crushing misfortunes. He had not been as rich and sound in position as the public had imagined him to be. The failure of a certain bank two or three years previously had given him a great shaking. The tick plague had ruined him as regarded his Queensland property, and the drought had made matters nearly as bad for him in New South Wales. The burning of his wool last year, and the failure of the agents in whose hands he had placed it, this had pushed him farther into the mire, and now the recent "going bung" of a building society—his sole remaining prop—had run him entirely ashore.

He had sequestrated his estate, and as soon as practicable was going through the courts as an insolvent. The personal estate allowed him from the debris of his wealth he intended to settle on his aunts, and he hoped it might be sufficient to support them. Himself, he had the same prospects as the boundary-riders on Five-Bob Downs.

I had nothing to say. Not that Harold was a much-to-be-pitied man when one contrasted his lot with that of millions of his fellows as deserving as he; but, on the other hand, considering he had been reared in wealth and as the master of it since his birth, to be suddenly rendered equal with a laborer was pretty hard lines.

"Oh, Harold, I am so sorry for you!" I managed to stammer at last.

"Don't worry about me. There's many a poor devil, crippled and ill, though rolling in millions, who would give all his wealth to stand in my boots today," he said, drawing his splendid figure to its full height, while a look of stern pride settled on the strong features. Harold Beecham was not a whimpering cur. He would never tell anyone his feelings on the subject; but such a sudden reverse of fortune, tearing from him even his home, must have been a great blow to him.

"Syb, I have been expecting this for some years; now that it is done with, it is a sort of grim relief. The worst of all is that I've had to give up all hope of winning you. That is the worst of all. If you didn't care for me when I was thought to be in a position to give you all that girls like, you could never look at me now that I'm a pauper. I only hope you will get some fellow who will make you as happy as I would have tried to had you let me."

I sat and wondered at the marvelous self-containment of the man before me. With this crash impending, just imagine the worry he must have gone through! But never had the least suspicion that he was troubled found betrayal on his brow.

"Good-bye, Syb," he said; "though I'm a nobody now, if I could ever be of use to you, don't be afraid to ask me."

I remember him wringing the limp hand I mechanically stretched out to him and then slowly revaulting the fence. The look of him riding slowly along with his broad shoulders drooping despondently waked me to my senses. I had been fully engrossed with the intelligence of Harold's misfortune—that I was of sufficient importance to concern him in any way had not entered my head; but it suddenly dawned on me that Harold had said that I was, and he was not in the habit of uttering idle nothings.

While fortune smiled on him I had played with his manly love, but now that she frowned had let him go without even a word of friendship. I had been poor myself, and knew what awaited him in the world. He would find that they who fawned on him most would be first to turn their backs on him now. He would be rudely disillusioned regarding the fables of love and friendship, and would become cynical, bitter, and skeptical of there being any disinterested good in human nature. Suffering the cold heart-weariness of this state myself, I felt anxious at any price to save Harold Beecham from a like fate. It would be a pity to let one so young be embittered in that way.

There was a short cut across the paddocks to a point of the road where he would pass; and with these thoughts flashing through my mind, hatless and with flying hair, I ran as fast as I could, scrambling up on the fence in a breathless state just as he had passed.

"Hal, Hal!" I called. "Come back, come back! I want you."

He turned his horse slowly.

"Well, Syb, what is it?"

"Oh, Hal, dear Hal! I was thinking too much to say anything; but you surely don't think I'd be so mean as to care a pin whether you are rich or poor—only for your own sake? If you really want me, I will marry you when I am twenty-one if you are as poor as a crow."

"It is too good to be true. I thought you didn't care for me. Sybylla, what do you mean?"

"Just what I say," I replied, and without further explanation, jumping off the fence I ran back as fast as I had come.

When half-way home I stopped, turned, looked, and saw Harold cantering smartly homewards, and heard him whistling a merry tune as he went.

After all, men are very weak and simple in some ways.

I laughed long and sardonically, apostrophizing myself thus:

"Sybylla Penelope Melvyn, your conceit is marvelous and unparalleled! So you actually imagined that you were of sufficient importance to assist a man through life—a strong, healthy young man too, standing six feet three and a half in his socks, a level-headed business man, a man of high connections, spotless character, and influential friends, an experienced bushman, a man of sense, and, above all, a man—a man! The world was made for men.

"Ha ha! You, Sybylla, thought this! You, a chit in your teens, an ugly, poor, useless, unimportant, little handful of human flesh, and, above, or rather below, all, a woman—only a woman! It would indeed be a depraved and forsaken man who would need your services as a stay and support! Ha ha! The conceit of you!"

CHAPTER TWENTY-FIVE

Because?

The Beechams were vacating Five-Bob almost immediately—before Christmas. Grannie, aunt Helen, and uncle Jay-Jay went down to say good-bye to the ladies, who were very heart-broken about being uprooted from Five-Bob, but they approved of their nephew settling things at once and starting on a clean sheet. They intended taking up their residence—hiding themselves, they termed it—in Melbourne. Harold would be detained in Sydney some time during the settling of his affairs, after which he intended to take anything that turned up. He had been offered the management of Five-Bob by those in authority, but could not bring himself to accept managership where he had been master. His great desire, now that Five-Bob was no longer his, was to get as far away from old associations as possible.

He had seen his aunts off, superintended the muster of all stock on the place, dismissed all the female and most of the male employees, and surrendered the reins of government, and as Harold Augustus Beecham, boss of Five-Bob, on Monday, the 21st of December 1896, was leaving the district for ever. On Sunday, the 20th of December, he came to bid us good-bye and to arrive at an understanding with me concerning what I had said to him the Sunday before. Grannie, strange to say, never suspected that there was likely to be anything between us. Harold was so undemonstrative, and had always come and gone as he liked at Caddagat: she overlooked the possibility of his being a lover, and in our intercourse allowed us almost the freedom of sister and brother or cousins.

On this particular afternoon, after we had talked to grannie for a little while, knowing that he wished to interview me, I suggested that he should come up the orchard with me and get some gooseberries. Without demur from anybody we set off, and were scarcely out of hearing before Harold asked me had I really meant what I said.

"Certainly," I replied. "That is, if you really care for me, and think it wise to choose me of all my sex."

Ere he put it in words I read his answer in the clear brown eyes bent upon me.

"Syb, you know what I feel and would like, but I think it would be mean of me to allow you to make such a sacrifice."

I knew I was not dealing with a booby, but with a sensible clear-sighted man, and so studied to express myself in a way which would not for an instant give him the impression that I was promising to marry him because—what I don't know and it doesn't matter much, but I said:

"Hal, don't you think it is a little selfish of you to want to throw me over just because you have lost your money? You are young, healthy, have good character and influential connections, and plenty of good practical ability and sense, so, surely, you will know no such thing as failure if you meet the world bravely. Go and be the man you are; and if you fail, when I am twenty-one I will marry you, and we will help each other. I am young and strong, and am used to hard work, so poverty will not alarm me in the least. If you want me, I want you."

"Syb, you are such a perfect little brick that I couldn't be such a beggarly cur as to let you do that. I knew you were as true as steel under your funny little whims and contrariness; and could you really love me now that I am poor?"

I replied with vigor:

"Do you think I am that sort, that cares for a person only because he has a little money? Why! that is the very thing I am always preaching against. If a man was a lord or a millionaire I would not have him if I loved him not, but I would marry a poor cripple if I loved him. It wasn't because you owned Five-Bob Downs that I liked you, but because you have a big heart in which one would have room to get warm, and because you are true, and because you are kind and big and——" Here I could feel my voice getting shaky, and being afraid I would make a fool of myself by crying, I left off.

"Syb, I will try and fix matters up a bit, and will claim you in that time if I have a home."

"Claim me, home or not, if you are so disposed, but I will make this condition. Do not tell anyone we are engaged, and remember you are perfectly free. If you see a woman you like more than me, promise me on your sacred word that you will have none of those idiotic unjust ideas of keeping true to me. Promise."

"Yes, I will promise," he said easily, thinking then, no doubt, as many a one before him has thought, that he would never be called upon to fulfill his word.

"I will promise in return that I will not look at another man in a matrimonial way until the four years are up, so you need not be jealous and worry yourself; for, Hal, you can trust me, can you not?"

Taking my hand in his and looking at me with a world of love in his eyes, which moved me in spite of myself, he said:

"I could trust you in every way to the end of the world."

"Thank you, Harold. What we have said is agreed upon—that is, of course, as things appear now: if anything turns up to disturb this arrangement it is not irrevocable in the least degree, and we can lay out more suitable plans. Four years will not be long, and I will

be more sensible at the end of that time—that is, of
course, if I ever have any sense. We will not write or
have any communication, so you will be perfectly free
if you see anyone you like better than me to go in and
win. Do you agree?"

"Certainly; any little thing like that you can settle
according to your fancy. I'm set up as long as I get you
one way or another,—that's all I want. It was a bit
tough being cleared out from all the old ways, but if I
have you to stand by me it will be a great start. Say
what you said last Sunday, again. Syb, say you will be
my wife."

I had expected him to put it in that way, and believ-
ing in doing all or nothing, had laid out that I would
put my hand in his and promise what he asked. But
now the word wife finished me up. I was very fond of
Harold—fond to such an extent that had I a fortune I
would gladly have given it all to him: I felt capable of
giving him a life of servitude, but I loved him—big,
manly, lovable, wholesome Harold—from the crown
of his head to the sole of his foot he was good in my
sight, but lacking in that power over me which would
make me desirous of being the mother of his children.

As for explaining my feelings to him—ha! He would
laughingly call them one of my funny little whims. With
his orthodox, practical, plain, commonsense views of
these things, he would not understand me. What was
there to understand? Only that I was queer and different
from other women. But he was waiting for me to speak.
I had put my hand to the plow and could not turn
back. I could not use the word wife, but I put my hand
in his, looked at him steadily, and said—

"Harold, I meant what I said last Sunday. If you
want me—if I am of any use to you—I will marry you
when I attain my majority."

He was satisfied.

He bade us good-bye early that afternoon, as he intended departing from Five-Bob when the morrow was

young, and had two or three little matters to attend to previous to his departure.

I accompanied him a little way, he walking and leading his horse. We parted beneath the old willow-tree.

"Good-bye, Harold. I mean all I have said."

I turned my face upwards; he stooped and kissed me once—only once—one light, gentle, diffident kiss. He looked at me long and intently without saying a word, then mounted his horse, raised his hat, and rode away.

I watched him depart along the white dusty road, looking like a long snake in the glare of the summer sun, until it and he who traveled thereon disappeared among the messmate- and hickory-trees forming the horizon.

I stood gazing at the hills in the distance on which the blue dreaming mists of evening were gathering, until tears stole down my cheeks.

I was not given to weeping. What brought them? I hardly knew. It was not because Harold was leaving, though I would miss him much. Was it because I was disappointed in love? I persuaded myself that I loved Harold as much as I could ever love anyone, and I could not forsake him now that he needed me. But, but, but, I did not want to marry, and I wished that Harold had asked anything of me but that, because—because, I don't know what, and presently felt ashamed for being such a selfish coward that I grudged to make a little sacrifice of my own inclinations to help a brother through life.

"I used to feel sure that Harry meant to come up to the scratch, but I suppose he's had plenty to keep him going lately without bothering his head about a youngster in short frocks and a pigtail," remarked uncle Jay-Jay that night.

"Well, Sybylla, poor Harry has gone: we will all—even you included—miss him very much, I am sure. I used to think that he cared for you. It may be that he has not spoken to us on account of his financial failure, and it may be that I made a mistake," said aunt Helen when she was bidding me good night.

I held my peace.

CHAPTER TWENTY-SIX

Boast Not Thyself of Tomorrow

We felt the loss of the Beechams very, very much. It was sad to think of Five-Bob—pleasant, hospitable Five-Bob—as shut up, with no one but a solitary caretaker there pending the settling of the Beecham insolvency; with flowers running to seed unheeded in the wide old garden, grass yellowing on the lawns, fruit wasting in wain-loads in the great orchard, kennels, stables, fowl-houses, and cow-yards empty and deserted. But more than all, we missed the quiet, sunburnt, gentlemanly, young giant whose pleasant countenance and strapping figure were always welcome at Caddagat.

Fortunately, Christmas preparations gave us no rest for the soles of our feet, and thus we had little time to moon about such things: in addition, uncle Jay-Jay was preparing for a trip, and fussed so that the whole place was kept in a state of ferment.

We had fun, feasting, and company to no end on Christmas Day. There were bank clerks and young fellows out of offices from Gool-Gool, jackeroos and governesses in great force from neighboring holdings, and we had a merry time.

On Boxing Day uncle Jay-Jay set out on a tour to New Zealand, intending to combine business with pleasure, as he meant to bring back some stud stock if he could make a satisfactory bargain. Boxing Day had fallen on a Saturday that year, and the last of our guests departed on Sunday morning. It was the first time we had had any quietude for many weeks, so in the afternoon I went out to swing in my hammock and meditate upon things in general. Taking with me a bountiful supply of figs, apricots, and mulberries, I laid myself out for a deal of enjoyment in the cool dense shade under the leafy kurrajong- and cedar-trees.

To begin with, Harold Beecham was gone, and I missed him at every turn. I need not worry about being engaged to be married, as four years was a long, long time. Before that Harold might take a fancy to someone else, and leave me free; or he might die, or I might die, or we both might die, or fly, or cry, or sigh, or do one thing or another, and in the meantime that was not the only thing to occupy my mind: I had much to contemplate with joyful anticipation.

Toward the end of February a great shooting and camping party, organized by grannie, was to take place. Aunt Helen, grannie, Frank Hawden, myself, and a number of other ladies and gentlemen, were going to have ten days or a fortnight in tents among the blue hills in the distance, which held many treasures in the shape of lyrebirds, musk, ferns, and such scenery as would make the thing perfection. After this auntie and I were to have our three months' holiday in Sydney, where, with Everard Grey in the capacity of showman, we were to see everything from Manly to Parramatta, the Cyclorama to the Zoo, the theaters to the churches, the restaurants to the jails, and from Anthony Hordern's to Paddy's Market. Who knows what might happen then? Everard had promised to have my talents tested by good judges. Might it not be possible for me to attain one of my ambitions—enter the musical profession? Joyful dream! Might I not be able to yet assist Harold in another way than matrimony?

Yes, life was a pleasant thing to me now. I forgot all my wild unattainable ambitions in the little pleasures of everyday life. Such a thing as writing never entered my head. I occasionally dreamed out a little yarn which, had it appeared on paper, would have brimmed over with pleasure and love—in fact, have been redolent of life as I found it. It was nice to live in comfort, and among ladies and gentlemen—people who knew how to conduct themselves properly, and who paid one every attention without a bit of fear of being twitted with "laying the jam on."

I ate another fig and apricot, a mulberry or two, and was interrupted in the perusal of my book by the clatter of galloping hoofs approaching along the road. I climbed on to the fence to see who it could be who was coming at such a breakneck pace. He pulled the rein opposite me, and I recognized a man from Dog-trap. He was in his shirt-sleeves; his horse was all in a lather, and its scarlet nostrils were wide open, and its sides heaving rapidly.

"I say, miss, hunt up the men quickly, will you?" he said hurriedly. "There's a tremenjous fire on Wyam-beet, and we're short-handed. I'm goin' on to knock them up at Bimbalong."

"Hold hard," I replied. "We haven't a man on the place, only Joe Slocombe, and I heard him say he would ride down the river and see what the smoke was about; so he will be there. Mr. Hawden and the others have gone out for the day. You go back to the fire at once; I'll rouse them up at Bimbalong."

"Right you are, miss. Here's a couple of letters. My old moke flung a shoe and went dead lame at Dogtrap; an' wile I was saddlun another, Mrs. Butler stuffed 'em in me pocket."

He tossed them over the fence, and, wheeling his mount, galloped the way he had come. The letters fell, address upward, on the ground—one to myself and one to grannie, both in my mother's handwriting. I left them where they lay. The main substance of mother's letters to me was a hope that I was a better girl to my

grannie than I had been to her—a sentiment which did
not interest me.

"Where are you off to?" inquired grannie, as I
rushed through the house.

I explained.

"What horse are you going to take?"

"Old Tadpole. He's the only one available."

"Well, you be careful and don't push him too quickly
up that pinch by Flea Creek, or he might drop dead
with you. He's so fat and old."

"All right," I replied, snatching a bridle and running
up the orchard, where old Tadpole had been left in
case of emergency. I clapped a side-saddle on his back,
a hat on my head, jumped on just as I was, and galloped for my life in the direction of Bimbalong, seven
miles distant. I eased my horse a little going up Flea
Creek pinch, but with this delay reached my destination
in half an hour, and sent the men galloping in the direction of the fire. I lingered for afternoon tea, and returned at my leisure.

It was sundown when I got in sight of Caddagat.
Knowing the men would not be home for some time, I
rode across the paddock to yard the cows. I drove them
home and penned the calves, unsaddled my horse and
returned him to the orchard, then stood upon the hillside and enjoyed the scene. It had been a fearfully hot
day, with a blasting, drought-breathed wind; but the
wind had dropped to sleep with the sunlight, and now
the air had cooled. Blue smoke wreathed hill and hollow
like a beauteous veil. I had traversed drought-baked
land that afternoon, but in the immediate vicinity of
Caddagat house there was no evidence of an unkind
season. Irrigation had draped the place with beauty,
and I stood ankle-deep in clover. Oh, how I loved the
old irregularly built house, with here and there a patch
of its low iron roof peeping out of a mass of greenery,
flowers, and fruit—the place where I was born—home!
Save for the murmur of the creek, the evening was
wrapped in silence—sweet-breathed, balmly-browed,
summer quietude. I stretched out my hand and stained

my fingers, next my lips and teeth, with the sweet dark fruit of a mulberry-tree beside me. The shadows deepened; I picked up my saddle, and, carrying it houseward, put it in its place in the harness-room among the fig- and apricot-trees—laden to breaking point with ripe and ripening fruit. The two servant girls had departed on their Christmas holiday that morning, so grannie and auntie were the only members of the family at home. I could not see or hear them anywhere, so, presuming they were out walking, I washed my hands, lit a lamp, and sat down to my tea, where it had been left for me on the dining-table. I remembered—wonderful aberration from my usual thoughtlessness—that the book I had left in the hammock had a beautiful cover which the dew would spoil, so I left my tea to bring it in. Two little white squares struck my eye in the gathering dusk. I picked them up also, and, bringing them to the light, opened the one addressed to me, and read:

No doubt what I have to write will not be very palatable to you; but it is time you gave up pleasuring and began to meet the responsibilities of life. Your father is lazier if anything, and drinks more than ever. He has got himself into great debt and difficulties, and would have been sold off again but for Peter M'Swat. You will remember Peter M'Swat? Well, he has been good enough to lend your father £500 at 4 per cent, which means £20 per year interest. Your father would have no more idea of meeting this amount than a cat would have. But now I am coming to the part of the matter which concerns you. Out of friendship to your father, Mr. M'Swat is good enough to accept your services as governess to his children, in lieu of interest on the money. I have told him you will be in Yarnung on Friday the 8th of January 1897, where he will meet you. Be careful to remember the date. I am sorry I could not give you more notice; but he wants his children to commence school as soon as possible, and he deserves every consideration in the matter. Perhaps you will not find it as pleasant as Caddagat; but he has been very good, and offers you a fair number of holidays, and what he will give you is equal to £20. That is a lot in these times, when he could easily get so many better girls than you are in every way for half the money, and make your father pay the interest, and thereby be £10 in pocket. You will have to help Mrs. M'Swat with the work and sewing; but that will do you good, and I hope you will try hard to give every satisfaction. I have also written to your grandmother.

That letter wiped away every vestige of my appetite for the dainties before me. M'Swat's! Send—me—to M'Swat's! I could not believe it! It must be a nightmare! M'Swat's!

Certainly, I had never been there; but all those who had gave graphic descriptions of the total ignorance of Mrs. M'Swat. Why, the place was quite tabooed on account of its squalor and dirt!

The steel of my mother's letter entered my soul. Why had she not expressed a little regret at the thing she was imposing on me? Instead, there was a note of satisfaction running through her letter that she was able to put an end to my pleasant life at Caddagat. She always seemed to grudge me any pleasure. I bitterly put it down as accruing from the curse of ugliness, as, when mentioning Gertie, it was ever, "I have let Gertie go to such and such an entertainment. We could not very well afford it, but the poor little girl does not have many pleasures for her years." I was smaller than Gertie, and only eleven months older; but to me it was "You must think of something besides pleasure."

The lot of ugly girls is not joyful, and they must be possessed of natures very absurdly sanguine indeed ever to hope for any enjoyment in life.

It was cruel, base, horrible of my mother to send me to M'Swat's. I would not go—not for £50 a day! I would not go! I would not! not for any consideration.

I stamped about in a fever of impatience until grannie appeared, when I handed both letters to her, and breathlessly awaited her verdict.

"Well, child, what do you say?"

"Say? I won't go! I can't! I won't! Oh, grannie, don't send me there—I would rather die."

"My dear child, I would not be willing to part with you under any circumstances, but I cannot interfere between a mother and her child. I would not have allowed any one to do it with me, and believe in acting the same toward any other mother, even though she is my own daughter. However, there is time to get a reply before you would have to start, so I will write and see what can be done."

The dear old lady, with her prompt businesslike propensities, sat down and wrote there and then. I wrote also—pleaded with my mother against her decree, begged her to leave me at Caddagat, and assured her I could never succeed at M'Swat's.

I did not sleep that night, so arose betimes to await the first traveler, whom I asked to post the letters.

We got an answer to them sooner than we expected —at least grannie did. Mother did not deign to write to me, but in her letter to grannie I was described as an abominably selfish creature, who would not consider her little brothers and sisters. I would never be any good; all I thought of was idleness and ease. Most decidedly I could not get out of going to M'Swat's, as mother had given her word.

"I am sorry for you," said grannie, "but it cannot be helped. You can stay there for two or three years, and then I can have you here again."

I was inconsolable, and would not listen to reason. Ah! that uncle Jay-Jay had been at home to rescue me from this. Then aunt Helen brought her arguments to bear upon me, and persuaded me to think it was necessary for the benefit of my little brothers and sisters that I should take up this burden, which I knew would be too much for me.

It was a great wrench to be torn away from Caddagat —from refinement and comfort—from home! As the days till my departure melted away, how I wished that it were possible to set one's weight against the grim wheel of time and turn it back! Nights I did not sleep, but drenched my pillow with tears. Ah, it was hard to leave grannie and aunt Helen, whom I worshiped, and turn my back on Caddagat!

I suppose it is only a fancy born of the wild deep love I bear it, but to me the flowers seem to smell more sweetly there; and the shadows, how they creep and curl! oh, so softly and caressingly around the quaint old place, as the great sun sets amid the blue peaks; and the never-ceasing rush of the crystal fern-banked stream—I see and hear it now, and the sinking sun as it turns to a sheet of flame the mirror hanging in the backyard in the laundry veranda, before which the station hands were wont to comb and wash themselves. Oh, the memories that crowd upon me! Methinks I can smell the roses that clamber up the veranda posts and peep over the garden gate. As I write my eyes grow misty, so that I cannot see the paper.

The day for my departure arrived—hot, 110 degrees in the shade. It was a Wednesday afternoon. Frank Hawden was to take me as far as Gool-Gool that evening, and see me on to the coach next day. I would arrive in Yarnung about twelve or one o'clock on Thursday night, where, according to arrangement, Mr. M'Swat would be waiting to take me to a hotel, thence to his home next day.

My trunks and other belongings were stowed in the buggy, to which the fat horses were harnessed. They stood beneath the dense shade of a splendid kurrajong, and lazily flicked the flies off themselves while Frank Hawden held the reins and waited for me.

I rushed frantically around the house taking a last look at nooks and pictures dear to me, and then aunt Helen pressed my hand and kissed me, saying:

"The house will be lonely without you, but you must

brighten up, and I'm sure you will not find things half as bad as you expect them."

I looked back as I went out the front gate, and saw her throw herself into a chair on the veranda and cover her face with her hands. My beautiful noble aunt Helen! I hope she missed me just a little, felt just one pang of parting for I have not got over that parting yet.

Grannie gave me a warm embrace and many kisses. I climbed on to the front seat of the buggy beside my escort, he whipped the horses—a cloud of dust, a whirr of wheels, and we were gone—gone from Caddagat!

We crossed the singing stream: on either bank great bushes of blackthorn—last native flower of the season —put forth their wealth of magnificent creamy bloom, its rich perfume floating far on the hot summer air. How the sunlight blazed and danced and flickered on the familiar and dearly loved landscape! Over a rise, and the house was lost to view, then good-bye to the crystal creek. The trees of Five-Bob Downs came within eye-range far away on our left. What merry nights I had spent there amid music, flowers, youth, light, love, and summer warmth, when the tide of life seemed full! Where now was Harold Beecham and the thirty or more station hands, who but one short month before had come and gone at his bidding, hailing him boss?

It was all over! My pleasant life at Caddagat was going into the past, fading as the hills which surrounded it were melting into a hazy line of blue.

CHAPTER TWENTY-SEVEN

My Journey

The coach was a big vehicle, something after the style of a bus, the tilt and seats running parallel with the wheels. At the rear end, instead of a door, was a great tail-board, on the principle of a spring-cart. This was let down, and, after we scrambled over it into our seats, it was fixed half-mast, all the luggage piled thereon, and firmly roped into position. When this was completed, to any one on the ground only the heads of passengers were visible above the pile. Had the coach capsized we would have been in a nice fix, as the only means of exit was by crawling up through the back of the box-seat, which rose breast-high—an awkward feat.

Frank Hawden and I parted good friends. I leaned out and waved my handkerchief, until a bend of the road hid him from sight.

It was noon, the thermometer registered 112 degrees in the shade, and the dust was simply awful. It rose in such thick gray clouds that often it was impossible to discern the team of five which pulled us, and there was danger of colliding with passing vehicles. We were very much crowded, there being sixteen passengers. When we settled down and got started, I discovered that I was the only representative of my sex, and that I was sandwiched between a perky youth in his teens and a Chinaman, while a black fellow and a man with a red beard sat opposite. A member of Parliament, farther up the seat, who had been patronizing New Year's Day races in a portion of his electorate, bawled loudly to his companion about "the doin's of the 'Ouse." In the perky youth I discovered a professional jockey; and when he found that I was a daughter of Dick Melvyn, the one-time great horse-breeder, he became very friendly. He gave me a couple of apples out of his tin box under the seat, from whence he also produced his whip for my inspection, and was good enough to say:

"If you can't stand the stink of that bloomin' chow, miss, just change seats with me. I've knocked about, so that I can easy stand some tough smells without much inconvenience."

I cautioned him to talk lower for fear of hurting the Chinaman's feelings: this amused him immensely. He laughed very much, and, leaning over to the red-bearded man, repeated the joke:

"I say, this young lady is afraid I might hurt the chow's feelin's. Golly! Fancy a bloomin' chow havin' any!"

The other man also thought it a great joke. I changed seats with the jockey, which put me beside a young gentleman of a literary turn of mind, with whom I had some conversation about books when the dust, rumble of wheels, and turf talk of my other neighbor permitted. They were all very kind to me—gave me fruit, procured me drinks of water, and took turns in nursing a precious hat, for which, on account of the crush, no safe place could be found among the other luggage.

Before we had gone half our journey the horses knocked up. All the men were forced to walk up hills for miles and miles in the dust and heat, which did not conduce to their amiability, and many and caustic were the remarks and jokes made upon the driver. He wore out two whips upon his team, until the labor and excessive heat sent the perspiration rolling in rivulets down his face, leaving muddy tracks in the thick coating of dust there. The jockey assisted with his loaded instrument of trade, some of the passengers thrashed with sticks, and all swore under their breath, while a passing bullock-driver used his whip with such deadly effect, that the sweat which poured off the poor beasts was mingled with blood.

"Why the deuce don't you have proper horses?" demanded the red-bearded passenger.

The man explained that a ministerial party had chartered his best team to go on a tour of inspection to a mine; a brother coachman had been "stuck up" for horses, and borrowed a couple from him, whereupon he was forced to do with animals which had been turned out for a spell, and the heat and overloading accounted for a good part of the contretemps. However, we managed to catch our train, but had to rush for it without waiting for refreshments. Nice articles we looked—our hair gray with dust, and our faces grimy. The men took charge of me as carefully as though I had been specially consigned to their care. One procured my ticket, another secured me a seat, while a third took charge of my luggage; and they were just as thoughtful when we had to change trains. Off we went. Grannie had packed me quite a large box full of dainties. I produced it, the men provided drinks, and we had quite a pleasant picnic, with all the windows down to catch a little air.

I love the rush and roar of the train, and wished on this occasion that it might go on and on for ever, never giving me time to think or stop. But, alas, at 1:20 we pulled up at Yarnung, where a man came inquiring for a young lady named Melvyn. My fellow passengers collected my belongings, and I got out.

"Good-bye, gentlemen; thank you very much for your kindness."

"Good-bye, miss; you're welcome. Some of us might meet again yet. Ta-ta!"

A shriek, a jerk, and the great train rushed on into the night, leaving me there on the insignificant little platform, feeling how lonely and unhappy, no one knew or cared.

Mr. M'Swat shouldered most of my luggage, I took the remainder, and we trudged off in the dark without a word on either side. The publican had given M'Swat the key, so that we might enter without disturbing the household, and he escorted me to a bedroom, where I tumbled into bed with expedition.

CHAPTER TWENTY-EIGHT

To Life

It is indelibly imprinted on my memory in a manner which royal joy, fame, pleasure, and excitement beyond the dream of poets could never efface, not though I should be cursed with a life of five-score years. I will paint it truthfully—letter for letter as it was.

It was twenty-six miles from Yarnung to Barney's Gap, as M'Swat's place was named. He had brought a light wagonette and pair to convey me thither.

As we drove along, I quite liked my master. Of course, we were of caliber too totally unlike ever to be congenial companions, but I appreciated his sound common sense in the little matters within his range, and his bluntly straightforward, fairly good-natured, manner. He was an utterly ignorant man, with small ideas according to the sphere which he fitted, and which fitted him; but he was "a man for a' that, an' a' that."

He and my father had been boys together. Years and years ago M'Swat's father had been blacksmith on my father's station, and the little boys had played together, and, in spite of their then difference in station, had formed a friendship which lived and bore fruit at this hour. I wished that their youthful relations had been inimical, not friendly.

We left the pub in Yarnung at nine, and arrived at our destination somewhere about two o'clock in the afternoon.

I had waxed quite cheerful, and began to look upon the situation in a sensible light. It was necessary that I should stand up to the guns of life at one time or another, and why not now? M'Swat's might not be so bad after all. Even if they were dirty, they would surely be willing to improve if I exercised tact in introducing a few measures. I was not afraid of work, and would do many things. But all these ideas were knocked on the head, like a dairyman's surplus calves, when on entering Barney's Gap we descended a rough road to the house, which was built in a narrow gully between two steep stony hills, which, destitute of grass, rose like grim walls of rock, imparting a desolate and prison-like aspect.

Six dogs, two pet lambs, two or three pigs, about twenty fowls, eight children which seemed a dozen, and Mrs. M'Swat bundled out through the back door at our approach. Those children, not through poverty— M'Swat made a boast of his substantial banking account—but on account of ignorance and slatternliness, were the dirtiest urchins I have ever seen, and were so ragged that those parts of them which should have been covered were exposed to view. The majority of them had red hair and wide hanging-open mouths. Mrs. M'Swat was a great, fat, ignorant, pleasant-looking woman, shockingly dirty and untidy. Her tremendous, flabby, stockingless ankles bulged over her unlaced hobnailed boots; her dress was torn and unbuttoned at the throat, displaying one of the dirtiest necks I have seen. It did not seem to worry her that the infant she held under her arm like a roll of cloth howled killingly, while the other little ones clung to her skirts, attempting to hide their heads in its folds like so many emus.

She greeted me with a smacking kiss, consigned the baby to the charge of the eldest child, a big girl of fourteen, and seizing upon my trunks as though they were feather-weight, with heavy clodhopping step disappeared into the house with them. Returning, she invited me to enter, and following in her wake, I was followed by the children through the dirtiest passage into the dirtiest room, to sit upon the dirtiest chair, to gaze upon the other dirtiest furniture of which I have ever heard. One wild horrified glance at the dirt, squalor, and total benightedness that met me on every side, and I trembled in every limb with suppressed emotion and the frantic longing to get back to Caddagat which possessed me. One instant showed me that I could never, never live here.

"Have ye had yer dinner?" my future mistress inquired in a rough uncultivated voice. I replied in the negative.

"Sure, ye'll be dyin' of hunger; but I'll have it in a twinklin'."

She threw a crumpled and disgustingly filthy cloth three-cornered ways on to the dusty table and clapped thereon a couple of dirty knives and forks, a pair of cracked plates, two poley cups and chipped saucers. Next came a plate of salt meat, red with saltpeter, and another of dark, dry, sodden bread. She then disappeared to the kitchen to make the tea, and during her absence two of the little boys commenced to fight. One clutched the tablecloth, and over went the whole display with a bang—meat-dish broken, and meat on the dusty floor; while the cats and fowls, ever on the alert for such occurrences, made the most of their opportunities. Mrs. M'Swat returned carrying the tea, which was spilling by the way. She gave those boys each a clout on the head which dispersed them roaring like the proverbial town bull, and alarmed me for the safety of their ear-drums. I wondered if their mother was aware of their having ear-drums. She grabbed the meat, and wiping it on her greasy apron, carried it around in her hand until she found a plate for it, and by that time the children had collected the other things. A cup was broken, and another, also a poley, was put in its stead.

Mr. M'Swat now appeared, and after taking a nip out of a rum bottle which he produced from a cupboard in the corner, he invited me to sit up to dinner.

There was no milk. M'Swat went in entirely for sheep, keeping only a few cows for domestic purposes: these, on account of the drought, had been dry for some months. Mrs. M'Swat apologized for the lack of sugar, stating she was quite out of it and had forgotten to send for a fresh supply.

"You damned fool, to miss such a chance wen I was goin' to town with the wagonette! I mightn't be goin' in again for munce [months]. But sugar don't count much. Them as can't do without a useless luxury like that for a spell will never make much of a show at gettin' on in the wu-r-r-r-ld," concluded Mr. M'Swat, sententiously.

The children sat in a row and, with mouths open and interest in their big wondering eyes, gazed at me unwinkingly till I felt I must rush away somewhere and shriek to relieve the feeling of overstrained hysteria which was overcoming me. I contained myself sufficiently, however, to ask if this was all the family.

"All but Peter. Where's Peter, Mary Ann?"

"He went to the Red Hill to look after some sheep, and won't be back till dark."

"Peter's growed up," remarked one little boy, with evident pride in this member of the family.

"Yes; Peter's twenty-one, and hes a mustache and shaves," said the eldest girl, in a manner indicating that she expected me to be struck dumb with surprise.

"She'll be surprised wen she sees Peter," said a little girl in an audible whisper.

Mrs. M'Swat vouchsafed the information that three had died between Peter and Lizer, and this was how the absent son came to be so much older than his brothers and sisters.

"So you have had twelve children?" I said.

"Yes," she replied, laughing fatly, as though it were a joke.

"The boys found a bees' nest in a tree an' have been robbin' it the smornin'," continued Mrs. M'Swat.

"Yes; we have ample exemplification of that," I responded. It was honey here and honey there and honey everywhere. It was one of the many varieties of dirt on the horrible foul-smelling tablecloth. It was on the floor, the door, the chairs, the children's heads, and the cups. Mrs. M'Swat remarked contentedly that it always took a couple of days to wear "off of" things.

After "dinner" I asked for a bottle of ink and some paper, and scrawled a few lines to grannie and my mother, merely reporting my safe arrival at my destination. I determined to take time to collect my thoughts before petitioning for release from Barney's Gap.

I requested my mistress to show me where I was to sleep, and she conducted me to a fairly respectable little bedroom, of which I was to be sole occupant, unless I felt lonely and would like Rose Jane to sleep with me. I looked at pretty, soft-eyed, dirty little Rose Jane, and assured her kind-hearted mother I would not be the least lonely, as the sickening despairing loneliness which filled my heart was not of a nature to be cured by having as a bedmate a frowzy wild child.

Upon being left alone I barred my door and threw myself on the bed to cry—weep wild hot tears that scalded my cheeks, and sobs that shook my whole frame and gave me a violent pain in the head.

Oh, how coarse and grating were the sounds to be heard around me! Lack, nay, not lack, but utter freedom from the first instincts of cultivation, was to be heard even in the great heavy footfalls and the rasping sharp voices which fell on my ears. So different had I been listening in a room at Caddagat to my grannie's brisk pleasant voice, or to my aunt Helen's low refined accents; and I am such a one to see and feel these differences.

However, I pulled together in a little while, and called myself a fool for crying. I would write to grannie

and mother explaining matters, and I felt sure they
would heed me, as they had no idea what the place was
like. I would have only a little while to wait patiently,
then I would be among all the pleasures of Caddagat
again; and how I would revel in them, more than ever,
after a taste of a place like this, for it was worse than
I had imagined it could be, even in the nightmares
which had haunted me concerning it before leaving
Caddagat.

The house was of slabs, unlimed, and with very low
iron roof, and having no sign of a tree near it, the heat
was unendurable. It was reflected from the rocks on
either side, and concentrated in this spot like an oven,
being 122 degrees in the veranda now. I wondered
why M'Swat had built in such a hole, but it appears
it was the nearness of the point to water which recommended it to his judgment.

With the comforting idea that I would not have long
to bear this, I bathed my eyes, and walked away from
the house to try and find a cooler spot. The children
saw me depart but not return, to judge from a discussion of myself which I heard in the dining-room, which
adjoined my bed-chamber.

Peter came home, and the children clustered around
to tell the news.

"Did she come?"

"Yes."

"Wot's she like?"

"Oh, a rale little bit of a thing, not as big as Lizer!"

"And, Peter, she hes teeny little hands, as wite as
snow, like that woman in the picter ma got off of the
tea."

"Yes, Peter," chimed in another voice; "and her feet
are that little that she don't make no nise wen she
walks."

"It ain't only becos her feet are little, but cos she's
got them beautiful shoes like wot's in picters," said
another.

"Her hair is tied with two great junks of ribbing, one
up on her head an' another near the bottom; better

than that bit er red ribbing wot Lizer keeps in the box
agin the time she might go to town some day."

"Yes," said the voice of Mrs. M'Swat, " her hair is
near to her knees, and a plait as thick as yer arm; and
wen she writ a couple of letters in a minute, you could
scarce see her hand move it was that wonderful quick;
and she uses them big words wot you couldn't understand without bein' eddicated."

"She has tree brooches, and a necktie better than
your best one wots you keeps to go seeing Susie Duffy
in," and Lizer giggled slyly.

"You shut up about Susie Duffy, or I'll whack yuz
up aside of the ear," said Peter angrily.

"She ain't like ma. She's fat up here, and goes in
like she'd break in the middle, Peter."

"Great scissors! she must be a flyer," said Peter. "I'll
bet she'll make you sit up, Jimmy."

"I'll make *her* sit up," retorted Jimmy, who came
next to Lizer. "She thinks she's a toff, but she's only old
Melvyn's darter, that pa has to give money to."

"Peter," said another, "her face ain't got them
freckles on like yours, and it ain't dark like Lizer's.
It's reel wite, and pinky round here."

"I bet she won't make me knuckle down to her, no
matter wot color she is," returned Peter, in a surly tone.

No doubt it was this idea which later in the afternoon induced him to swagger forward to shake hands
with me with a flash insolent leer on his face. I took
pains to be especially nice to him, treating him with
deference, and making remarks upon the extreme heat
of the weather with such pleasantness that he was
nonplussed, and looked relieved when able to escape. I
smiled to myself, and apprehended no further trouble
from Peter.

The table for tea was set exactly as it had been before, and was lighted by a couple of tallow candles
made from bad fat, and their odor was such as my
jockey traveling companion of the day before would
have described as a tough smell.

"Give us a toon on the peeany," said Mrs. M'Swat

after the meal, when the dishes had been cleared away by Lizer and Rose Jane. The tea and scraps, of which there was any amount, remained on the floor, to be picked up by the fowls in the morning.

The children lay on the old sofa and on the chairs, where they always slept at night until their parents retired, when there was an all-round bawl as they were wakened and bundled into bed, dirty as they were, and very often with their clothes on.

I acceded to Mrs. M'Swat's request with alacrity, thinking that while forced to remain there I would have one comfort, and would spend all my spare time at the piano. I opened the instrument, brushed a little of the dust from the keys with my pocket-handkerchief, and struck the opening chords of Kowalski's "Marche Hongroise."

I have heard of pianos sounding like a tin dish, but this was not as pleasant as a tin dish by long chalks. Every note that I struck stayed down not to rise, and when I got them up the jarring, clanging, discordant clatter they produced beggars description. There was not the slightest possibility of distinguishing any tune on the thing. Worthless to begin with, it had stood in the dust, heat, and wind so long that every sign that it had once made music had deserted it.

I closed it with a feeling of such keen disappointment that I had difficulty in suppressing tears.

"Won't it play?" inquired Mr. M'Swat.

"No; the keys stay down."

"Then, Rose Jane, go ye an' pick 'em up while she tries again."

I tried again, Rose Jane fishing up the keys as I went along. I perceived instantly that not one had the least ear for music or idea what it was; so I beat on the demented piano with both hands, and often with all fingers at once, and the bigger row I made the better they liked it.

CHAPTER TWENTY-NINE

To Life—continued

Mr. M'Swat very kindly told me I need not begin my duties until Monday morning, and could rest during Saturday and Sunday. Saturday, which was sickeningly hot and sultry, and which seemed like an eternity, I spent in arranging my belongings, brushing the dust from my traveling dress, and in mending a few articles. Next morning rain started to fall, which was a great God-send, being the first which had fallen for months, and the only rain I saw during my residence at Barney's Gap.

That was a hideous Sabbath. Without a word of remonstrance from their parents, the children entertained themselves by pushing each other into the rain, the smaller ones getting the worst of it, until their clothing was saturated with water. This made them very cold, so they sat upon the floor and yelled outrageously.

It was the custom of Peter to spend his Sundays in riding about, but today, being deterred by the rain, he slept some of the time, and made a muzzle for one of his dogs between whiles.

From breakfast to the midday meal I shut myself in my bedroom and wrote letters to my mother and grandmother. I did not rant, rave, or say anything which I ought not to have said to my elders. I wrote those letters very coolly and carefully, explaining things just as they were, and asked grannie to take me back to Caddagat, as I could never endure life at Barney's Gap. I told my mother I had written thus, and asked her if she would not let grannie take me again, would she get me some other situation?—what I did not care, so long as it brought emancipation from the M'Swat's. I stamped and addressed these missives, and put them by till a chance of posting should arise.

Mr. M'Swat could read a little by spelling the long words and blundering over the shorter ones, and he spent the morning and all the afternoon in perusal of the local paper—the only literature with which Barney's Gap was acquainted. There was a long list of the prices of stock and farm produce in this edition, which perfectly fascinated its reader. The ecstasy of a man of fine, artistic, mental caliber, when dipping for the first time into the work of some congenial poet, would be completely wiped out in comparison to the utter soul-satisfaction of M'Swat when drinking in the items of that list.

"By damn, pigs was up last Toosday! Thames the things to make prawfit on," he would excitedly exclaim; or—"Wheat's rose a shillun a bushel! By dad, I must double my crops this year." When he had plodded to the end, he started at the beginning again.

His wife sat the whole afternoon in the one place, saying and doing nothing. I looked for something to read, but the only books in the house were a Bible, which was never opened, and a diary kept most religiously by M'Swat. I got permission to read this, and opening it, saw:

September

1st. Fine. Wint to boggie creak for a cow.
2nd. Fine. Got the chestnut mair shode.
3rd. Fine. On the jury.
4th. Fine. Tail the lams 60 yeos 52 wethers.
5th. Cloudy. Wint to Duffys.
6th. Fine. Dave Duffy called.
7th. Fine. Roped the red filly.

8th. Showery. Sold the gray mair's fole.
9th. Fine. Wint to the Red hill after a horse.
10th. Fine. Found tree sheap ded in sqre padick.

I closed the book and put it up with a sigh. The little record was a perfect picture of the dull narrow life of its writer. Week after week that diary went on the same—drearily monotonous account of a drearily monotonous existence. I felt I would go mad if forced to live such a life for long.

"Pa has lots of diaries. Would I like to read them?"

They were brought and put before me. I inquired of Mr. M'Swat which was the liveliest time of the year, and being told it was shearing and threshing, I opened one first in November:

November 1896

1st. Fine. Started to muster sheep.
2nd. Fine. Counten sheep very dusty 20 short.
3rd. Fine. Started shering. Joe Harris cut his hand bad and wint hoam.
4th. Showery. Shering stopped on account of rane.

Then I skipped to December:

December 1896

1st. Fine and hot. Stripped the weet 60 bages.
2nd. Fine. Killed a snake very hot day.
3rd. Fine. Very hot alle had a boagy in the river.
4th. Fine. Got returns of woll 7½ fleece 5¼ bellies.
5th. Fine. Awful hot got a serkeler from Tatersal by the poast.
6th. Fine. Saw Joe Harris at Duffys.

There was no entertainment to be had from the diaries, so I attempted a conversation with Mrs. M'Swat.

"A penny for your thoughts."

"I wuz jist watchin' the rain and thinkin' it would put a couple a bob a head more on sheep if it keeps on."

What was I to do to pass the day? I was ever very restless, even in the midst of full occupation. Uncle Jay-Jay used to accuse me of being in six places at once, and of being incapable of sitting still for five minutes consecutively; so it was simply endurance to live that long, long day—nothing to read, no piano on which to play hymns, too wet to walk, no one with whom to converse, no possibility of sleeping, as in an endeavor to kill a little of the time I had gone to bed early and got up late. There was nothing but to sit still, tormented by maddening regret. I pictured what would be transpiring at Caddagat now; what we had done this time last week, and so on, till the thing became an agony to me.

Among my duties before school I was to set the table, make all the beds, dust and sweep, and "do" the girls' hair. After school I had to mend clothes, sew, set the table again, take a turn at nursing the baby, and on washing-day iron. This sounds a lot, but in reality was nothing, and did not half occupy my time. Setting the table was a mere sinecure, as there was nothing much to put on it; and the only ironing was a few articles outside my own, as Mr. M'Swat and Peter did not wear white shirts, and patronized paper collars. Mrs. M'Swat did the washing and a little scrubbing, also boiled the beef and baked the bread, which formed our unvaried menu week in and week out. Most peasant mothers with a family of nine have no time for idleness, but Mrs. M'Swat managed things so that she spent most of the day rolling on her frowsy bed playing with her dirty infant, which was as fat and good-tempered as herself.

On Monday morning I marshaled my five scholars (Lizer, aged fourteen; Jimmy, twelve; Tommy, Sarah, and Rose Jane, younger) in a little back skillion, which was set apart as a school-room and store for flour and rock salt. Like all the house, it was built of slabs, which, erected while green, and on account of the heat, had shrunk until many of the cracks were sufficiently wide to insert one's arm. On Monday—after the rain —the wind, which disturbed us through them, was piercingly cold, but as the week advanced summer and drought regained their pitiless sway, and we were often sunburnt by the rough gusts which filled the room with such clouds of dust and grit that we were forced to cover our heads until it passed.

A policeman came on Tuesday to take some returns, and to him I entrusted the posting of my letters, and then eagerly waited for the reply which was to give me glorious release.

The nearest post-office was eight miles distant, and thither Jimmy was dispatched on horseback twice a week. With trembling expectancy every mail-day I watched for the boy's return down the tortuous track to the house, but it was always, "No letters for the school-missus."

A week, a fortnight, dragged away. Oh, the slow horror of those never-ending days! At the end of three weeks Mr. M'Swat went to the post unknown to me, and surprised me with a couple of letters. They bore the handwriting of my mother and grandmother—what I had been wildly waiting for,—and now that they had come at last I had not the nerve to open them while any one was observing me. All day I carried them in my bosom till my work was done, when I shut myself in my room and tore the envelopes open to read first my grannie's letter, which contained two:

My dear child,

I have been a long time answering your letter on account of waiting to consult your mother. I was willing to take you back, but your mother is not agreeable, so I cannot interfere between you. I enclose your mother's letter, so you can see how I stand in the matter. Try and do good where you are. We cannot get what we would like in this world, and must bow to God's will. He will always, &c.

Mother's Letter to Grannie

My dear Mother,

I am truly grieved that Sybylla should have written and worried you. Take no notice of her; it is only while she is unused to the place. She will soon settle down. She has always been a trial to me, and it is no use of taking notice of her complaints, which no doubt are greatly exaggerated, as she was never contented at home. I don't know where her rebellious spirit will eventually lead her. I hope M'Swat's will tame her; it will do her good. It is absolutely necessary that she should remain there, so do not say anything to give her other ideas &c.

Mother's Letter to Me

My dear Sybylla,

I wish you would not write and worry your poor old grandmother, who has been so good to you. You must try and put up with things; you cannot expect to find it like holidaying at Caddagat. Be careful not to give offense to any one, as it would be awkward for us. What is wrong with the place? Have you too much work to do? Do you not get sufficient to eat? Are they unkind to you, or what? Why don't you have sense and not talk of getting another place, as it is utterly impossible; and unless you remain there, how are we to pay the interest on that money? I've always been a good mother to you, and the least you might do in return is this, when you know how we are situated. Ask God &c.

Full of contempt and hatred for my mother, I tore her letters into tiny pieces and hurled them out the window. Oh, the hard want of sympathy they voiced! She had forced me to this place: it would have been different had I wanted to come of my own accord, and then sung out for a removal immediately; but no, against my earnest pleadings she had forced me here, and now would not heed my cry. And to whom in all the world can we turn when our mother spurns our prayer?

There never was any sympathy between my mother and myself. We are too unlike. She is intensely matter-of-fact and practical, possessed of no ambitions or aspirations not capable of being turned into cash value. She is very ladylike, and though containing no spice of either poet or musician, can take a part in conversation on such subjects, and play the piano correctly, because in her young days she was thus cultivated; but had she been born a peasant, she would have been a peasant, with no longings unattainable in that sphere. She no more understood me than I understand the works of a watch. She looked upon me as a discontented, rebellious, bad child, possessed of evil spirits, which wanted trouncing out of me; and she would have felt that she was sinning had she humored me in any way, so after cooling I did not blame her for her letters. She was doing her duty according to her lights. Again, it was this way, grannie did not come to my rescue on this occasion on account of her attitude toward my father. The Bossiers were not at enmity with him, but they were so disgusted with his insobriety that they never visited Possum Gully, and did not assist us as much as they would have done had my father's failure been attributable to some cause more deserving of sympathy.

After reading my letters I wept till every atom of my body writhed with agonized emotion. I was aroused by Mrs. M'Swat hammering at my door and inquiring:

"What ails ye, child? Did ye git bad noos from home?"

I recovered myself as by a miracle, and replied, no; that I was merely a little homesick, and would be out presently.

I wrote again to my mother, but as I could not truthfully say I was hungry or ill-treated, for, according to their ability, the M'Swats were very kind to me, she took no notice of my plaint, but told me that instead of complaining of monotony, it would suit me better if I cleared up the house a little.

Acting upon this advice, I asked Mr. M'Swat to put a paling fence around the house, as it was useless trying to keep the house respectable while the fowls and pigs ran in every time the door was opened.

He was inclined to look with favor upon this proposition, but his wife sat upon it determinedly—said the fowls would lose the scraps. "Would it not be possible to throw them over the fence to the fowls?" I asked; but this would cause too much waste, she considered.

Next I suggested that the piano should be tuned, but they were united in their disapproval of such a fearful extravagance. "The peeany makes a good nise. What ails it?"

Then I suggested that the children should be kept tidier, for which I was insulted by their father. I wanted them to be dressed up like swells, and if he did that he would soon be a pauper like my father. This I found was the sentiment of the whole family regarding me. I was only the daughter of old hard-up Melvyn, consequently I had little weight with the children, which made things very hard for me as a teacher.

One day at lunch I asked my mistress if she would like the children to be instructed in table-manners. "Certainly," her husband replied, so I commenced.

"Jimmy, you must never put your knife in your mouth."

"Pa does at any rate," replied Jimmy.

"Yes," said pa; "and I'm a richer man today than them as didn't do it."

"Liza, do not put a whole slice of bread to your mouth like that, and cram so. Cut it into small pieces."

"Ma doesn't," returned Liza.

"Ye'll have yer work cut out with 'em," laughed Mrs. M'Swat, who did not know how to correct her family herself, and was too ignorant to uphold my authority.

That was my only attempt at teaching manners there.

In the face of such odds it was a bootless task, and as there were not enough knives and forks to go around, I could not inculcate the correct method of handling those implements.

Mrs. M'Swat had but one boiler in which to do all her cooking, and one small tub for the washing, and there was seldom anything to eat but bread and beef; and this was not because they were poor, but because they did not know, or want to know, any better.

Their idea of religion, pleasure, manners, breeding, respectability, love, and everything of that ilk, was the possession of money, and their one idea of accumulating wealth was by hard sordid dragging and grinding.

A man who rises from indigence to opulence by business capabilities must have brains worthy of admiration, but the man who makes a fortune as M'Swat of Barney's Gap was making his must be dirt mean, grasping, narrow-minded, and soulless—to me the most uncongenial of my fellows.

I wrote once more to my mother, to receive the same reply. One hope remained. I would write to aunt Helen. She understood me somewhat, and would know how I felt.

Acting on this inspiration, I requested her to plead for me. Her answer came as a slap in the face, as I had always imagined her above the common cant of ordinary religionists. She stated that life was full of trials. I must try and bear this little cross patiently, and at the end of a year they might have me back at Caddagat. A year! A year at Barney's Gap! The possibility of such a thing made me frantic. I picked up my pen and bitterly reproached my aunt in a letter to which she did not deign to reply; and from that day to this she has rigidly ignored me—never so much as sending me the most commonplace message, or casually using my name in her letters to my mother.

Aunt Helen, is there such a thing as firm friendship when even yours—best of women—quibbled and went under at the hysterical wail from the overburdened heart of a child?

My predecessor, previous to her début at Barney's Gap, had spent some time in a lunatic asylum, and being a curious character, allowed the children to do as they pleased, consequently they knew not what it meant to be ruled, and were very bold. They attempted no insubordination while their father was about the house, but when he was absent they gave me a dog's life, their mother sometimes smiling on their pranks, often lazily heedless of them, but never administering any form of correction.

If I walked away from the house to get rid of them, they would follow and hoot at me; and when I reproved them they informed me they were not going "to knuckle under to old Melvyn's darter, the damnedest fool in the world, who's lost all his prawperty, and has to borry money off of pa."

Did I shut myself in my room, they shoved sticks in the cracks and made grimaces at me. I knew the fallacy of appealing to their father, as they and their mother would tell falsehoods, and my word would not be taken in contradiction of theirs. I had experience of this, as the postmistress had complained of Jimmy, to be insulted by his father, who could see no imperfection in his children.

M'Swat was much away from home at that time. The drought necessitated the removal of some of his sheep, for which he had rented a place eighty miles coastward. There he left them under the charge of a man, but he repaired thither frequently to inspect them. Sometimes he was away from home a fortnight at a stretch. Peter would be away at work all day, and the children took advantage of my defenseless position. Jimmy was the ringleader. I could easily have managed the others had he been removed. I would have thrashed him well at the start but for the letters I constantly received from home warning me against offense to the parents, and knew that to set my foot on the children's larrikinism would require measures that would gain their mother's ill-will at once. But when M'Swat left home for three weeks Jim got so bold that I resolved to take decisive steps toward subjugating him. I procured a switch—a very small one, as his mother had a great objection to corporal punishment—and when, as usual, he commenced to cheek me during lessons, I hit him on the coat-sleeve. The blow would not have brought tears from the eyes of a toddler, but this great calf emitted a wild yope, and opening his mouth let his saliva pour on to his slate. The others set up such blood-curdling yells in concert that I was a little disconcerted, but I determined not to give in. I delivered another tap, whereupon he squealed and roared so that he brought his mother to his rescue like a ton of bricks on stilts, a great fuss in her eyes which generally beamed with a cowful calm.

Seizing my arm she shook me like a rat, broke my harmless little stick in pieces, threw it in my face, and patting Jimmy on the shoulder, said:

"Poor man! She sharn't touch me Jimmy while I know. Sure you've got no sense. You'd had him dead if I hadn't come in."

I walked straight to my room and shut myself in, and did not teach any more that afternoon. The children rattled on my door-handle and jeered:

"She thought she'd hit me, but ma settled her. Old poor Melvyn's darter won't try no more of her airs on us."

I pretended not to hear. What was I to do? There was no one to whom I could turn for help. M'Swat would believe the story of his family, and my mother would blame me. She would think I had been in fault because I hated the place.

Mrs. M'Swat called me to tea, but I said I would not have any. I lay awake all night and got desperate. On the morrow I made up my mind to conquer or leave. I would stand no more. If, in all the wide world and the whole of life this was the only use for me, then I would die—take my own life if necessary.

Things progressed as usual next morning. I attended to my duties and marched my scholars into the school-

room at the accustomed hour. There was no decided
insubordination during the morning, but I felt Jimmy
was waiting for an opportunity to defy me. It was a
fearful day, possessed by a blasting wind laden with
red dust from Riverina, which filled the air like a fog.
The crockery ware became so hot in the kitchen that
when taking it into the dining-room we had to handle
it with cloths. During the dinner-hour I slipped away
unnoticed to where some quince-trees were growing and
procured a sharp rod, which I secreted among the flour-
bags in the schoolroom. At half-past one I brought
my scholars in and ordered them to their work with a
confident air. Things went without a ripple until three
o'clock, when the writing lesson began. Jimmy struck
his pen on the bottom of the bottle every time he re-
plenished it with ink.

"Jimmy," I gently remonstrated, "don't jab your pen
like that—it will spoil it. There is no necessity to shove
it right to the bottom."

Jab, jab, went Jimmy's pen.

"Jimmy, did you hear me speak to you?"

Jab went the pen.

"James, I am speaking to you!"

Jab went the pen again.

"James," I said sternly, "I give you one more
chance."

He deliberately defied me by stabbing into the ink-
bottle with increased vigor. Liza giggled triumphantly,
and the little ones strove to emulate her. I calmly produced my switch and brought it smartly over the shoulders of my refractory pupil in a way that sent the dust
in a cloud from his dirty coat, knocked the pen from
his fingers, and upset the ink.

He acted as before—yelled ear-drum-breakingly,
letting the saliva from his distended mouth run on his
copy-book. His brothers and sisters also started to roar,
but bringing the rod down on the table, I threatened
to thrash every one of them if they so much as whim-
pered; and they were so dumbfounded that they sat
silent in terrified surprise.

Jimmy continued to bawl. I hit him again.

"Cease instantly, sir."

Through the cracks Mrs. M'Swat could be seen approaching. Seeing her, Jimmy hollered anew. I expected her to attack me. She stood five feet nine inches, and weighed about sixteen stones; I measured five feet one inch, and turned the scale at eight stones—scarcely a fair match; but my spirit was aroused, and instead of feeling afraid, I rejoiced at the encounter which was imminent, and had difficulty to refrain from shouting "Come on! I'm ready, physically and mentally, for you and a dozen others such."

My curious ideas regarding human equality gave me confidence. My theory is that the cripple is equal to the giant, and the idiot to the genius. As, if on account of his want of strength the cripple is subservient to the giant, the latter, on account of that strength, is compelled to give in to the cripple. So with the dolt and the man of brain, so with Mrs. M'Swat and me.

The fact of not only my own but my family's dependence on M'Swat sank into oblivion. I merely recognized that she was one human being and I another. Should I have been deferential to her by reason of her age and maternity, then from the vantage which this gave her, she should have been lenient to me on account of my chit-ship and inexperience. Thus we were equal.

Jimmy hollered with renewed energy to attract his mother, and I continued to rain blows across his shoulders. Mrs. M'Swat approached to within a foot of the door, and then, as though changing her mind, retraced her steps and entered the hot low-roofed kitchen. I knew I had won, and felt disappointed that the conquest had been so easy. Jimmy, seeing he was worsted, ceased his uproar, cleaned his copy-book on his sleeve, and sheepishly went on with his writing.

Whether Mrs. M'Swat saw she had been in fault the day before I know not; certain it is that the children ever after that obeyed me, and I heard no more of the matter; neither, as far as I could ascertain, did the "ruction" reach the ears of M'Swat.

"How long, how long!" was my cry, as I walked out ankle-deep in the dust to see the sun, like a ball of blood, sink behind the hills on that February evening.

CHAPTER THIRTY

Where Ignorance is Bliss, 'Tis Folly to be Wise

When by myself, I fretted so constantly that the traces it left upon me became evident even to the dull comprehension of Mrs. M'Swat.

"I don't hold with too much pleasure and disherpation, but you ain't had overmuch of it lately. You've stuck at home pretty constant, and ye and Lizer can have a little fly around. It'll do yous good," she said.

The dissipation, pleasure, and flying around allotted to "Lizer" and me were to visit some of the neighbors. Those, like the M'Swats, were sheep-farming selectors. They were very friendly and kind to me, and I found them superior to my employers, in that their houses were beautifully clean; but they lived the same slow life, and their soul's existence fed on the same small ideas. I was keenly disappointed that none of them had a piano, as my hunger for music could be understood only by one with a passion for that art.

I borrowed something to read, but all that I could get in the way of books were a few *Young Ladies' Journals,* which I devoured ravenously, so to speak.

When Lizer's back would be turned, the girls would ask me how I managed to live at Barney's Gap, and expressed themselves of the opinion that it was the most horrible hole in the world, and Mrs. M'Swat the dirtiest creature living, and that they would not go there for £50 a week. I made a point of never saying anything against Mrs. M'Swat; but I fumed inwardly that this life was forced upon me, when girls with no longings or aspirations beyond being the wife of a Peter M'Swat recoiled from the thought of it.

My mother insisted upon my writing to her regularly, so once a week I headed a letter "Black's Camp," and condemned the place, while mother as unfailingly replied that these bad times I should be thankful to God that I was fed and clothed. I knew this as well as any one, and was aware there were plenty of girls willing to jump at my place; but they were of different temperament to me, and when one is seventeen, that kind of reasoning does not weigh very heavily.

My eldest brother, Horace, twin brother of my sister Gertie, took it upon himself to honor me with the following letter:

Why the deuce don't you give up writing those letters to mother? We get tongue-pie on account of them, and it's not as if they did you any good. It only makes mother more determined to leave you where you are. She says you are that conceited you think you ought to have something better, and you're not fit for the place you have, and she's glad it is such a place, and it will do you the world of good and take the nonsense out of you—that it's time you got a bit of sense. Sullivan's Ginger. After she gets your letters she does jaw, and wishes she never had a child, and what a good mother she is, and what bad devils we are to her. You are a fool not to stay where you are. I wish I could get away to M'Swat or Mack Pot, and I would jump at the chance like a good un. The boss still sprees and loafs about town till some one has to

go and haul him home. I'm about full of him, and
I'm going to leave home before next Christmas, or
my name ain't what it is. Mother says the kiddies
would starve if I leave; but Stanley is coming on
like a haystack, I tell him, and he does kick up,
and he ought to be able to plow next time. I
plowed when I was younger than him. I put in
fourteen acres of wheat and oats this year, and I
don't think I'll cut a wheelbarrow-load of it. I'm
full of the place. I never have a single penny to my
name, and it ain't father's drinking that's all to
blame; if he didn't booze it wouldn't be much
better. It's the slowest hole in the world, and I'll
chuck it and go shearing or droving. I hate this
dairying, it's too slow for a funeral: there would
be more life in trapping 'possums out on Timlinbilly. Mother always says to have patience, and
when the drought breaks and good seasons come
round again things will be better, but it's no good
of trying to stuff me like that. I remember when
the seasons were wet. It was no good growing anything, because every one grew so much that there
was no market, and the sheep died of foot-rot and
you couldn't give your butter away, and it is not
much worse to have nothing to sell than not be
able to sell a thing when you have it. And the long
and short of it is that I hate dairying like blue
murder. It's as tame as a clucking hen. Fancy a
cove sitting down every morning and evening pulling at a cow's tits fit to bust himself, and then
turning an old separator, and washing it up in a
dish of water like a blooming girl's work. And if
you go to a picnic, just when the fun commences
you have to nick off home and milk, and when you
tog yourself on Sunday evening you have to undress again and lay into the milking, and then you
have to change everything on you and have a bath,
or your best girl would scent the cow-yard on you,
and not have you within cooee of her. We won't
know what rain is when we see it; but I suppose it

will come in floods and finish the little left by the drought. The grasshoppers have eaten all the fruit and even the bark off the trees, and the caterpillars made a croker of the few tomatoes we kept alive with the suds. All the cockeys round here and dad are applying to the Government to have their rents suspended for a time. We have not heard yet whether it will be granted, but if Gov. doesn't like it, they'll have to lump it, for none of us have a penny to bless ourselves with, let alone dub up for taxes. I've written you a long letter, and if you growl about the spelling and grammar I won't write to you any more, so there, and you take my tip and don't write to mother on that flute any more, for she won't take a bit of notice.

Yr loving brother,
Horace.

So! Mother had no pity for me, and the more I pleaded with her the more determined she grew upon leaving me to suffer on, so I wrote to her no more. However, I continued to correspond with grannie, and in one of her letters she told me that Harry Beecham (that was in February) was still in Sydney settling his affairs; but when that was concluded he was going to Queensland. He had put his case in the hands of squatters he had known in his palmy days, and the first thing that turned up in managing or overseeing he was to have; but for the present he had been offered the charge of 1600 head of bullocks from a station up near the Gulf of Carpentaria overland to Victoria. Uncle Jay-Jay was not home yet: he had extended his tour to Hong Kong, and grannie was afraid he was spending too much money, as in the face of the drought she had difficulty in making both ends meet, and feared she would be compelled to go on the banks. She grieved that I was not becoming more reconciled to my place. It was dull, no doubt, but it would do my reputation no harm, whereas, were I in a lively situation, there

might be numerous temptations hard to resist. Why
did I not try to look at it in that way?

She sent a copy of the *Australasian,* which was a
great treat to me, also to the children, as they were
quite ignorant of the commonest things in life, and the
advent of this illustrated paper was an event to be re-
corded in the diary in capital letters. They clustered
around me eagerly to see the pictures. In this edition
there chanced to be a page devoted to the portraits of
eleven Australian singers, and our eyes fell on Madame
Melba, who was in the middle. As what character she
was dressed I do not remember, but she looked magnificent. There was a crown upon her beautiful head,
the plentiful hair was worn flowing, and the shapely
bosom and arms exposed.

"Who's that?" they inquired.

"Madame Melba; did you ever hear her name?"

"Who's Madame Melba? What's she do? Is she a
queen?"

"Yes, a queen, and a great queen of song"; and being inspired with great admiration for our own Australian cantatrice, who was great among the greatest
prima-donnas of the world, I began to tell them a
little of her fame, and that she had been recently
offered £40,000 to sing for three months in America.

They were incredulous. Forty thousand pounds! Ten
times as much as "pa" had given for a paid-up selection
he had lately bought. They told me it was no use of me
trying to tell them fibs. No one would give a woman
anything to sing, not even one pound. Why, Susie
Duffy was the best singer on the Murrumbidgee, and
she would sing for any one who asked her, and free
of charge.

At this juncture Jimmy, who had been absent, came
to see the show. After gazing for a few seconds he
remarked what the others had failed to observe. "Why,
the woman's naked!"

I attempted to explain that among rich people in
high society it was customary to dress like that in the
evening, and that it looked very pretty.

Mrs. M'Swat admonished me for showing the children low pictures.

"She must be a very bold woman," said Jimmy; and Lizer pronounced her mad because, as she put it, "It's a wonder she'd be half-undressed in her photo; you'd think she oughter dress herself up complete then."

Lizer certainly acted upon this principle, as a photo of her, which had been taken by a traveling artist, bore evidence that for the occasion she had arrayed herself in two pairs of ill-fitting cuffs, Peter's watch and chain, strings, jackets, flowers, and other gewgaws galore.

"There ain't no such person as Madame Melber; it's only a fairy-tale," said Mrs. M'Swat.

"Did you ever hear of Gladstone?" I inquired.

"No; where is that place?"

"Did you ever hear of Jesus Christ?"

"Sure, yes; he's got something to do with God, ain't he?"

After that I never attempted to enlighten them regarding our celebrities.

Oh, how I envied them their ignorant contentment! They were as ducks on a duck-pond; but I was as a duck forced for ever to live in a desert, ever wildly longing for water, but never reaching it outside of dreams.

CHAPTER THIRTY-ONE

Mr. M'Swat and I Have a Bust-up

Men only, and they merely on business, came to Barney's Gap—women tabooed the place. Some of them told me they would come to see me, but not Mrs. M'Swat, as she always allowed the children to be as rude to them as they pleased. With the few individuals who chanced to come M'Swat would sit down, light his pipe, and vulgarly and profusely expectorate on the floor, while they yarned and yarned for hours and hours about the price of wool, the probable breeding capacity of the male stock they kept, and of the want of grass—never a word about their country's politics or the events of the day; even the news of the "Mountain Murders" by Butler had not penetrated here. I wondered if they were acquainted with the names of their Governor and Prime Minister.

It was not the poor food and the filthy way of preparing it that worried me, or that Mr. M'Swat used "damn" on an average twice in five minutes when conversing, or that the children for ever nagged about my father's poverty and tormented me in a thousand other ways,—it was the dead monotony that was killing me.

I longed feveredly for something to happen. Agony is a tame word wherewith to express what that life meant to me. Solitary confinement to a gypsy would be something on a par.

Every night unfailingly when at home M'Swat sat in the bosom of his family and speculated as to how much richer he was than his neighbors, what old Reece lived on, and who had the best breed of sheep and who was the smartest at counting these animals, until the sordidness of it turned me dizzy, and I would steal out under the stars to try and cool my heated spirit. This became a practice with me, and every night I would slip away out of hearing of the household to sing the songs I had heard at Caddagat, and in imagination to relive every day and hour there, till the thing became too much for me, and I was scarcely responsible for my actions. Often I knelt on the parched ground beneath the balmy summer sky to pray—wild passionate prayers that were never answered.

I was under the impression that my nightly ramble was not specially noticed by any one, but I was mistaken. Mr. M'Swat, it appears, suspected me of having a lover, but was never able to catch me red-handed.

The possibility of a girl going out at night to gaze at the stars and dream was as improbable a thought for him as flying is to me, and having no soul above mud, had I attempted an explanation he would have considered me mad, and dangerous to have about the place.

Peter, junior, had a sweetheart, one Susie Duffy, who lived some miles on the other side of the Murrumbidgee. He was in the habit of courting her every Sunday and two or three nights during the week, and I often heard the clang of his stirrup-irons and the clink of hobble-chain when he returned late; but on one occasion I stayed out later than usual, and he passed me going home. I stood still and he did not see me, but his horse shied violently. I thought he would imagine I was a ghost, so called out:

"It is I."

"Well, I'll be hanged! What are ye doin' at this time ev night. Ain't yuz afraid of ghosts?"

"Oh dear no. I had a bad headache and couldn't sleep, so came out to try if a walk would cure it," I explained.

We were a quarter of a mile or so from the house, so Peter slackened his speed that I might keep pace with him. His knowledge of etiquette did not extend as far as dismounting. There is a great difference between rudeness and ignorance. Peter was not rude; he was merely ignorant. For the same reason he let his mother feed the pigs, clean his boots, and chop wood, while he sat down and smoked and spat. It was not that he was unmanly, as that this was the only manliness he had known.

I was alone in the schoolroom next afternoon when Mr. M'Swat sidled in, and after stuttering and hawing a little, delivered himself of:

"I want to tell ye that I don't hold with a gu-r-r-r-l going out of nights for to meet young men: if ye want to do any coortin' yuz can do it inside, if it's a decent young man. I have no objections to yer hangin' yer cap up to our Peter, only that ye have no prawperty—in yerself I like ye well enough, but we have other views for Peter. He's almost as good as made it sure with Susie Duffy, an' as ole Duffy will have a bit ev prawperty I want him to git her, an' wouldn't like ye to spoil the fun."

Peter was "tall and freckled and sandy, face of a country lout," and, like Middleton's rouse-about, "hadn't any opinions, hadn't any ideas," but possessed sufficient instinct and common bushcraft with which, by hard slogging, to amass money. He was developing a moustache, and had a "gu-r-r-r-l"; he wore tight trousers and long spurs; he walked with a sidling swagger that was a cross between shyness and flashness, and took as much pride in his necktie as any man; he had a kind heart, honest principles, and would not hurt a fly; he worked away from morning till night, and contentedly did his duty like a bullock in the sphere in which God had placed him; he never had a bath while I knew him, and was a man according to his lights. He knew there was such a thing as the outside world, as I know there is such a thing as algebra; but it troubled him no more than algebra troubles me.

This was my estimation of Peter M'Swat, junior. I respected him right enough in his place, as I trust he respected me in mine, but though fate thought fit for the present to place us in the one groove, yet our lives were unmixable commodities as oil and water, which lay apart and would never meet until taken in hand by the omnipotent leveler—death.

Marriage with Peter M'Swat!

Consternation and disgust held me speechless, and yet I was half inclined to laugh at the preposterousness of the thing, when Peter's father continued:

"I'm sorry if you've got smitten on Peter, but I know you'll be sensible. Ye see I have a lot of childre, and when the place is divided among 'em it won't be much. I tell ye wot, old Duffy has a good bit of money and only two childre, Susie and Mick. I could get you to meet Mick—he mayn't be so personable as our Peter," he reflected, with evident pride in his weedy firstborn, and he got no farther, for I had been as a yeast-bottle bubbling up, and now went off bang!

"Silence, you ignorant old creature! How dare you have the incomparable impertinence to mention my name in conjunction with that of your boor of a son. Though he were a millionaire I would think his touch contamination. You have fallen through for once if you imagine I go out at night to meet any one—I merely go away to be free for a few minutes from the suffocating atmosphere of your odious home. You must not think that because you have grasped and slaved and got a little money that it makes a gentleman of you; and never you *dare* to again mention my name in regard to matrimony with any one about here"; and with my head high and shoulders thrown back I marched to my room, where I wept till I was weak and ill.

This monotonous sordid life was unhinging me, and there was no legitimate way of escape from it. I formed wild plans of running away, to do what I did not care so long as it brought a little action, anything but this torturing maddening monotony; but my love for my little brothers and sisters held me back. I could not do anything that would put me for ever beyond the pale of their society.

I was so reduced in spirit that had Harold Beecham appeared then with a matrimonial scheme to be fulfilled at once, I would have quickly erased the fine lines I had drawn and accepted his proposal; but he did not come, and I was unacquainted with his whereabouts or welfare. As I remembered him, how lovable and superior he seemed in comparison with the men I met nowadays: not that he was any better than these men in their place and according to their lights, but his lights—at least not his lights, for Harold Beecham was nothing of a philosopher, but the furniture of the drawing-room which they illuminated—was more artistic. What a prince of gentlemanliness and winning gallantries he was in his quiet way!

This information concerning him was in a letter I received from my grandmother at Easter:

Who should surprise us with a visit the other day but Harold Beecham. He was as thin as a whipping post, and very sunburnt [I smiled, imagining it impossible for Harold to be any browner than of yore]. He has been near death's door with the measles—caught them in Queensland while droving, and got wet. He was so ill that he had to give up charge of that 1600 head of cattle he was bringing. He came to say good-bye to us, as he is off to Western Australia next week to see if he can mend his fortunes there. I was afraid he was going to be like young Charters, and swear he would never come back unless he made a pile, but he says he will be back next Christmas three years for certain, if he is alive and kicking, as he says himself. Why he intends returning at that stipulated time I don't know, as he never was very communi-

cative, and is more unsociable than ever now. He
is a man who never shows his feelings, but he must
feel the loss of his old position deeply. He seemed
surprised not to find you here, and says it was a
pity to set you teaching, as it will take all the life
and fun out of you, and that is the first time I ever
heard him express an opinion in any one's business but his own. Frank Hawden sends kind regards, &c.

Teaching certainly had the effect upon me antic-
ipated by Harold Beecham, but it was not the teaching
but the place in which I taught which was doing the
mischief—good, my mother termed it.

I was often sleepless for more than forty-eight hours
at a stretch, and cried through the nights until my
eyes had black rings around them, which washing failed
to remove. The neighbors described me as "a sorrow-
ful lookin' delicate creetur', that couldn't larf to save
her life"—quite a different character to the girl who at
Caddagat was continually chid for being a romp, a hoy-
den, a boisterous tomboy, a whirlwind, and for excessive laughter at anything and everything. I got into
such a state of nervousness that I would jump at the
opening of a door or an unexpected footfall.

When cooling down, after having so vigorously delivered Mr. M'Swat a piece of my mind, I felt that I
owed him an apology. According to his lights (and that
is the only fair way of judging our fellows) he had
acted in a kind of fatherly way. I was a young girl
under his charge, and he would have in a measure
been responsible had I come to harm through going
out in the night. He had been good-natured, too, in
offering to help things along by providing an eligible,
and allowing us to "spoon" under his surveillance.
That I was of temperament and aspirations that made
his plans loathsome to me was no fault of his—only
a heavy misfortune to myself. Yes; I had been in the
wrong entirely.

With this idea in my head, sinking ankle-deep in the dust, and threading my way through the pigs and fowls which hung around the back door, I went in search of my master. Mrs. M'Swat was teaching Jimmy how to kill a sheep and dress it for use; while Lizer, who was nurse to the baby and spectator of the performance, was volubly and ungrammatically giving instructions in the art. Peter and some of the younger children were away felling stringybark-trees for the sustenance of the sheep. The fall of their axes and the murmur of the Murrumbidgee echoed faintly from the sunset. They would be home presently and at tea; I reflected it would be "The old yeos looks terrible skinny, but the hoggets is fat yet. By crikey! They did go into the bushes. They chawed up stems and all—some as thick as a pencil."

This information in that parlance had been given yesterday, the day before, would be given today, tomorrow, and the next day. It was the boss item on the conversational program until further orders.

I had a pretty good idea where to find Mr. M'Swat, as he had lately purchased a pair of stud rams, and was in the habit of admiring them for a couple of hours every evening. I went to where they usually grazed, and there, as I expected, found Mr. M'Swat, pipe in mouth, with glistening eyes, surveying his darlings.

"Mr. M'Swat, I have come to beg your pardon."

"That's all right, me gu-r-r-r-l. I didn't take no notice to anything ye might spit out in a rage."

"But I was not in a rage. I meant every word I said, but I want to apologize for the rude way in which I said it, as I had no right to speak so to my elders. And I want to tell you that you need not fear me running away with Peter, even supposing he should honor me with his affections, as I am engaged to another man."

"By dad, I'll be hanged!" he exclaimed, with nothing but curiosity on his wrinkled dried tobacco-leaf-looking face. He expressed no resentment on account of my behavior to him.

"Are ye to be married soon? Has he got any

prawperty? Who is he? I suppose he's respectable. Ye're very young."

"Yes; he is renowned for respectability, but I am not going to marry him till I am twenty-one. He is poor, but has good prospects. You must promise me not to tell anyone, as I wish it kept a secret, and only mention it to you so that you need not be disturbed about Peter."

He assured me that he would keep the secret, and I knew I could rely on his word. He was greatly perturbed that my intended was poor.

"Never ye marry a man widout a bit er prawperty, me gu-r-r-r-l. Take my advice—the divil's in a poor match, no matter how good the man may be. Don't ye be in a hurry; ye're personable enough in yer way, and there's as good fish in the seas as ever come out of 'em. Yer very small; I admire a good lump of a woman meself—but don't ye lose heart. I've heerd some men say they like little girls, but, as I said, I like a good lump of a woman meself."

"And you've got a good lump of a squaw," I thought to myself.

Do not mistake me. I do not for an instant fancy myself above the M'Swats. Quite the reverse; they are much superior to me. Mr. M'Swat was upright and clean in his morals, and in his little sphere was as sensible and kind a man as one could wish for. Mrs. M'Swat was faithful to him, contented and good-natured, and bore uncomplainingly, year after year, that most cruelly agonizing of human duties—childbirth, and did more for her nation and her Maker than I will ever be noble enough to do.

But I could not help it that their life was warping my very soul. Nature fashions us all; we have no voice in the matter, and I could not change my organization to one which would find sufficient sustenance in the mental atmosphere of Barney's Gap.

CHAPTER THIRTY-TWO

Ja-Ja to Barney's Gap

It chanced at last, as June gave place to July and July to August, that I could bear it no longer. I would go away even if I had to walk, and what I would do I did not know or care, my one idea being to leave Barney's Gap far and far behind. One evening I got a lot of letters from my little brothers and sisters at home. I fretted over them a good deal, and put them under my pillow; and as I had not slept for nights, and was feeling weak and queer, I laid my head upon them to rest a little before going out to get the tea ready. The next thing I knew was that Mrs. M'Swat was shaking me vigorously with one hand, holding a flaring candle in the other, and saying:

"Lizer, shut the winder quick. She's been lyin' here in the draught till she's froze, and must have the nightmare, the way she's been singin' out that queer, an' I can't git her woke up. What ails ye, child? Are ye sick?"

I did not know what ailed me, but learned subsequently that I laughed and cried very much, and pleaded hard with grannie and some Harold to save me, and kept reiterating, "I cannot bear it, I cannot bear it," and altogether behaved so strangely that Mr. M'Swat became so alarmed that he sent seventeen miles for the nearest doctor. He came next morning, felt my

226

pulse, asked a few questions, and stated that I was suffering from nervous prostration.

"Why, the child is completely run down, and in a fair way to contract brain fever!" he exclaimed. "What has she been doing? It seems as though she had been under some great mental strain. She must have complete rest and change, plenty of diversion and nourishing food, or her mind will become impaired."

He left me a bottle of tonic and Mr. and Mrs. M'Swat many fears. Poor kind-hearted souls, they got in a great state, and understood about as much of the cause of my breakdown as I do of the inside of the moon. They ascribed it to the paltry amount of teaching and work I had done.

Mrs. M'Swat killed a fowl and stewed it for my delectation. There was part of the inside with many feathers to flavor the dish, and having no appetite, I did not enjoy it, but made a feint of so doing to please the good-natured cook.

They intended writing at once to give my parents notice when I would be put on the train. I was pronounced too ill to act as scribe; Lizer was suggested, and then Jimmy, but M'Swat settled the matter thus:

"Sure, damn it! I'm the proper one to write on an important business matther like this here."

So pens, ink, and paper were laid on the diningroom table, and the great proclamation went forth among the youngsters, "Pa is goin' to write a whole letter all by hisself."

My door opened with the dining-room, and from my bed I could see the proceeding. Mr. M'Swat hitched his trousers well through the saddle-strap which he always wore as a belt, took off his coat and folded it on the back of a chair, rolled his shirt-sleeves up to his elbows, pulled his hat well over his eyes, and "shaped up" to the writing material, none of which met with his approval. The ink was "warter," the pens had not enough "pint," and the paper was "trash"; but on being assured it was the good stuff he had purchased especially for himself, he buckled to the fray,

producing in three hours a half-sheet epistle, which in
grammar, composition, and spelling quite eclipsed the
entries in his diary. However, it served its purpose, and
my parents wrote back that, did I reach Goulburn on
a certain day, a neighbor who would be in town then
would bring me home.

Now that it was settled that I had no more to teach
the dirty children, out of dirty books, lessons for
which they had great disinclination, and no more to
direct Lizer's greasy fingers over the yellow keys of
that demented piano in a vain endeavor to teach her
"choones," of which her mother expected her to learn
on an average two daily, it seemed as though I had
a mountain lifted off me, and I revived magically, got
out of bed and packed my things.

I was delighted at the prospect of throwing off the
leaden shackles of Barney's Gap, but there was a little
regret mingled with my relief. The little boys had not
been always bold. Did I express a wish for a parrot-
wing or water-worn stone, or such like, after a time I
would be certain, on issuing from my bedroom, to find
that it had been surreptitiously laid there, and the
little soft-eyed fellows would squabble for the privilege
of bringing me my post, simply to give me pleasure.
Poor little Lizer, and Rose Jane too, copied me in style
of dress and manners in a way that was somewhat
ludicrous but more pathetic.

They clustered around to say good-bye. I would be
sure to write. Oh yes, of course, and they would write
in return and tell me if the bay mare got well, and
where they would find the yellow turkey-hen's nest.
When I got well I must come back, and I wouldn't
have as much work to do, but go for more rides to
keep well, and so on. Mrs. M'Swat very anxiously impressed it upon me that I was to explain to my mother
that it was not her (Mrs. M'S.'s) fault that I "ailed"
from overwork, as I had never complained and always
seemed well.

With a kindly light on his homely sunburnt face,
M'Swat said, as he put me on the train:

"Sure, tell yer father he needn't worry over the money. I'll never be hard on him, an' if ever I could help ye, I'd be glad."

"Thank you; you are very good, and have done too much already."

"Too much! Sure, damn it, wot's the good er bein' alive if we can't help each other sometimes. I don't mind how much I help a person if they have a little gratitood, but, damn it, I can't abear ingratitood."

"Good-bye, Mr. M'Swat, and thank you."

"Good-bye, me gu-r-r-r-l, and never marry that bloke of yours if he don't git a bit er prawperty, for the divil's in a poor match."

CHAPTER THIRTY-THREE

Back at Possum Gully

They were expecting me on the frosty evening in September, and the children came bounding and shouting to meet me, when myself and luggage were deposited at Possum Gully by a neighbor, as he passed in a great hurry to reach his own home ere it got too dark. They bustled me to a glowing fire in no time.

My father sat reading, and, greeting me in a very quiet fashion, continued the perusal of his paper. My mother shut her lips tightly, saying exultingly, "It seems it was possible for you to find a worse place than home"; and that little speech was the thorn on the rose of my welcome home. But there was no sting in Gertie's greeting, and how beautiful she was growing, and so tall! It touched me to see she had made an especial dainty for my tea, and had put things on the table which were only used for visitors. The boys and little Aurora chattered and danced around me all the while. One brought for my inspection some soup-plates which had been procured during my absence; another came with a picture-book; and nothing would do them but that I must, despite the darkness, straightaway go out and admire a new fowl-house which "Horace and Stanley built all by theirselves, and no one helped them one single bit."

After Mrs. M'Swat it was a rest, a relief, a treat, to hear my mother's cultivated voice, and observe her lady-like and refined figure as she moved about; and, what a palace the place seemed in comparison to Barney's Gap! simply because it was clean, orderly, and bore traces of refinement; for the stamp of indigent circumstances was legibly imprinted upon it, and many things which had been considered "done for" when thirteen months before I had left home, were still in use.

I carefully studied my brothers and sisters. They had grown during my absence, and were all big for their age, and though some of them not exactly handsome, yet all pleasant to look upon—I was the only wanting in physical charms—also they were often discontented, and wished, as children will, for things they could not have; but they were natural, understandable children, not like myself, cursed with a fevered ambition for the utterly unattainable.

> *Oh, were I seated high as my ambition,*
> *I'd place this foot on naked necks of monarchs!*

At the time of my departure for Caddagat my father had been negotiating with beer regarding the sale of his manhood; on returning I found that he had completed the bargain, and held a stamped receipt in his miserable appearance and demeanor. In the broken-down man, regardless of manners, one would have failed to recognize Dick Melvyn, "Smart Dick Melvyn," "Jolly-good-fellow Melvyn," "Thorough Gentleman," and "Manly Melvyn" of the handsome face and ingratiating manners, one-time holder of Bruggabrong, Bin Bin East, and Bin Bin West. He never corrected his family nowadays, and his example was most deleterious to them.

Mother gave me a list of her worries in private after tea that night. She wished she had never married: not only was her husband a failure, but to all appearances her children would be the same. I wasn't worth my salt or I would have remained at Barney's Gap; and there was Horace—heaven only knew where he would end. God would surely punish him for his disrespect to his father. It was impossible to keep things together much longer, etc., etc.

When we went to bed that night Gertie poured all her troubles into my ear in a jumbled string. It was terrible to have such a father. She was ashamed of him. He was always going into town, and stayed there till mother had to go after him, or some of the neighbors were so good as to bring him home. It took all the money to pay the publican's bills, and Gertie was ashamed to be seen abroad in the nice clothes which grannie sent, as the neighbors said the Melvyns ought to pay up the old man's bills instead of dressing like swells; and she couldn't help it, and she was sick and tired of trying to keep up respectability in the teeth of such odds.

I comforted her with the assurance that the only thing was to feel right within ourselves, and let people say whatsoever entertained their poor little minds. And I fell asleep thinking that parents have a duty to children greater than children to parents, and they who do not fulfill their responsibility in this respect are as bad in their morals as the debauchee, corrupt the community as much as a thief, and are among the ablest underminers of their nation.

On the morrow, the first time we were alone, Horace

seized the opportunity of holding forth on *his* woes. It was no use, he was choke full of Possum Gully: he would stick to it for another year, and then he would chuck it, even if he had to go on the wallaby. He wasn't going to be slaving for ever for the boss to swallow the proceeds, and there was nothing to be made out of dairying. When it wasn't drought it was floods and caterpillars and grasshoppers.

Among my brothers and sisters I quickly revived to a certain extent, and mother asserted her opinion that I had not been ill at all, but had made up my mind to torment her; had not taken sufficient exercise, and might have had a little derangement of the system but nothing more. It was proposed that I should return to Barney's Gap. I demurred, and was anathematized as ungrateful and altogether corrupt, that I would not go back to M'Swat, who was so good as to lend my father money out of pure friendship; but for once in my life I could not be made submit by either coercion or persuasion. Grannie offered to take one of us to Caddagat; mother preferred that Gertie should go. So we sent the pretty girl to dwell among her kindred in a land of comfort and pleasure.

I remained at Possum Gully to tread the same old life in its tame narrow path, with its never-ending dawn-till-daylight round of tasks; with, as its entertainments, an occasional picnic or funeral or a day in town, when, should it happen to be Sunday, I never fail to patronize one of the cathedrals. I love the organ music, and the hush which pervades the building; and there is much entertainment in various ways if one goes early and watches the well-dressed congregation filing in. The costumes and the women are pretty, and, in his own particular line, the ability of the verger is something at which to marvel. Regular attendants, of course, pay for and have reserved their seats, but it is in classing the visitors that the verger displays his talent. He can cull the commoners from the parvenu aristocrats, and put them in their respective places as skillfully as an expert horse-dealer can draft his stock at a sale. Then, when the audience is complete, in the middle and front of the edifice are to be found they of the white hands and fine jewels; and in the topmost seat of the synagogue, praying audibly, is one who has made all his wealth by devouring widows' houses; while pushed away to the corners and wings are they who earn their bread by the sweat of their brow; and those who cannot afford good linen are too proud to be seen here at all.

"The choir sings and the organ rings," the uninteresting prayers are rattled off ("O come, let us worship, and fall down: and kneel before the Lord, our Maker"); a sermon, mostly of the debts of the concern, of the customs of the ancients, or of the rites and ceremonies of up-to-date churchism, is delivered, and the play is done, and as I leave the building a great hunger for a little Christianity fills my heart.

Oh that a preacher might arise and expound from the Book of books a religion with a God, a religion with a heart in it—a Christian religion, which would abolish the cold legend whose center is respectability, and which rears great buildings in which the rich recline on silken hassocks while the poor perish in the shadow thereof.

Through the hot dry summer, then the heartless winter and the scorching summer again which have spent themselves since Gertie's departure, I have struggled hard to do my duty in that state of life unto which it had pleased God to call me, and sometimes I have partially succeeded. I have had no books or papers, nothing but peasant surroundings and peasant tasks, and have encouraged peasant ignorance—ignorance being the mainspring of contentment, and contentment the bed-rock of happiness; but it is all to no purpose. A note from the other world will strike upon the chord of my being, and the spirit which has been dozing within me awakens and fiercely beats at its bars, demanding some nobler thought, some higher aspiration, some wider action, a more saturnalian pleasure, something more than the peasant life can ever yield. Then I hold my spirit tight till wild passionate longing sinks down, down to sickening dumb despair, and had I the privilege extended to Job of old—to curse God and die—I would leap at it eagerly.

CHAPTER THIRTY-FOUR

But Absent Friends are Soon Forgot

We received a great many letters from Gertie for a little while after she went up the country, but they grew shorter and farther between as time went on.

In one of grannie's letters there was concerning my sister: "I find Gertie is a much younger girl for her age than Sybylla was, and not nearly so wild and hard to manage. She is a great comfort to me. Every one remarks upon her good looks."

From one of Gertie's letters:

Uncle Julius came home from Hong Kong and America last week, and brought such a lot of funny presents for every one. He had a lot for you, but he has given them to me instead as you are not here. He calls me his pretty little sunbeam, and says I must always live with him.

I sighed to myself as I read this. Uncle Jay-Jay had said much the same to me, and where was I now? My thoughts were ever turning to the people and old place I love so well, but Gertie's letters showed me that I was utterly forgotten and unmissed.

Gertie left us in October 1897, and it was somewhere about January 1898 that all the letters from Caddagat were full to overflowing with the wonderful news of Harold Beecham's reinstatement at Five-Bob Downs, under the same conditions as he had held sway there in my day.

From grannie's letters I learned that some old sweetheart of Harold's father had bequeathed untold wealth to this her lost love's son. The wealth was in bonds and stocks principally, and though it would be some time ere Harold was actually in possession of it, yet he had no difficulty in getting advancements to any amount, and had immediately repurchased Five-Bob.

I had never dreamed of such a possibility. True, I had often said were Harold a character in fiction instead of real life, some relative would die opportunely and set him up in his former position, but, here, this utterly unanticipated contingency had arisen in a manner which would affect my own life, and what were my feelings regarding the matter?

I think I was not fully aware of the extent of my lack of wifely love for Harold Beecham, until experiencing the sense of relief which stole over me on holding in my hand the announcement of his return to the smile of fortune.

He was rich; he would not need me now; my obligation to him ceased to exist; I was free. He would no longer wish to be hampered with me. He could take his choice of beauty and worth; he might even purchase a princess did his ambition point that way.

One of Gertie's letters ran:

That Mr. Beecham you used to tell me so much about has come back to live at Five-Bob. He has brought his aunts back. Every one went to welcome them, and there was a great fuss. Aunt Helen says he (Mr. B.) is very conservative; he has everything just as it used to be. I believe he is richer than ever. Every one is laughing about his luck. He was here twice last week, and has just left this evening. He is very quiet. I don't know how you thought him so wonderful. I think he is too slow, I have great work to talk to him, but he is very kind, and I like him. He seems to remember you well, and often says you were a game youngster, and could ride like old Nick himself.

I wrote to the owner of Five-Bob desiring to know if what I heard concerning his good fortune was correct, and he replied by return post:

My dear little Syb,

Yes, thank goodness it is all true. The old lady left me nearly a million. It seems like a fairy yarn, and I will know how to value it more now. I would have written sooner, only you remember our bargain, and I was just waiting to get things fixed up a little, when I'm off at great tracks to claim you in the flesh, as there is no need for us to wait above a month or two now if you are agreeable. I am just run to death. It takes a bit of jigging to get things straight again, but it's simply too good to believe to be back in the same old beat. I've seen Gertie a good many times, and find your descriptions of her were not at all overdrawn. I won't send any love in this, or there would be a "bust up" in the post-office, because I'd be sure to overdo the thing, and I'd have all the officials on to me for damages. Gather up your goods and chattels, because I'll be along in a week or two to take possession of you.

> Yr. devoted
> Hal.

I screwed the letter in two and dropped it into the kitchen-fire.

I knew Harold meant what he had said. He was a strong-natured man of firm determinations, and having made up his mind to marry me would never for an instant think of anything else; but I could see what he could not see himself—that he had probably tired of me, and was becoming enamoured of Gertie's beauty.

The discordance of life smote hard upon me, and the letter I wrote was not pleasant. It ran:

To H. A. BEECHAM, Esq.,
    Five-Bob Downs Station,
        Gool-Gool, N.S.W.
Sir,
    Your favor duly to hand. I heartily rejoice at your good fortune, and trust you may live long and have health to enjoy it. Do not for an instant consider yourself under any obligations to me, for you are perfectly free. Choose some one who will reflect more credit on your taste and sense.
                With all good wishes,
                    Faithfully yrs,
                        S. Penelope Melvyn.

As I closed and directed this how far away Harold Beecham seemed! Less than two years ago I had been familiar with every curve and expression of his face, every outline of his great figure, every intonation of his strong cultivated voice; but now he seemed as the shadow of a former age.

He wrote in reply: What did I mean? Was it a joke—just a little of my old tormenting spirit? Would I explain immediately? He couldn't get down to see me for a fortnight at the least.

I explained, and very tersely, that I had meant what I said, and in return received a letter as short as my own:

Dear Miss Melvyn,
    I regret your decision, but trust I have sufficient

manhood to prevent me from thrusting myself
upon any lady, much less you.

Your sincere friend,
Harold Augustus Beecham.

He did not demand a reason for my decision, but
accepted it unquestionably. As I read his words he grew
near to me, as in the days gone by.

I closed my eyes, and before my mental vision there
arose an overgrown old orchard, skirting one of the
great stock-routes from Riverina to Monaro. A glorious
day was languidly smiling good night on abundance
of ripe and ripening fruit and flowers. The scent of
stock and the merry cry of the tennis-players filled the
air. I could feel Harold's wild jolting heart-beats, his
burning breath on my brow, and his voice husky with
rage in my ear. As he wrote that letter I could fancy
the well-cut mouth settling into a sullen line, as it had
done on my birthday when, by caressing, I had won it
back to its habitual pleasant expression; but on this
occasion I would not be there. He would be angry
just a little while—a man of his strength and importance
could not long hold ill-will toward a woman, a girl,
a child! as weak and insignificant as I. Then when I
should meet him in the years to come, when he would
be the faithful and loving husband of another woman,
he would be a little embarrassed perhaps; but I would
set him at his ease, and we would laugh together re
what he would term our foolish young days, and he
would like me in a brotherly way. Yes, that was how it
would be. The tiny note blackened in the flames.

So much for my romance of love! It had ended in a
bottle of smoke, as all my other dreams of life bid fair
to do.

I think I was not fully aware how near I had been
to loving Harold Beecham until experiencing the sense
of loss which stole over me on holding in my hand the
acceptance of his dismissal. It was a something gone

out of my life, which contained so few somethings, that I crushingly felt the loss of any one.

Our greatest heart-treasure is a knowledge that there is in creation an individual to whom our existence is necessary—some one who is part of our life as we are part of theirs, some one in whose life we feel assured our death would leave a gap for a day or two. And who can be this but a husband or wife? Our parents have other children and themselves, our brothers and sisters marry and have lives apart, so with our friends; but one's husband would be different. And I had thrown behind me this chance; but in the days that followed I knew that I had acted wisely.

Gertie's letters would contain: "Harold Beecham, he makes me call him Harry, took me to Five-Bob last week, and it was lovely fun."

Again it would be: "Harry says I am the prettiest little girl ever was, Caddagat or anywhere else, and he gave me such a lovely bracelet. I wish you could see it."

Or this:

We all went to church yesterday. Harry rode with me. There is to be a very swell ball at Wyambeet next month, and Harry says I am to keep nearly all my dances for him. Frank Hawden sailed for England last week. We have a new jackeroo. He is better-looking than Frank, but I don't like him as well.

Grannie's and aunt Helen's letters to my mother corroborated these admissions. Grannie wrote:

Harry Beecham seems to be very much struck with Gertie. I think it would be a good thing, as he is immensely rich, and a very steady young fellow into the bargain. They say no woman could live with him on account of his temper; but he has always been a favorite of mine, and we cannot expect a man without some faults.

Aunt Helen remarked:

Don't be surprised if you have young Beecham down there presently on an "asking papa" excursion. He spends a great deal of time here, and has been inquiring the best route to Possum Gully. Do you remember him? I don't think he was here in your day. He is an estimable and likeable young fellow, and I think will make a good husband apart from his wealth. He and Gertie present a marked contrast.

Sometimes on reading this kind of thing I would wax rather bitter. Love, I said, was not a lasting thing; but knowledge told me that it was for those of beauty and winsome ways, and not for me. I was ever to be a lonely-hearted waif from end to end of the world of love—an alien among my own kin.

But there were other things to worry me. Horace had left the family roof. He averred he was "full up of life under the old man's rule. It was too slow and messed up." His uncle, George Melvyn, his father's eldest brother, who had so often and so kindly set us up with cows, had offered to take him, and his father had consented to let him go. George Melvyn had a large station outback, a large sheep-shearing machine, and other improvements. Thence, strong in the hope of sixteen years, Horace set out on horseback one springless spring morning ere the sun had risen, with all his earthly possessions strapped before him. Bravely the horse stepped out for its week's journey, and bravely its rider sat, leaving me and the shadeless, wooden sun-baked house on the side of the hill, with the regretlessness of teens—especially masculine teens. I watched him depart until the clacking of his horse's hoofs grew faint on the stony hillside and his form disappeared amid the she-oak scrub which crowned the ridge to the westward. He was gone. Such is life. I sat down and buried my face in my apron, too miserable even for tears. Here was another article I ill could spare wrenched from my poorly and sparsely furnished existence.

True, our intercourse had not always been carpeted with rose-leaves. His pitiless scorn of my want of size and beauty had often given me a sleepless night; but I felt no bitterness against him for this, but merely cursed the Potter who had fashioned the clay that was thus described.

On the other hand, he was the only one who had ever stood up and said a word of extenuation for me in the teeth of a family squall. Father did not count; my mother thought me bad from end to end; Gertie, in addition to the gifts of beauty and lovableness, possessed that of holding with the hare and running with the hound; but Horace once had put in a word for me that I would never forget. I missed his presence in the house, his pounding of the old piano with four dumb notes in the middle, as he bawled thereto rollicking sea and comic songs; I missed his energetic dissertations on spurs, whips, and blood-horses, and his spirited rendering of snatches of Paterson and Gordon, as he came in and out, banging doors and gates, teasing the cats and dogs and tormenting the children.

CHAPTER THIRTY-FIVE

The 3rd of December 1898

It was a very hot day. So extreme was the heat that to save the lives of some young swallows my father had to put wet bags over the iron roof above their nest. A galvanized-iron awning connected our kitchen and house: in this some swallows had built, placing their nest so near the iron that the young ones were baking with the heat until rescued by the wet bagging. I had a heavy day's work before me, and, from my exertions of the day before, was tired at the beginning. Bush-fires had been raging in the vicinity during the week, and yesterday had come so close that I had been called out to carry buckets of water all the afternoon in the blazing sun. The fire had been allayed, after making a gap in one of our boundary fences. Father and the boys had been forced to leave the harvesting of the miserable pinched wheat while they went to mend it, as the small allowance of grass the drought gave us was precious, and had to be carefully preserved from neighbors' stock.

I had baked and cooked, scrubbed floors and white-washed hearths, scoured tinware and cutlery, cleaned windows, swept yards, and discharged numerous miscellaneous jobs, and half-past two in the afternoon found me very dirty and very tired, and with very much more yet to do.

One of my half-starved poddy calves was very ill, and I went out to doctor it previous to bathing and tidying myself for my finishing household duties.

My mother was busy upon piles and piles of wearying mending, which was one of the most hopeless of the many slaveries of her life. This was hard work, and my father was slaving away in the sun, and mine was arduous labor, and it was a very hot day, and a drought-smitten and a long day, and poddy calves ever have a tendency to make me moralize and snarl. This was life, my life and my parents' life, and the life of those around us, and if I was a good girl and honored my parents I would be rewarded with a long stretch of it. Yah!

These pagan meditations were interrupted by a foot-fall slowly approaching. I did not turn to ascertain who it might be, but trusted it was no one of importance, as the poddy and I presented rather a grotesque appearance. It was one of the most miserable and sickly of its miserable kind, and I was in the working uniform of the Australian peasantry. My tattered skirt and my odd and bursted boots, laced with twine, were spattered with white-wash, for coolness my soiled cotton blouse hung loose, an exceedingly dilapidated sun-bonnet surmounted my head, and a bottle of castor-oil was in my hand.

I supposed it was one of the neighbors or a tea-agent, and I would send them to mother.

The footsteps had come to a halt beside me.

"Could you tell me if——"

I glanced upward. Horrors! There stood Harold Beecham, as tall and broad as of yore, even more sunburnt than ever, and looking very stylish in a suit of gray and a soft fashionable dinted-in hat; and it was the first time I had ever seen him in a white shirt and high collar.

I wished he would explode, or I might sink into the ground, or the calf would disappear, or that something might happen.

On recognizing me his silence grew profound, but

an unmistakable expression of pity filled his eyes and stung me to the quick.

I have a faculty of self-pity, but my pride promptly refuses the slightest offer of sympathy from another.

I could feel my heart grow as bitterly cold as my demeanor was icily stiff, when I stood up and said curtly:

"This is a great surprise, Mr. Beecham."

"Not an unpleasant one, I hope," he said pleasantly.

"We will not discuss the matter. Come inside out of the heat."

"I'm in no hurry, Syb, and couldn't I help you with that poor little devil?"

"I'm only trying to give it another chance of life."

"What will you do with it if it lives?"

"Sell it for half a crown when it's a yearling."

"It would pay better to shoot the poor little beggar now."

"No doubt it would the owner of Five-Bob, but we have to be more careful," I said tartly.

"I didn't mean to offend you."

"I'm not offended," I returned, leading the way to the house, imagining with a keen pain that Harold Beecham must be wondering how for an instant he could have been foolish enough to fancy such an object two years ago.

Thank goodness I have never felt any humiliation on account of my mother, and felt none then, as she rose to greet Harold upon my introduction. She was a lady, and looked it, in spite of the piles of coarse mending, and the pair of trousers, almost bullet-proof with patches, out of which she drew her hand, roughened and reddened with hard labor, in spite of her patched and faded cotton gown, and the commonest and most poverty-stricken of peasant surroundings, which failed to hide that she had not been always thus.

Leaving them together, I expeditiously proceeded to relieve the livery-stable horse, on which Harold had come, of the valise, saddle, and bridle with which it was encumbered, and then let it loose in one of the grassless paddocks near at hand.

Then I threw myself on a stool in the kitchen, and felt, to the bone, the sting of having ideas above one's position.

In a few minutes mother came hurrying out.

"Good gracious, what's the matter? I suppose you didn't like being caught in such a pickle, but don't get in the dumps about it. I'll get him some tea while you clean yourself, and then you'll be able to help me by and by."

I found my little sister Aurora, and we climbed through the window into my bedroom to get tidy. I put a pair of white socks and shoes and a clean pinafore on the little girl, and combed her golden curls. She was all mine—slept with me, obeyed me, championed me; while I—well, I worshiped her.

There was a hole in the wall, and through it I could see without being seen.

Mother was dispensing afternoon tea and talking to Harold. It was pleasant to see that manly figure once again. My spirits rose considerably. After all, if the place was poor, it was very clean, as I had scrubbed it all that morning, and when I came to consider the matter, I remembered that men weren't such terrible creatures, and never made one feel the sting of one's poverty half as much as women do.

"Aurora," I said, "I want you to go out and tell Mr. Beecham something."

The little girl assented. I carefully instructed her in what she was to say, and dispatched her. She placed herself in front of Harold—a wide-eyed mite of four, that scarcely reached above his knee—and clasping her chubby hands behind her, gazed at him fearlessly and unwinkingly.

"Aurora, you mustn't stand staring like that," said mother.

"Yes, I must," she replied confidently.

"Well, and what's your name?" said Harold laughingly.

"Aurora and Rory. I belong to Sybyller, and got to tell you somesing."

"Have you? Let's hear it."

"Sybyller says you's Mr. Beecher; when you're done tea, you'd like me if I would to 'scort you to farver and the boys and 'duce you."

Mother laughed. "That's some of Sybylla's nonsense. She considers Rory her especial property, and delights to make the child attempt long words. Perhaps you would care to take a stroll to where they are at work, by and by."

Harold said he would go at once, and accepting Rory's escort, and with a few directions from mother, they presently set out—she importantly trudging beneath a big white sun-bonnet, and he looking down at her in amusement. Presently he tossed her high above his head, and depositing her upon his shoulder, held one sturdy brown leg in his browner hand, while she held on by his hair.

"My first impressions are very much in his favor," said mother, when they had got out of hearing. "But fancy Gertie the wife of that great man!"

"She is four inches taller than I am," I snapped. "And if he was as big as a gum-tree, he would be a man all the same, and just as soft on a pretty face as all the rest of them."

I bathed, dressed, arranged my hair, got something ready for tea, and prepared a room for our visitor. For this I collected from all parts of the house—a mat from one room, a toilet-set from another, and so on— till I had quite an elaborately furnished chamber ready for my one-time lover.

They returned at dusk, Rory again seated on Harold's shoulder, and two of the little boys clinging around him.

As I conducted him to his room I was in a different humor from that of the sweep-like object who had met him during the afternoon. I laughed to myself, for, as on a former occasion during our acquaintance, I felt I was master of the situation.

"I say, Syb, don't treat a fellow as though he was altogether a stranger," he said diffidently, leaning against the doorpost.

Our hands met in a cordial grasp as I said, "I'm awfully glad to see you, Hal; but, but——"

"But what?"

"I didn't feel over delighted to be caught in such a stew this afternoon."

"Nonsense! It only reminded me of the first time we met," he said with a twinkle in his eye. "That's always the way with you girls. You can't be civil to a man unless you're dressed up fit to stun him, as though you couldn't make fool enough of him without the aid of clothes at all."

"You'd better shut up," I said over my shoulder as I departed, "or you will be saying something better left unsaid, like at our first meeting. Do you remember?"

"Do I not? Great Scot, it's just like old times to have you giving me impudence over your shoulder like that!" he replied merrily.

"Like, yet unlike," I retorted with a sigh.

CHAPTER THIRTY-SIX

Once upon a Time, when the days were long and hot

Next day was Sunday—a blazing one it was too. I proposed that in the afternoon some of us should go to church. Father sat upon the idea as a mad one. Walk two miles in such heat for nothing! as walk we would be compelled to do, horseflesh being too precious in such a drought to fritter it away in idle jaunts. Surprising to say, however, Harold, who never walked anywhere when he could get any sort of a horse, uttered a wish to go. Accordingly, when the midday dinner was over, he, Stanley, and I set out. Going to church was quite the event of the week to the residents around Possum Gully. It was a small Dissenting chapel, where a layman ungrammatically held forth at 3 p.m. every Sunday; but the congregation was composed of all denominations, who attended more for the sitting about on logs outside, and yarning about the price of butter, the continuance of the drought, and the latest gossip, before and after the service, than for the service itself.

I knew the appearance of Harold Beecham would make quite a miniature sensation, and form food for no end of conjecture and chatter. In any company he was a distinguished-looking man, and particularly so among these hard-worked farmer-selectors, on whose careworn features the cruel effects of the drought were leaving additional lines of worry. I felt proud of my

248

quondam sweetheart. There was an unconscious air of physical lordliness about him, and he looked such a swell—not the black-clothed, clean-shaved, great display of white collar-and-cuffs swell appertaining to the office and city street, but of the easy sunburnt squatter type of swelldom, redolent of the sun, the saddle, the wide open country—a man who is a man, utterly free from the least suspicion of effeminacy, and capable of earning his bread by the sweat of his brow—with an arm ready and willing to save in an accident.

All eyes were turned on us as we approached, and I knew that the attentions he paid me out of simple courtesy—tying my shoe, carrying my book, holding my parasol—would be put down as those of a lover.

I introduced him to a group of men who were sitting on a log, under the shade of a stringybark, and leaving him to converse with them, made my way to where the women sat beneath a gum-tree. The children made a third group at some distance. We always divided ourselves thus. A young fellow had to be very far gone ere he was willing to run the gauntlet of all the chaff leveled at him had he the courage to single out a girl and talk to her.

I greeted all the girls and women, beginning at the great-grandmother of the community, who illustrated to perfection the grim sarcasm of the fifth commandment. She had worked hard from morning till night, until too old to do so longer, and now hung around with aching weariness waiting for the grave. She generally poured into my ears a wail about her "rheumatisms," and "How long it do be waiting for the Lord"; but today she was too curious about Harold to think of herself.

"Sure, Sybyller, who's that? Is he yer sweetheart? Sure he's as fine a man as iver I clapped me eyes on."

I proceeded to give his pedigree, but was interrupted by the arrival of the preacher, and we all went into the weatherboard iron-roofed house of prayer.

After service, one of the girls came up to me and

whispered, "That is your sweetheart, isn't it, Sybyller? He was looking at you all the time in church."

"Oh dear, no! I'll introduce him to you."

I did so, and watched him as they made remarks about the heat and drought. There was nothing of the cad or snob about him, and his short season of adversity had rubbed all the little crudities off his character, leaving him a man that the majority of both sexes would admire: women for his bigness, his gentleness, his fine brown moustache—and for his wealth; men, because he was a manly fellow.

I know he had walked to church on purpose to get a chance of speaking to me about Gertie, before approaching her parents on the matter; but Stanley accompanied us, and, boy-like, never relaxed in vigilance for an instant, so there was no opportunity for anything but matter-of-fact remarks. The heat was intense. We wiped the perspiration and flies from our face frequently, and disturbed millions of grasshoppers as we walked. They had devoured all the fruit in the orchards about, and had even destroyed many of the trees by eating the bark, and now they were stripping the briers of foliage. In one orchard we passed, the apricot, plum, and peach-stones hung naked on their leafless trees as evidence of their ravages. It was too hot to indulge in any but the most desultory conversation. We dawdled along. A tiger-snake crossed our path. Harold procured a stick and killed it, and Stanley hung it on the top wire of a fence which was near at hand. After this we discussed snakes for a few yards.

A blue sea-breeze, redolent of the bush-fires which were raging at Tocumwal and Bombala, came rushing and roaring over the ranges from the east, and enshrouded the scene in its heavy fog-like folds. The sun was obscured, and the temperature suddenly took such a great drop that I felt chilled in my flimsy clothing, and I noticed Harold draw his coat together.

Stanley had to go after the cows, which were little better than walking hides, yet were yarded morning and evening to yield a dribble of milk. He left us among some sallie-trees, in a secluded nook, walled in by briers, and went across the paddock to round-up the cows. Harold and I came to a halt by tacit consent.

"Syb, I want to speak to you," he said earnestly, and then came to a dead stop.

"Very well; 'tear into it,' as Horace would say; but if it is anything frightful, break it gently," I said flippantly.

"Surely, Syb, you can guess what it is I have to say."

Yes, I could guess, I *knew* what he was going to say, and the knowledge left a dull bitterness at my heart. I knew he was going to tell me that I had been right and he wrong—that he had found some one he loved better than me, and that some one being my sister, he felt I needed some explanation before he could go in and win; and though I had refused him for want of love, yet it gave me pain when the moment arrived that the only man who had ever pretended to love me was going to say he had been mistaken, and preferred my sister.

There was silence save for the whirr of the countless grasshoppers in the brier bushes. I knew he was expecting me to help him out, but I felt doggedly savage and wouldn't. I looked up at him. He was a tall grand man, and honest and true and rich. He loved my sister; she would marry him, and they would be happy. I thought bitterly that God was good to one and cruel to another —not that I wanted this man, but why was I so different from other girls?

But then I thought of Gertie, so pretty, so girlish, so understandable, so full of innocent winning coquetry. I softened. Could any one help preferring her to me, who was strange, weird, and perverse—too outspoken to be engaging, devoid of beauty and endearing little ways? It was **my** own misfortune and nobody's fault that my singular individuality excluded me from the ordinary run of youthful joyous-heartednesses, and why should I be nasty to these young people?

I was no heroine, only a common little bush-girl, so had to make the best of the situation without any fooling. I raised my eyes from the scanty baked wisps of grass at my feet, placed my hand on Hal's arm, and tiptoeing so as to bring my five-foot stature more on a level with his, said:

"Yes, Hal, I know what you want to say. Say it all. I won't be nasty."

"Well, you see you are so jolly touchy, and have snubbed me so often, that I don't know how to begin; and if you know what I'm going to say, won't you give me an answer without hearing it?"

"Yes, Hal; but you'd better say it, as I don't know what conditions——"

"Conditions!"——catching me up eagerly at the word. "If it is only conditions that are stopping you, you can make your own conditions if you will marry me."

"Marry you, Harold! What do you mean? Do you know what you are saying?" I exclaimed.

"There!" he replied: "I knew you would take it as an insult. I believe you are the proudest girl in the world. I know you are too clever for me; but I love you, and could give you everything you fancied."

"Hal, dear, let me explain. I'm not insulted, only surprised. I thought you were going to tell me that you loved Gertie, and would ask me not to make things unpleasant by telling her of the foolish little bit of flirtation there had been between us."

"Marry Gertie! Why, she's only a child! A mere baby, in fact. Marry Gertie! I never thought of her in that light; and did you think I was that sort of a fellow, Syb?" he asked reproachfully.

"No, Hal," I promptly made answer. "I did not think you were that sort of fellow; but I thought that was the only sort of fellow there was."

"Good heavens, Syb! Did you really mean those queer little letters you wrote me last February? I never for an instant looked upon them as anything but a little bit of playful contrariness. And have you forgotten me? Did you not mean your promise of two years ago, that you speak of what passed between us as a paltry bit of flirtation? Is that all you thought it?"

"No, I did not consider it flirtation; but that is what

I thought you would term it when announcing your affection for Gertie."

"Gertie! Pretty little Gertie! I never looked upon the child as anything but your sister, consequently mine also. She's a child."

"Child! She is eighteen. More than a year older than I was when you first introduced the subject of matrimony to me, and she is very beautiful, and twenty times as good and lovable as I could ever be even in my best moments."

"Yes, I know you are young in years, but there is nothing of the child in you. As for beauty, it is nothing. If beauty was all a man required, he could, if rich, have a harem full of it any day. I want some one to be true."

> *"The world is filled with folly and sin,*
> *And love must cling where it can, I say;*
> *For beauty is easy enough to win,*
> *But one isn't loved every day,"*

I quoted from Owen Meredith.

"Yes," he said, "that is why I want you. Just think a moment; don't say no. You are not vexed with me—are you, Syb?"

"Vexed, Hal! I am scarcely inhuman enough to be angry on account of being loved."

Ah, why did I not love him as I have it in me to love! Why did he look so exasperatingly humble? I was weak, oh, so pitifully weak! I wanted a man who would be masterful and strong, who would help me over the rough spots of life—one who had done hard grinding in the mill of fate—one who had suffered, who had understood. No; I could never marry Harold Beecham.

"Well, Syb, little chum, what do you say?"

"Say!"—and the words fell from me bitterly—"I say, leave me; go and marry the sort of woman you ought to marry. The sort that all men like. A good conventional woman, who will do the things she should at the proper time. Leave me alone."

He was painfully agitated. A look of pain crossed his face.

"Don't say that, Syb, because I was a beastly cad once: I've had all that knocked out of me."

"I am the cad," I replied. "What I said was nasty and unwomanly, and I wish I had left it unsaid. I am not good enough to be your wife, Hal, or that of any man. Oh, Hal, I have never deceived you! There are scores of good noble women in the world who would wed you for the asking—marry one of them."

"But, Syb, I want you. You are the best and truest girl in the world."

"Och! Sure, the blarney-stone is getting a good rub now," I said playfully.

Annoyance and amusement struggled for mastery in his expression as he replied:

"You're the queerest girl in the world. One minute you snub a person, the next you are the jolliest girl going, and then you get as grave and earnest as a fellow's mother would be."

"Yes, I am queer. If you had any sense, you'd have nothing to do with me. I'm more queer, too. I am given to something which a man never pardons in a woman. You will draw away as though I were a snake when you hear."

"What is it?"

"I am given to writing stories, and literary people predict I will yet be an authoress."

He laughed—his soft, rich laugh.

"That's just into my hand. I'd rather work all day than write the shortest letter; so if you will give me a hand occasionally, you can write as many yarns as you like. I'll give you a study, and send for a truck-load of writing-gear at once, if you like. Is that the only horror you had to tell me?"

I bowed my head.

"Well, I can have you now," he said gently, folding me softly in his arms with such tender reverence that I cried out in pain, "Oh, Hal, don't, don't!" and struggled free. I was ashamed, knowing I was not worthy of this.

He flushed a dusky red.

"Am I so hateful to you that you cannot bear my touch?" he asked half wistfully, half angrily.

"Oh no; it isn't that. I'm really very fond of you, if you'd only understand," I said half to myself.

"Understand! If you care for me, that is all I want to understand. I love you, and have plenty of money. There is nothing to keep us apart. Now that I know you care for me, I *will* have you, in spite of the devil."

"There will be a great tussle between you," I said mischievously, laughing at him. "Old Nick has a great hold on me, and I'm sure he will dispute your right."

At any time Harold's sense of humor was not at all in accordance with his size, and he failed to see how my remark applied now.

He gripped my hands in a passion of pleading, as two years previously he had seized me in jealous rage. He drew me to him. His eyes were dark and full of entreaty; his voice was husky.

"Syb, poor little Syb, I will be good to you! You can have what you like. You don't know what you mean when you say no."

No; I would not yield. He offered me everything—but control. He was a man who meant all he said. His were no idle promises on the spur of the moment. But no, no, no, no, he was not for me. My love must know, must have suffered, must understand.

"Syb, you do not answer. May I call you mine? You must, you must, you must!"

His hot breath was upon my cheek. The pleasant, open, manly countenance was very near—perilously near. The intoxication of his love was overpowering me. I had no hesitation about trusting him. He was not distasteful to me in any way. What was the good of waiting for that other—the man who had suffered, who knew, who understood? I might never find him; and, if I did, ninety-nine chances to one he would not care for me.

"Syb, Syb, can't you love me just a little?"

There was a winning charm in his manner. Nature had endowed him liberally with virile fascination. My hard uncongenial life had rendered me weak. He was drawing me to him; he was irresistible. Yes; I would be his wife. I grew dizzy, and turned my head sharply backward and took a long gasping breath, another and another, of that fresh cool air suggestive of the grand old sea and creak of cordage and bustle and strife of life. My old spirit revived, and my momentary weakness fled. There was another to think of than myself, and that was Harold. Under a master-hand I would be harmless; but to this man I would be as a two-edged sword in the hand of a novice—gashing his fingers at every turn, and eventually stabbing his honest heart.

It was impossible to make him see my refusal was for his good. He was as a favorite child pleading for a dangerous toy. I desired to gratify him, but the awful responsibility of the after-effects loomed up and deterred me.

"Hal, it can never be."

He dropped my hands and drew himself up.

"I will not take your No till the morning. Why do you refuse me? Is it my temper? You need not be afraid of that. I don't think I'd hurt you; and I don't drink, or smoke, or swear very much; and I've never destroyed a woman's name. I would not stoop to press you against your will if you were like the ordinary run of women; but you are such a queer little party, that I'm afraid you might be boggling at some funny little point that could easily be wiped out."

"Yes; it is only a little point. But if you wipe it out you will knock the end out of the whole thing—for the point is myself. I would not suit you. It would not be wise for you to marry me."

"But I'm the only person concerned. If you are not afraid for yourself, I am quite satisfied."

We faced about and walked homeward in unbroken

silence—too perturbed to fall into our usual custom of chewing bush-leaves as we went.

I thought much that night when all the house was abed. It was tempting. Harold would be good to me, and would lift me from this life of poverty which I hated, to one of ease. Should I elect to remain where I was, till the grave there was nothing before me but the life I was leading now: my only chance of getting above it was by marriage, and Harold Beecham's offer was the one chance of a lifetime. Perhaps he could manage me well enough. Yes; I had better marry him.

And I believe in marriage—that is, I think it the most sensible and respectable arrangement for the replenishing of a nation which has yet been suggested. But marriage is a solemn issue of life. I was as suited for matrimony as any of the sex, but only with an exceptional helpmeet—and Harold was not he. My latent womanliness arose and pointed this out so plainly that I seized my pen and wrote:

Dear Harold,

I will not get a chance of speaking to you in the morning, so write. Never mention marriage to me again. I have firmly made up my mind—it must be No. It will always be a comfort to me in the years to come to know that I was loved once, if only for a few hours. It is not that I do not care for you, as I like you better than any man I have ever seen; but I do not mean ever to marry. When you lost your fortune I was willing to accede to your request, as I thought you wanted me; but now that you are rich again you will not need me. I am not good enough to be your wife, for you are a good man; and better, because you do not know you are good. You may feel uncomfortable or lonely for a little while, because, when you make up your mind, you are not easily thwarted; but you will find that your fancy for me will soon pass. It is only a fancy, Hal. Take a look in the glass, and you will see reflected there the figure of a stalwart man who is purely virile, possessing not the slightest attribute of the weaker sex, therefore your love is merely a passing flame. I do not impute fickleness to you, but merely point out a masculine characteristic, and that you are a man, and only a man, pure and unadulterated. Look around, and from the numbers of good women to be found on every side choose one who will make you a fitter helpmeet, a more conventional comrade, than I could ever do. I thank you for the inestimable honor you have conferred upon me; but keep it till you find some one worthy of it, and by and by you will be glad that I have set you free.

Good-bye, Hal!

> Your sincere and affec. friend,
> Sybylla Penelope Melvyn.

Then I crept into bed beside my little sister, and though the air inside had not cooled, and the room was warm, I shivered so that I clasped the chubby, golden-haired little sleeper in my arms that I might feel something living and real and warm.

"Oh, Rory, Rory!" I whispered, raining upon her lonely-hearted tears. "In all the world is there never a comrade strong and true to teach me the meaning of this hollow, grim little tragedy—life? Will it always be this ghastly aloneness? Why am I not good and pretty and simple like other girls? Oh, Rory, Rory, why was I ever born? I am of no use or pleasure to any one in all the world!"

CHAPTER THIRTY-SEVEN

He that despiseth little things, shall fall little by little

I

The morning came, breakfast, next Harold's departure.
I shook my head and slipped the note into his hand as
we parted. He rode slowly down the road. I sat on the
step of the garden gate, buried my face in my hands,
and reviewed the situation. I could see my life stretch-
ing out ahead of me, barren and monotonous as the
thirsty track along which Harold was disappearing. Today it was washing, ironing tomorrow, next day baking,
after that scrubbing—thus on and on. We would occasionally see a neighbor or a tea-agent, a tramp or an
Assyrian hawker. By hard slogging against flood, fire,
drought, pests, stock diseases, and the sweating occasioned by importation, we could manage to keep bread
in our mouths. By training and education I was fitted
for nought but what I was, or a general slavey, which
was many degrees worse. I could take my choice. Life
was too much for me. What was the end of it, what
its meaning, aim, hope, or use?

In comparison to millions I knew that I had received
more than a fair share of the goods of life; but knowing another has leprosy makes our cancer none the
easier to bear.

My mother's voice, sharp and cross, roused me.

"Sybylla, you lazy unprincipled girl, to sit scheming there while your poor old mother is at the wash-tub. You sit idling there, and then by and by you'll be groaning about this terrible life in which there's time for nothing but work."

How she fussed and bothered over the clothes was a marvel to me. My frame of mind was such that it seemed it would not signify if all our clothes went to the dogs, and the clothes of our neighbors, and the clothes of the whole world, and the world itself for the matter of that.

"Sybylla, you are a dirty careless washer. You've put Stanley's trousers in the boil and the color is coming out of them, and your father's best white handkerchief should have been with the first lot, and here it is now."

Poor mother got crosser as she grew weary with the fierce heat and arduous toil, and as I in my abstraction continued to make mistakes, but the last straw was the breaking of an old cup which I accidentally pushed off the table.

I got it hot. Had I committed an act of premeditated villainy I could not have received more lecturing. I deserved it—I was careless, cups were scarce with us, and we could not afford more; but what I rail against is the grindingly uneventful narrowness of the life in which the unintentional breaking of a common cup is good for a long scolding.

Ah, my mother! In my life of nineteen years I can look back and see a time when she was all gentleness and refinement, but the polish has been worn off it by years and years of scrubbing and scratching, and washing and patching, and poverty and husbandly neglect, and the bearing of burdens too heavy for delicate shoulders. Would that we were more companionable, it would make many an oasis in the desert of our lives. Oh that I could take an all-absorbing interest in patterns and recipes, bargains and orthodoxy! Oh that you could understand my desire to feel the rolling billows of the ocean beneath, to hear the pealing of a great

organ through dimly lit arches, or the sob and wail of a
violin in a brilliant crowded hall, to be swept on by
the human stream.

Ah, thou cruel fiend—Ambition! Desire!

> *Soul of the leaping flame,*
>   *Heart of the scarlet fire,*
> *Spirit that hath for name*
>   *Only the name—Desire!*

To hot young hearts beating passionately in strong
breasts, the sweetest thing is motion.

No, that part of me went beyond my mother's understanding. On the other hand, there was a part of my
mother—her brave cheerfulness, her trust in God, her
heroic struggle to keep the home together—which went
soaring on beyond my understanding, leaving me a
coward weakling, groveling in the dust.

Would that hot dreary day never close? What advantage when it did? The next and the next and many
weeks of others just the same were following hard after.

If the souls of lives were voiced in music, there are
some that none but a great organ could express, others
the clash of a full orchestra, a few to which nought
but the refined and exquisite sadness of a violin could
do justice. Many might be likened unto common pianos,
jangling and out of tune, and some to the feeble piping
of a penny whistle, and mine could be told with a
couple of nails in a rusty tin-pot.

Why do I write? For what does any one write? Shall I
get a hearing? If so—what then?

I have voiced the things around me, the small-minded
thoughts, the sodden round of grinding tasks—a monotonous, purposeless, needless existence. But patience,
O heart, surely I can make a purpose! For the present,
of my family I am the most suited to wait about common public-houses to look after my father when he is
inebriated. It breaks my mother's heart to do it; it

is dangerous for my brothers; imagine Gertie in such a position! But me it does not injure, I have the faculty for doing that sort of thing without coming to harm, and if it makes me more bitter and godless, well, what matter?

II

The next letter I received from Gertie contained:

I suppose you were glad to see Harry. He did not tell me he was going, or I would have sent some things by him. I thought he would be able to tell me lots about you that I was dying to hear, but he never said a word, only that you were all well. He went traveling some weeks ago. I missed him at first because he used to be so kind to me; but now I don't, because Mr. Creyton, whom Harry left to manage Five-Bob, comes just as often as Harry used to, and is lots funnier. He brings me something nice every time. Uncle Jay-Jay teases me about him.

Happy butterfly-natured Gertie! I envied her. With Gertie's letter came also one from grannie, with further mention of Harold Beecham.

We don't know what to make of Harold Beecham. He was always such a steady fellow, and hated to go away from home even for a short time, but now he has taken an idea to rush away to America, and is not coming home till he has gone over the world. He is not going to see anything, because by cablegrams his aunts got he is one place today and hundreds of miles away tomorrow. It is some craze he has suddenly taken. I was asking Augusta if there was ever any lunacy in the family, and she says not that she knows of. It was a very unwise act to leave full management to Creyton and Benson in the face of such a drought. One warning and marvelous escape such as he has had ought to be enough for a man with any sense. I told him he'd be poor again if he didn't take care, but he said he didn't mind if all his property was blown into atoms, as it had done him more harm than good, whatever he means by talking that way. Insanity is the only reason I can see for his conduct. I thought he had his eye on Gertie, but I questioned her, and it appears he has never said anything to her. I wonder what was his motive for going to Possum Gully that time?

Travel was indeed an unexpected development on the part of Harold Beecham. He had such a marked aversion to anything of that sort, and never went even to Sydney or Melbourne for more than a few days at a stretch, and that on business or at a time of stock shows.

There were many conjectures re the motive of his visit to Possum Gully, but I held my peace.

CHAPTER THIRTY-EIGHT

A Tale that is told and a Day that is done

There are others toiling and straining
    'Neath burdens graver than mine;
They are weary, yet uncomplaining—
    I know it, yet I repine:
I know it, how time will ravage,
    How time will level, and yet
I long with a longing savage,
    I regret with a fierce regret.

A. L. GORDON
POSSUM GULLY, 25th *March,* 1899

Christmas, only distinguished from the fifty-two slow
Sundays of the year by plum-pudding, roast turkey,
and a few bottles of home-made beer, has been once
more; New Year, ushered in with sweet-scented mid-
summer wattle and bloom of gum- and box-tree has
gone; February has followed, March is doing likewise,
and my life is still the same.

What the future holds I know not, and am tonight
so weary that I do not care.

> *Time rules us all. And life, indeed, is not*
> *The thing we planned it out, ere hope was dead;*
> *And then, we women cannot choose our lot.*

Time is thorough in his work, and as that arch-cheat, Hope, gradually becomes a phantom of the past, the neck will grow inured to its yoke.

Tonight is one of the times when the littleness—the abject littleness—of all things in life comes home to me.

After all, what is there in vain ambition? King or slave, we all must die, and when death knocks at our door, will it matter whether our life has been great or small, fast or slow, so long as it has been true—true with the truth that will bring rest to the soul?

> *But the toughest lives are brittle,*
> *And the bravest and the best*
> *Lightly fall—it matters little;*
> *Now I only long for rest.*

To weary hearts throbbing slowly in hopeless breasts the sweetest thing is rest.

And my heart is weary. Oh, how it aches tonight—not with the ache of a young heart passionately crying out for battle, but with the slow dead ache of an old heart returning vanquished and defeated!

Enough of pessimistic snarling and grumbling! Enough! Enough! Now for a lilt of another theme:

I am proud that I am an Australian, a daughter of the Southern Cross, a child of the mighty bush. I am thankful I am a peasant, a part of the bone and muscle of my nation, and earn my bread by the sweat of my brow, as man was meant to do. I rejoice I was not born a parasite, one of the blood-suckers who loll on velvet and satin, crushed from the proceeds of human sweat and blood and souls.

Ah, my sunburnt brothers!—sons of toil and of

Australia! I love and respect you well, for you are brave and good and true. I have seen not only those of you with youth and hope strong in your veins, but those with pathetic streaks of gray in your hair, large families to support, and with half a century sitting upon your work-laden shoulders. I have seen you struggle uncomplainingly against flood, fire, disease in stock, pests, drought, trade depression, and sickness, and yet have time to extend your hands and hearts in true sympathy to a brother in misfortune, and spirits to laugh and joke and be cheerful.

And for my sisters a great love and pity fills my heart. Daughters of toil, who scrub and wash and mend and cook, who are dressmakers, paperhangers, milkmaids, gardeners, and candlemakers all in one, and yet have time to be cheerful and tasty in your homes, and make the best of the few oases to be found along the narrow dusty track of your existence. Would that I were more worthy to be one of you—more a typical Australian peasant—cheerful, honest, brave!

I love you, I love you. Bravely you jog along with the rope of class distinction drawing closer, closer, tighter, tighter around you: a few more generations and you will be as enslaved as were ever the moujiks of Russia. I see it and know it, but I cannot help you. My ineffective life will be trod out in the same round of toil,—I am only one of yourselves, I am only an unnecessary, little, bush commoner, I am only a—woman!

The great sun is sinking in the west, grinning and winking knowingly as he goes, upon the starving stock and drought-smitten wastes of land. Nearer he draws to the gum-tree scrubby horizon, turns the clouds to orange, scarlet, silver flame, gold! Down, down he goes. The gorgeous, garish splendor of sunset pageantry flames out; the long shadows eagerly cover all; the kookaburras laugh their merry mocking good-night; the clouds fade to turquoise, green, and gray; the stars peep shyly out; the soft call of the mopoke arises in the gullies! With much love and good wishes to all— Good night! Good-bye!

AMEN